Books by Nicola Skinner

BLOOM: THE SURPRISING SEEDS OF SORREL FALLOWFIELD

STORM

STORM

STORM

NICOLA SKINNER

Illustrated by Flavia Sorrentino

HarperCollins *Children's Books*

First published in Great Britain by
HarperCollins *Children's Books* in 2020
Published in this edition in 2021
HarperCollins *Children's Books* is a division of HarperCollins*Publishers* Ltd,
HarperCollins Publishers
1 London Bridge Street
London SE1 9GF

The HarperCollins website address is:
www.harpercollins.co.uk

2

HarperCollins*Publishers*
1st Floor, Watermarque Building, Ringsend Road
Dublin 4, Ireland

ISBN 978–0–00–829536–3

Typeset in Goudy Old Style 12pt
Printed and bound in England by CPI Group (UK) Ltd, Croydon CR0 4YY

MIX
Paper from
responsible sources
FSC™ C007454

This book is produced from independently certified FSC™ paper
to ensure responsible forest management.

For more information visit: www.harpercollins.co.uk/green

All of this book is dedicated to Ben and Polly.
Except for a few chapters towards the end,
which are for Meg and Saul.

Poltergeist: a type of ghost or spirit responsible for loud, chaotic and destructive disturbances. A noisy ghost.

From the German *poltern* (to make sound) and *geist* (ghost).

Some people think we don't exist.
They're wrong.

PART 1

- 1 -
A BiT EGGY

WHEN YOU'RE BORN, you're a baby. That's something we can all agree on. But you're not *just* a baby. No.

You're a story.

A beautiful, bouncing, gurgling story.

A tale to be treasured.

And not just one story either. You're all of the stories, all of the time. You're an adventure, a love story, a thriller, occasionally a horror – yes, I am looking at you, you naughty little scamp – all rolled into one. And every day is story time now *you've* arrived.

Basically, babies are page-turners, and will only get more fascinating with each passing day. Or that's what their parents think anyway.

Even if no one else does.

Parents *love* talking about their children, don't they? Stick around any school gate long enough and all you'll hear is: 'my treasure this' and 'my darling that'. And what do they love to talk about the *most*?

Our beginning.

Also known as *the Birth*.

This part is special.

It is sacred.

It is long.

Have a look around. Go on.

Are there parents nearby? Is their conversation turning towards childbirth? Do any of them have a funny misty-eyed look on their face? Is anyone – this is the clincher – *clearing their throat?*

If the answer to any of that is *yes*, then I ask you this. Have you got an escape route? If you have, run to it. Now.

If not, tough luck. Did you have something planned for the day? Not any more you don't. Because when a parent breaks into a birth story, it takes a while and there's nowhere to hide.

You will hear:

a. When the contractions started.

b. Which hospital they decided to drive to.

c. What song was on the radio in the car.

d. Whether that glitchy traffic light had been fixed.

Not to mention:

a. How much the parking cost.
b. Whether that was reasonable.
c. What pain relief was available.
d. And how much the baby weighed.

(This last bit captivates them all, for some mysterious reason. Like farmers and their prize-winning turnips, parents are obsessed with how much their babies weigh. Why? Who knows? Ask *them*, if you don't mind waving goodbye to another day of your life.)

Anyway, you'd better pay attention. Make sure you listen closely and nod thoughtfully in all the right places, as if you're having a fantastic time. If you don't listen hard enough, they'll somehow know, with that uncanny parental sixth sense, and *start all over again from the top*. Then it will be YOU asking for pain relief.

For your ears.

And I'll tell you another thing. For your entire life, how you were born will be used to explain you. Why you *are* how you *are*. Parents will say stuff like 'Oh, it's no wonder our Jasper is so good at

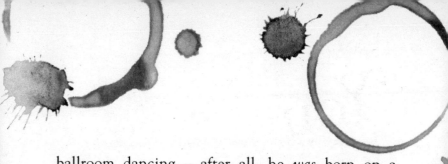

ballroom dancing – after all, he *was* born on a Tuesday just after I'd had a ham sandwich' or 'Well, of *course* Deidre's a dawdler – she was born just shy of the M25!', and all the other parents will nod solemnly like this makes total sense, pour themselves another cup of tea, and say, 'Tell me again what she weighed.'

Mine were the same. They'd bring up the way I was born at the drop of a hat. Especially when I was cross. And they'd always say the same thing: 'Well, that's what happens when you're born in a storm.'

This, of course, would only make things worse. I mean, it's very difficult to discuss the injustice of the recycling rota when your parents just keep bringing up the weather.

From eleven years ago.

It didn't end there either. Once they started, there was no stopping them. My birth story was so well rehearsed in our house it was like a duet. My parents had their lines and they knew them well.

'You

were

born

RAGING,

Frances Frida Ripley.'

That's how Dad would start. 'Salty from the get-go, you were.' (Frances Frida Ripley is me by the way. Hi. Except I'd rather you didn't call me Frances, if that's okay. Frankie's fine.)

Then Mum would interrupt. 'Well, love, that's not completely true. Frankie was a *very* peaceful baby girl. A little wet, a bit cold, perhaps, but so calm. So still. You looked as if you didn't have a care in the world.'

That would have been the hypothermia kicking in, Mum.

'Yeah, you were peaceful, for all of a second,' Dad would add. 'Right up until the moment you took your first breath.' Tiny smiles would fly between them, like birds swooping home. '*That* was when you started raging. And you haven't really stopped since.' Then, at a look from Mum, he'd mutter, 'But we wouldn't have you any other way, of course' and lope off towards his painting shed.

But here's my take on it: what did they expect? Of *course* I lost my temper when I was born. I mean, they were the ones who decided to have a baby on a freezing beach! On top of some pebbles! In the middle of winter! In a *storm*! No wonder I got a bit eggy. Any sensible baby would.

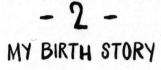

- 2 -
MY BIRTH STORY

ANYWAY, IT WASN'T my fault. It was their idea to head down to the beach that day, even though Mum was heavily pregnant with me. Even after they saw the thick black storm clouds circling our small village.

They *could* have done something sensible instead, like driving to the nearest hospital on a test run, making a careful note of how much the parking cost and whether that was reasonable. Perhaps then I would have turned into a very different child and this would be a very different story.

But they weren't practical people.

'I wanted to paint the storm,' Dad said. 'Stand inside it. See its colours.'

Dad said stuff like this regularly. He was an artist. He was nuts about colours. For his day job, he painted pet portraits. Didn't matter if they were scaly, hairy, sweet or scary, if you had £275 to splash out on a nine-inch by twelve-inch painting of your pet (unframed) then Dad, also known as Dougie Ripley, also known as –

Cliffstones' One and Only
PET PORTRAIT PAINTER!

– was your man.

In his spare time though, he painted the sea.

'I'll never get close to showing the sea the way she looks in my head,' he'd say to us – us being me and Birdie (my six-year-old sister).

'Why paint it then?' we'd ask.

In reply he'd tap the side of his nose and smile his wonky smile. 'It's the pull of it,' he'd say then. 'You can't deny the pull of it.'

Whatever that meant.

And don't even get me started on Mum. She was practically nine months pregnant on the day of the storm. She could have sat about on the sofa complaining about her swollen ankles, like any normal pregnant woman. She *could* have said, 'No, Douglas Ripley, we are not going to the beach in the middle of a hurricane, not on your nelly. Now drive me to the nearest hospital so I can have this baby, and put the radio on because apparently that's important.'

But she didn't.

'I was sick of staring at our four walls, Frankie, and I thought the sea air would make me feel better. You weren't due for another week anyway, so you can take that look off your face for starters.'

Here's what they didn't take:

1. A phone.
2. A car.
3. Anything practical in case one of them gave birth.

Here's what they took:

a. A moth-eaten picnic blanket.
b. Mum's favourite coral lipstick.
c. Dad's easel and paints.

Anyway, unsurprisingly, Mum went into labour just after they got to the shingle beach down by the harbour. No one else was around, what with it being January. And the storm. And having normal brains.

And without 1, 2 and 3,
it finally dawned on Mum and
Dad that *I* was going to be born right
on top of a. The moth-eaten picnic blanket.
So they threw it on top of some lumpy pebbles
and hoped for the best. Which was completely
against NHS guidelines at the time, especially under
the bit called 'Good Places to Have a Baby'.

I was not swaddled in a comfy hospital blanket and
cooed over by nurses. Instead I was bundled into a
damp hoodie and seagulls squawked over my head. To
cap it all off, I opened my mouth for some milk but got
a mouthful of salt spray instead. And that was my first
taste of the world:

A LUNGFUL OF STORM.

According to Mum, it moulded me for ever. 'You changed, right then and there,' she'd say. 'I watched the storm come over you, as sudden as a fever. You clenched your tiny fist and you raged up at the sky, like you were having a competition about who could be louder.'

A coral smile would flash on her lips, quick as a fish. 'And sometimes I think a bit of that storm's been stuck inside you ever since.'

Then she'd wander off in the direction of her study, stopping on the way to make her one billionth coffee of the day. Then, *just* as I'd begin to think I'd got away with it, she'd say, 'Oh, and don't forget to put the recycling out.'

And that was my birth story.

But here's an inescapable fact about being born. You might live until you're 101, experience wild success and mountain peaks and dancing monkeys, but however you live and whatever you do, the story of your life will end with a death.

Yours.

That's the deal. Because the thing about human stories is: they all finish more or less the same way. On the final page. The *end*.

But because you're dead you never normally hear that bit. Normally.

BUZZ BUZZ

- 3 -
BUZZES

THAT LAST CHRISTMAS – *our* last Christmas – I grew strange to myself. My emotions felt wilder, my moods harder to control. I'd slam doors and cry for weird reasons.

'Hormones,' Mum would sigh to Dad when she thought I couldn't hear.

I'd heard about those. I wasn't completely sure what they looked like, but I had a feeling they weren't good. Like dark things flapping about inside me. Like the massive wasps' nest we'd found behind the wall in Birdie's bedroom once.

Recently I'd been wondering if there was just a thin wall between me and my hormones too. That if you peeled back my skin there'd be an angry, quivering nest deep within my bones and all my words would turn to buzzes that no one understood.

Other words I heard a lot: *Hot-tempered.*
Temperamental. Moody. Volatile. Quite bolshie, for an
eleven-year-old. They were written in my school reports.
They were uttered in parent meetings. They were said
about me so often that sometimes I didn't know where
I ended and those words began.

And I'm not saying that to excuse all of this – I'm
just saying it. In the interests of a balanced debate.

It was the last day of the Christmas holidays. I was in
Mum's study. My best friend Ivy was on the phone.

'Can you come for lunch at the Crab Pot?' she
asked.

The Crab Pot was the new restaurant down by the
harbour. I'd never actually been inside, but I'd heard
good things. Its white chocolate cheesecake was the
talk of the village. Ivy said it was delicious.

So did Thea Thrubwell.

Thea Thrubwell had been hanging around us for an
entire term. She looked like she was angling to become
Ivy's best friend *instead of me*. I felt like I'd been signed
up for an invisible competition that no one was talking
about, but which I was frankly losing.

Thea was in Ivy's Guides group, and I wasn't.

(I'd been thrown out because of a disagreement with my Guides leader. Well, I called it a disagreement – she called it arson. But I never *meant* to start a fire during the annual Scouts and Guides fundraiser disco. It was those tea lights that were faulty and, like I told the investigating officer at the time, you didn't need a Fire Safety Badge to see *that*.)

Thea had a pony.

Thea had shiny brown hair that didn't go frizzy in the rain.

Thea hadn't burnt down any buildings.

Allegedly.

'Oh, and Thea Thrubwell is coming too. Is that okay?' said Ivy.

Obviously, it was not okay.

'I guess that's okay,' I said.

Thea Thrubwell was bringing her family too, which was just *great*.

'Our mums get on really well,' said Ivy. 'They do yoga together in the hall. Well, they *did*, until it was shut for the refurb—'

'Mmm.'

'Okay. See you at See Pee then.'

'Where?'

Ivy laughed. 'It's just what we call it. It's the initials for Crab Pot. CP?'

'Oh, yeah. Great. See you at the Pot. That's just what we call it, me and, er, them.'

I put the phone down and took a few deep breaths. Then I walked to the sitting room.

Arthur Christmas was on the telly for what felt like the hundredth time. Birdie was doing her new jigsaw puzzle. Mum was flicking through a magazine with one eye on the screen. (And the only yoga *she* was doing was stretching for the bottle of Prosecco by her feet and pouring it into her chipped QUEEN MUM mug.) Dad was fiddling about with paper and kindling in the fireplace.

'Can we go to the Crab Pot for lunch?' I said.

'That pricey place in the harbour?' Dad looked as enthusiastic as if I'd suggested grabbing a bite at the local crematorium. 'I guess. One day.'

'No, can we go *today*? Ivy's going with her family and invited us along too. I said we'd go.'

'You should have checked with us first,' said Dad, lighting a ball of newspaper in the grate.

'I'm checking with you now.'

Mum and Dad looked at each other.

I felt my THROAT TWITCH.
THIS WAS ALWAYS
THE BEGINNING.

When I felt words

down

there,

SLIPPERY STRONG,
wanting to jump

up

like

Salmon.

'It's a nice idea, love,' said Mum, lifting my hopes, only to dash them again by adding, 'but we need more notice than that. Also, there's no point eating out when we've got so many leftovers. All that turkey isn't going to eat itself. Another time.'

'But if you want a fancy lunch *out*,' said Dad, missing the point entirely, 'how about an al-fresco lunch in the garden? It's got the best view in the village, and it's totally free – you can't argue with that.'

He really did think everything was brilliant if you did it in terrible weather. Even then, he was staring outside at the drizzly rain and churning ocean as if it was the most beautiful thing he'd ever seen.

Our house was called Sea View for a reason. A three-hundred-year-old, small fisherman's cottage built at the top of the highest hill behind Cliffstones, it offered panoramic views of – you guessed it – the sea, from every single room at the back of the house. When Mum and Dad had bought it, it hadn't had any electricity or running water. As they were fond of reminding us, our house was a labour of love. They'd spent almost every evening and weekend doing it up. Dad had been up on the roof the day of their wedding, and they spent their honeymoon putting in window frames.

And although Dad often talked about it like it was the greatest masterpiece he'd ever done, to be honest with you, I didn't think it was completely finished. It was rickety. It was rackety. It was freezing in the winter if we ran out of gas or wood. The roof was always leaking somewhere. And it wasn't that clean and tidy either. According to Ivy's parents, Mum and Dad were 'free spirits'. Now, I don't know what free spirits do elsewhere, but in my house, they stayed up late listening to terrible folk music, took us camping in woods *with no toilets*, and were generally allergic to housework.

Those coffee cups dotted on every surface in Mum's study would sit there for *weeks*, quietly growing little personalities of their own, until she decided to do something radical about them, like take them to the kitchen. The piles of paperwork on her desk were so layered they could qualify for their own archaeological dig.

Dad wasn't much better: he wore the same jeans until they fell apart, had permanently grubby fingernails, and trailed a smell of paint, turps and rollie cigarettes wherever he went. And, as you've just seen, he had *very* random ideas about what we should do with our spare time, and it wasn't eating lunch at the Crab Pot. According to him, if you wanted to do something cool, all you had to do was paint in a storm, give birth somewhere inappropriate or (and this was scraping the barrel) literally look out of a window.

'Drink in the colours, girls!' was the rallying cry in our house. 'Take in those views!'

As you can imagine, this could get annoying. As far as I could tell, the sea came in three different colours: blue, green and grey. It was like being told to constantly admire a bruise.

- 4 -
FREAK EARTHQUAKE

I RENEWED MY efforts in the Crab Pot Campaign. 'But I haven't seen Ivy for ages!' I said. 'Not for the entire holidays! Please can we go? Please?'

'You'll see her tomorrow,' said Mum, 'when the new term starts.'

I glanced around the room in desperation and saw, above the Christmas cards on the mantelpiece, someone equally unimpressed. Me. Glaring back at me from the mirror.

Mum always said I'd grow into my face, but that was easy for her to say. Her jaw and mouth seemed to get on with each other, and even though her hair was *also* a mass of tight curls, just like mine, hers never went frizzy.

Dad told me to embrace my uniqueness. I was unconvinced. It was all right for *him* to have thick black eyebrows that almost met in the middle, ruddy cheeks and a strong wide jaw that shoved everything else out of the way so it could bask in the spotlight all by itself. *He* spent most of his life in his shed in the garden, plus he could grow a beard.

I'd definitely got the dregs of the gene pool, no question. Birdie looked more like Mum, with her hazelnut eyes and silky hair that in no way looked as if it had been accidentally electrocuted.

Dad shuffled the pages of his newspaper. I caught a glimpse of the headline. FREAK EARTHQUAKE ON COA—

Mum sipped from her mug and wiggled her toes. 'It's special, the last day of a holiday, isn't it? All of us, at home, nowhere we have to be.'

'It's not that special when you've been at home all week,' I muttered.

Dad shot me a warning, disappointed glance. In our house, you could lose your socks and homework, you could even lose your book bag *at least once a week*, mentioning no names, but *hi, Birdie* – but you could never, *ever*, lose your temper.

'Shouting creates negative energy and harmful interpersonal toxicity,' Dad would say. 'Plus it does our heads in.'

'Frankie,' he said now, once.

Birdie's face creased with worry. She patted the carpet. 'Do my puzzle with me, Frankie,' she offered. 'It's got sunflowers on. Look.'

She gave me a little smile.

My brain flickered like the lights on the tree. On.

Off.

On . . .

Off.

Where it would end up was anyone's guess.

Perhaps I will sit down. Perhaps I will do that puzzle. Perhaps Mum's right, and today's a day for family, and family only.

But then I remembered that easy way Ivy had said, '*It's just what we call it. The CP?*'

She and Thea were so tight now, they were a 'we'. She didn't even have to say her name. Me and Ivy had been like that once. If I missed this lunch, would she ever invite me again? Would Thea Thrubwell speed ahead to the finishing line in our invisible competition for ever?

I rotated my scowl back towards my parents and regarded them with frustration. There was something they weren't saying. This wasn't about leftovers. This

wasn't about sacred family time. This was about *money*.
My bones went

BUZZ

BUZZ

BUZZ

And – I've had some time to think about this, so am
fairly confident with this theory – that's when things
began to go horribly wrong.

- 5 -
A DYING ART

DAD'S OUTPUT WASN'T being consumed in line with current market trends, according to his bank manager. Or as Dad put it, pet portraiture was a noble, misunderstood and dying art. Or as Mum put it, we were broke.

Because, for some mystifying reason, not enough people in our village – or *any* village, actually – were gazing at their pets and thinking: *Do you know what I'd love to do, oh sweet guinea pig of mine? Immortalise you in paint, and fiddlesticks to the cost.*

Dad blamed the internet. For just £9.99, people could upload a photo of their pet from any battered mobile and a mere two days later receive a tea towel, T-shirt *and* key ring printed with that pet's face. Getting all of that for under a tenner seemed, to most of the British public, a better deal than the £275 Dad charged for *one* painting. Which took him a month to paint, not two days.

And he wouldn't even change the price to £274.99, for crying out loud.

'Mum?' I turned pleading eyes on her. Mum worked in catering recruitment and found work for chefs and waitresses. 'You had a bumper month in December, you said!'

But she was shaking her head. 'Well, yes, technically, but we've set aside my commission to spend on stuff that keeps us alive, like food and heating—'

'Which doesn't even *work*—'

'Oi,' said Dad. 'Lower your voice. The energy fields in this room literally just died. I felt it inside me. Very sad.'

I rolled my eyes as loudly as I could.

'I heard that,' he muttered.

'Oh, please stop,' wailed Birdie.

'Yes, pack it in,' said Mum. 'My favourite film is starting in a minute—'

'OH, I'M SORRY,'

I snapped.

'SORRY for RUINING YOUR LIFE with MY ACTUAL NEEDS —'

'That's *enough*.' Dad made some vague sweeping gestures around the room, as if he was trying to shoo the energy fields out of harm's way. 'Go away, Frankie,' he said, 'until you've calmed down.'

'But—'

'Now.'

I glared at him, realised there was no point, and stomped up the stairs towards my bedroom, those words in my mouth writhing with frustration. What happens to strong emotions if you're not allowed to feel them? Where do they *go*?

Because adults are always at it, aren't they? Sorting out and tidying up our feelings, squishing them into other shapes if they don't like the look of them, as if they're made of Play-Doh or something, right from the moment we're born. 'Hush Little Baby, Don't You Cry' is essentially just one long lecture about keeping quiet, but set to music. Then when we get older, it's always 'Don't be cross!', 'Calm down!', 'Buck *up*' and

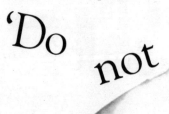

'Do not

set fire to the village hall, even if it is by accident.'

If we're sad, we're told to be happy, but if we laugh, it's a bit too loud. If we're excited, we're told to be quiet. And then they say, 'Everything all right? *You're very quiet.*' It's a losing game all right.

No one ever says: 'You know that big, bad, loud feeling you're experiencing? Well, you go right ahead. Feel away. Don't let us stop you. Look at you, clever girl, expressing your wonderfully complex personality by shouting, going bright red and slamming doors. We admire your efforts to be so in tune with your inner self and applaud your enthusiasm in this area. Here, have a trophy.'

No. They don't. Trust me. I did my research in the field, put it that way.

- 6 -
I COULD HAVE
HANDLED THIS BETTER

TWENTY MINUTES LATER, there was a knock on my bedroom door.

'What?' I said.

Mum poked her head round. Her cheeks were flushed from the fire Dad had lit downstairs, and her mid-morning Prosecco.

'I do know how important friends are, Frankie. Especially at your age. And me and Dad both recognise that you need opportunities to enjoy peer-to-peer interactions.'

I nodded, not entirely sure what she was talking about, but encouraged anyway.

'And your birthday *is* coming up . . .' she added, smiling.

'Seven sleeps.'

'So if it means that much to you, as an early birthday

treat, we'll go to the Crack Bot for lunch. I mean the Crat Pop. The Crab thingy.'

She looked at me in a meaningful way. 'But it's *not* because you shouted at us. I know, underneath it all, you're trying to control your temper. We know it's a challenge for you, and I love you for making an effort, I do. But honestly, Frankie, sometimes I wish you'd find something more important to get angry *about*.'

I leapt off my bed and hugged her. 'Thank you,' I muttered into her woodsmoke curls.

She paused for a moment, as if she wanted to say something else. After a while, she hugged me back. 'Now go and say sorry to Birdie, please, because she hates it when you get cross, and then let's get dressed for our posh lunch.' She glanced out of my window and smiled. 'It's stopped raining. Looks like the sun's trying to come out.'

So I went and made amends. It wasn't a good apology. I was desperate to get going. I mumbled out 'Sorry' and 'Didn't mean it'. But Birdie didn't seem to mind. She just said, 'It's all right' in that husky voice of hers and hugged me tightly, because that's what she was like. Hopeless at bearing grudges. It was hard to believe we were sisters sometimes.

I had to prise her arms away in the end, saying I needed to get dressed. When she asked if I would put a braid in her hair, I said, 'Not *now*' and ran to my room to get changed.

Not, admittedly, my best moment as her big sister. If I'd known how things were going to turn out, I'd have done it all differently. I'd have cuddled her back as tightly as I could. Plaited her hair for hours. Told her how much I loved her, and why.

Then I'd have stood at the front door and said, 'I've changed my mind! Let's not go anywhere *near* the harbour. We'll stay at home all day – what a *great* idea. Consider yourselves under house arrest!'

But I didn't say any of that. Instead I stood in the porch with a face on, and said, 'What's taking you all so long?'

I *hurried* them.

Me. I did that.

Me.

We walked up and down Legkiller Road so much back then I could have navigated it blindfold. It was our path to school, to the harbour and the village. Its real name was Kegmiller Road, but everyone called it Legkiller because of how steep it was. Its other distinguishing features were nettles, brambles, cow pats and potholes, and to reach it you had to cross a rutted field with a scary bull in it called Alan.

But I was so happy about lunch that it might as well have been paved with candyfloss. I practically skipped down it. Within minutes, we crested the hill, and began the slow descent down to the village.

'It's so quiet,' Dad muttered. 'Can't even hear the birds singing.'

It was true. The silence around us felt heavy. There was a weird pressure on my eardrums, and by the look of pain on Birdie's face as she rubbed her ears, I wasn't the only one. And when we got down to Harbour Street, which was *packed* with people enjoying the weak winter sun, all its usual sounds felt muffled. Even the screaming gulls and jangling boat masts that provided a noisy soundtrack to every harbour visit were subdued. It felt like Cliffstones was holding its breath.

We went into the restaurant. The others were already sitting at a table by the window.

'You made it!' said Ivy, giving me a hug.

'Course.' Over Ivy's shoulder, I gave Thea Thrubwell a big beaming smile, a real face-stretcher, and was rewarded by a baffled stare back. *Not the cosy twosome you were expecting, Thrubwell?*

'Sorry it's rather dark,' said the waiter as he took our coats. 'There's just been a power cut.'

'Oh dear,' said Mum.

'Nothing to worry about,' he added. 'Be up and running in a jiffy.'

'Well, as long as the Prosecco doesn't get dangerously warm,' she said.

Outside, a small white terrier by the harbour wall began to bark.

'Sea looks odd, doesn't it?' said Dad, settling himself into his chair.

The dog's yapping grew more frantic. It kept turning around in frenzied circles, then snarling at the sea. The teenager holding its lead looked confused.

'Yes,' said Mrs Thrubwell. 'Glassy.'

'Heard about the earthquake?' said someone. 'France, wasn't it?'

'Only saw the headlines,' said Dad. 'Didn't realise it was—'

'Yes. Not too far away from us either, as the crow flies.'

The little white dog was almost beside itself by now.

The teenager had stopped laughing at it in confusion and was trying to drag it away from the harbour wall. Some people were pointing at the horizon and their mouths were open and their eyes were wide.

'What's everyone looking at?' muttered Mum, squinting into the sunshine.

'Is it *dolphins*?' gasped Birdie, jumping out of her seat. She had a thing about dolphins.

I looked.

It

wasn't

dolphins.

- 7 -
A BAD BATCH OF HOT CHOCOLATE

THERE'S BEEN AN *accident*.

My bed was wet. Oh no. *That* hadn't happened in a while. Not since I was five, at least. I was soaking in it. And not just in my pyjama bottoms either. It was *everywhere*.

My cheeks. My hair.

My eyelashes. Wait – I had wee in my actual eyelashes? *How is that even possible?* I had literally sprayed myself with my own wee overnight. *Did I drink too much hot chocolate last night, when we came back from . . .*

For a scary, sucked-out moment, my brain went blank . . . *The Crab Pot?* Course. Must have drunk too much hot chocolate when we got home. Although – had we got home?

I couldn't *remember*. Couldn't scrape together

any memory of saying goodbye, or walking back up Legkiller. What had we had for lunch, even? *How had the cheesecake tasted?* Nothing was there.

Wait.

No.

I did remember something. There had been a dog. Barking. *Is that really the only thing you remember?* said a voice inside my head.

I frowned and fidgeted uncomfortably in my puddle of wee. No. There were other bits and pieces. Not very nice.

Running?

'Faster, faster.' Mum's voice, hollow, black.

Why had we been running? I waited, holding my breath, to see if anything else would unspool. But nothing. My mind felt like a field at dusk, filled with secrets I couldn't see, things that rustled in the grasses.

I reached up to dab the wee out of my eyelashes. That's when I noticed my hands. They were in a bad shape, badly scratched. All my fingernails had been ripped off.

I felt the first nudge of fear touch me then. Cold wet nose, sniffing me out, not in any rush. *Hi there. Just wanted to let you know I'm around.*

Fortunately, not everything was terrible. I could hear the reassuring sound of someone mowing the lawn. Nothing can ever be that bad when someone is mowing the lawn. This is a scientific fact.

Although why was Dad cutting the grass in January? Just before school? Also, since when had our lawnmower been that loud? And – an unrelated issue, but still worth considering – what was that *gritty coating* on my gums?

I stuck my finger into my mouth to investigate and it came out dusted in sand.

Wee in my eyelashes. Sand in my mouth.

That was when I first knew, I think. That something quite bad had happened. It jumped through those long grasses in my skull so quickly I couldn't see its shape and didn't know its name. But it was there all right.

'Mum? Dad? Birdie? Anyone?'

I pushed myself to a sitting position on the bed. Another nasty surprise. I wasn't in my pyjamas. I was still wearing my clothes from yesterday. And they looked *awful*.

My blue jeans looked like they'd been put through the paper shredder in Mum's office, and just hung off my legs in strips. One of my trainers was missing, while the other was hanging off my feet, barely clinging on. And my new sparkly Christmas jumper, the one I'd been so excited about wearing to lunch, was damp, stretched and shapeless, with rips across both arms.

How had *that* happened? Had I fallen out of bed? Had my clothes caught on something? Or could I have ripped them myself, in my sleep?

That hot chocolate must have been a bad batch.

A very bad batch.

Someone should write and complain.

Exhausted, I let my head droop, and stared in confusion at my lap.

There were lots of tiny white things sticking out of my thighs, visible through the rips in my jeans. With battered fingers I tried to pull one out, noticing my skin had gone all pale and rubbery, like old yoghurt.

But maybe that's just what happens to your skin when you sleep in your own wee for a whole night?

After a few seconds of effort, one of the white things came out with a sucking *pop* and I held it in my hand.

It was a shell.

- 8 -
THEY MAY BE INJURED

THERE WERE LOADS of them, embedded into my skin, sticking out from my thighs. My legs were like those oranges studded with cloves hanging from our Christmas tree downstairs. And you'd think something like that would hurt, but it didn't.

That's because I'm numb with shock though, right?

'Mum? Dad? Birdie?' I shouted.

There was no reply.

They must all be outside, admiring that noisy new lawnmower. I ran to my bedroom window – vaguely aware I hadn't closed my curtains last night, weird – and looked outside.

But Dad wasn't in our garden, mowing the lawn.

Instead it was three helicopters making that roaring sound, slicing through a sky the colour of wet slate. Their beam lights flickered across the clouds.

I ran into Mum and Dad's bedroom. *Empty.*

I went into Birdie's bedroom. *Empty.*

I drew closer to her wonky, sea-facing window. The view outside was different. The sea looked like an overcrowded bath, filled with damaged toys. There were *buildings* in the sea. I saw the roof of Birdie's primary school. At least seven white caravans were in there too, moving up and down in the waves. Here and there were red and yellow boats, snapped in half like crayons broken by a petulant child.

I hurried downstairs, my gait lopsided from running with one shredded trainer and one bare foot.

'Mum? Dad? BIRDIE?'

I yelled for them in the kitchen, the sitting room and Mum's study. But they didn't come.

After searching the cottage three times, I had to face facts.

They're not here. They're missing.

I'll tell you something else that was missing. Their winter jackets and wellies – they weren't in the porch. My parka was also missing. The one I'd put on yesterday.

Had they gone out for a walk before school? Without me, but with my parka? WHY?

And how quiet it was. Mornings at home were

usually noisy, pop songs blaring out from the radio competing with Birdie shouting that she couldn't find her book bag, and the ancient coffee machine grinding through its first cycle of the day. But this morning, our house was more like an empty beach than a home. A beach at the end of the day – footprints washed clean by the tide, human existence rubbed away.

Then someone knocked on the front door.

Phew.

I skidded on the floorboards in my rush to get there, and then stopped. Why were they knocking anyway? They had *keys*.

'Hello?' boomed Mum.

'Anyone there?' roared Dad.

'Anyone hurt?' said a third deep voice.

They did not sound like themselves at all.

Unsure, I took a few steps away, in the direction of the staircase, and then sank down on to its bottom step. I wrapped my arms around myself. The door went *RATTLE RATTLE* and a few seconds later broke apart in a pile of large wooden splinters and a tall man who was definitely *Not Dad* pushed his way through its remains.

Behind him came a woman who was definitely

Not Mum and a shorter man who was definitely *Not Birdie*. These *Nots* wore padded waterproof trousers, the ones that make a swishy noise when you move, big fluorescent jackets and hard hats with the words *Coastal Rescue* on them. I felt a mixture of relief and fear. They didn't look like thieving murderers. On the other hand, they had just kicked our door in.

The three of them stood, gathered before me. The grey light that filled the unlit hallway cast shadows on their faces, making it harder for me to see their eyes. I shivered slightly.

'Hello?' said the woman.

'Hello,' I said.

'Anyone here?' she said, throwing anxious, quick glances around the hallway.

'I'm here,' I said from my step. 'But my parents and sister aren't. Can you help me find them?'

'Okay,' said the woman firmly, and I gave her a grateful smile. 'There's a car in the drive, so it's possible the residents are still at home. I spotted a child's bicycle in the garden so we could be searching for minors. It's possible they can't get to the door, so they may be injured. Let's find some visual ID so we know who we're looking for.'

The two men nodded.

'Right,' said the woman. 'Ed, find the fuse box and switch everything off.'

'Got it,' said *Not Dad*, the tall man.

The woman turned to the shorter man. 'Let's check downstairs first.'

'But I've looked everywhere,' I said. 'Three times at least. They're *definitely* not here.'

In spite of that, they hurried off in the direction of the sitting room.

They're double-checking, I thought, getting up from my step to follow them. *That's nice, I suppose*.

Off we went.

- 9 -
FAMILY PHOTO

ME AND THE three strangers regarded the jumble of blankets and cushions on the sofa, the overturned mugs on the floor, Dad's newspaper sprawled out on the carpet. I stood awkwardly in the doorway, hoping they couldn't smell the wee on me.

'I *have* already checked in here,' I reminded them, as gently as I could.

The man and woman said nothing.

Would it hurt them to reply? I mean, what happened to basic manners?

On the other hand, grown-ups could get that way when they were concentrating. It was like the sound of children's voices stopped their brains from working properly, so they'd demand silence when confronted with a knotty problem.

This happened quite often at school, and whenever our parents were trying to drive to a new campsite and had forgotten a map again. What I was dealing with here was a case of Grown-ups Needing Total Quiet for Their Thinking Time.

The fairy lights on the Christmas tree went dark.

The tall man appeared in the sitting room. 'Circuit's off,' he said. He walked up to the fireplace in his heavy black boots and began to rifle through the Christmas cards.

Hold on a minute!

On top of being ignored by the other two, this was too much. My throat went all scratchy. 'Those are *private.*'

His hand paused for a moment. 'Did you hear that?' he said.

The three of them went very still, as if straining to catch a far-off sound.

'Very funny,' I muttered. 'Point taken.'

Again, this was nothing new. What I was experiencing *here* was that old chestnut, Let's Pretend Our Ears Don't Work to Teach a Child Some Manners. It was boring, it wasn't funny, but it was clearly rather popular among the elderly.

'No,' said the woman, 'but check the kitchen.'

Two of them ran off while I stared at the man nosing

around our mantelpiece. There were deep shadows under his bloodshot eyes, as if he'd been on the go all night without any sleep.

Now I thought about it, the others looked pretty bad too. The way they moved had a heavy feel. They needed a couple of early nights if you asked me.

Tall Man lifted something off the mantelpiece. 'Come and have a look,' he shouted.

The other two ran back, all signs of exhaustion gone, and gazed down at the photo frame in his hands. I smiled when I realised what it was. Our *one* decent family photo.

It shows the four of us at a wedding. We're sitting in a row along a hay bale; me and Birdie in the middle, Mum and Dad on either side. We're flushed, catching our breath between dancing. Mum's looking straight at the camera and laughing. She's wearing that emerald-green dress she bought at the flea market in Swanage, red nail polish on her dirty bare feet, eyes all bright and shining.

The exceptional wonkiness of Dad's smile, always a handy barometer in letting us know how happy he is, is dialled all the way up to ten. He's gazing over my head and Birdie's at Mum, and looks quite handsome, his teeth white in a tanned face, his unruly hair sort of combed for once. Birdie and I have our arms around each other. There are cornflowers braided into our hair. They look like blue stars. Birdie's eyes are closed and she's got the goofiest grin on as she nestles into me.

The three strangers stared at that photo a bit too long. *We're just regular human beings, guys. Seriously. You should see all our other family albums – I look dreadful in those. This was a total fluke.*

And then I realised none of them was smiling. Just like that, the whole house changed. Like a drop of paint falling into water, sadness stained the room.

The woman pressed her lips tightly before releasing them again. 'We might be looking for a family then. One man, one woman and two young girls.'

'Er, you don't need to find *two*,' I said. 'Just one? *I'm right here*. It's my little sister
that's miss—'
And then
my voice
tailed off.

Because I'd finally realised.

Although you guessed a few chapters back, didn't you?

- 10 -
THE TRUTH

THE TRUTH DANCED in front of my eyes like it was written by a sparkler on Bonfire Night, teasingly incomplete, almost too bright to look at, fading to nothing at the end.

But could it really be true? I mean, what were the chances?

The three Coastal Rescue people ran upstairs, calling out in quick, clipped voices.

I staggered after them in a daze, as my brain began to sift through things. To test my theory, I sneaked up behind them on the upstairs landing and screamed as loud as I could.

Nothing.

Zip. Zilch. Not so much as a shudder.

The shorter man went into Birdie's bedroom.

'This might hurt,' I said, and tried to kick him on his backside.

He needn't have worried. My foot stopped just short of his swishy trousers, as if some invisible barrier protected him. He didn't even turn around.

Gasping, I ran to the upstairs bathroom and stared at the mirror above the sink. Staring back was something stormy, strong and tempestuous – but it wasn't me. It was one of Dad's seascapes that hung on the wall opposite.

I waved my battered hand in front of the mirror. Nothing.

One final test.

Taking a deep breath, I hurled myself down the stairs, making sure to bang my head against the banisters on the way. Didn't feel a thing.

I sat at the bottom of the staircase and dealt with the facts. I hadn't woken up in wee. I had woken up in seawater.

Now I remembered what that dog had barked at so desperately. What we'd tried to run from. Suddenly, in one dreadful moment, it all came flooding back to me. As it were.

At the beginning, when we saw the wave from our window table, the fear had come in quite slyly, like it was stapled on to the end of a joke. The wave was still quite far away, just by the end of the jetty, and that was surely as close as it would come.

Plus people in Cliffstones moved slowly; nothing was done in a rush. That was the Dorset way.

So at first, we didn't even think about escaping.

We'd just looked for a while. Gazed, while it gathered itself together, quietly, stealthily. We'd watched it. What we hadn't realised, of course, was that it was also watching us.

Glossy as a blackberry, the sea had pleated and rippled against itself, and then it had risen, a sea monster *made of the actual sea*, and as it built itself up into this new, nightmarish height, it seemed to say, '*Bet you didn't think I could do* this!' And then it no longer looked anything like the sea I'd known all my life – the paddling, running in and squealing sea, the bright blue crabbing sea, the postcard sea of our summers.

This was a different, alien sea. This was the sea *beneath*. The one that made you shudder and snatch your hand out when you glimpsed it from a boat.

It was only when the wave went *over* the jetty, instead of around it, and tipped the people right into itself in a horrible gathering, like a malevolent mother folding children into her skirt, that the stampede inside the restaurant began, even though it had been too late by then, of course.

Mum and Dad reached for us and we ran to the door but there was too much of a crush. Dad picked up a chair and threw it at the window and we'd scrambled out of that, cutting ourselves on the glass in our rush to escape.

I looked at the nicks on my hands. *Ah*.

But even when we were scrabbling out of the Crab Pot, even *then*, some disbelief lingered. The sea – *our* sea, our *friend* – would surely realise its mistake? Would drop back down to a less threatening height? And somehow it would stop oozing towards us, would slink back, *shrink* back, to a safe spot beyond the harbour wall, *back where it belonged*, saying in a watery and very sorry way, 'Whoops! My bad! Don't know what I was thinking of! Here's the people I swallowed earlier – do have them back, and let's pretend this never happened, shall we?' and we'd all gasp with relief and go about our day.

That was going to happen, any second.

Any *second*.

Once the four of us had struggled out of the broken window, we ran.

Dad, grey with fear,
attempted to gather up Birdie in his
arms as we stumbled along the pavement,
trying to dodge the scrum around us, but it
wasn't a smooth movement and she bobbed
awkwardly in his arms, her face one terrified
question mark. Over Dad's shoulder, her eyes
met mine and I tried to say sorry, but my mouth
was all twisted, and the wave was so close and so loud
she wouldn't have heard me anyway.

Mum gripped my hand in hers as we ran, making strange sobbing noises.

The wave was now just outside the harbour wall, just a few paces away.

It will turn back, I thought.

But it didn't turn back. It charged.

Leapt over the wall with greedy, outstretched, frothing, white fingers. Shut the little dog up for ever. Ripped hands out of hands, people from people. And that had been that. The bruise I'd always been told to admire had turned into a bruiser and finished us right off.

I couldn't remember coming back from the Crab Pot because I *hadn't* come back.

Not
alive
anyway.

I was dead.
I had drowned.
I held my fingernails up
to my face. I hadn't bitten them
off. They'd been *ripped* off. I took in
my ragged clothes, shredded trainers, those
shells sticking out of my legs. *Now* they made sense.

Born by the sea, died by the sea. Exit: me.

And if Dad had been with me right then and there, he'd probably have made it all about Art, by saying something meaningful in that philosophical way he had. Something like: 'Well, Franks, really that's got a bittersweet symmetry when you think about it' or 'Maybe we *do* always return to the source of our own beginnings.' But he wasn't with me and anyway he'd have been wrong.

I wasn't a work of art. I wasn't a thought-provoking allegory.

I was *dead*.

Well, technically, I was dead-*ish*.

- 11 -
HUMAN FLESH IS YUCK

I WAS DOING pretty well for myself, as far as death went. This was death with added features. I could still walk. Talk. Waggle my fingers in front of my face. The only thing I couldn't do, apparently, was communicate with the living. Or feel physical pain where pain should be. It was a strange sensation, not having to breathe. My lungs didn't work. My chest didn't rise. I was just rawness, stunned with bright shock.

I closed my eyes and listened, numb, as my brain whispered questions. Questions like: Why had only *I* come back? Was I a ghost? A spirit? A ghoul? If I was dead, was I meant to call my body a corpse now? I stared down at myself and shuddered. And then thought: *Does it matter what I call it?* I had died. We had died. The shock of it shrieked through me like a forest fire. My brain whispered: *What happens now?*

But, most importantly of all, *where* were the rest of

my family? And how was I meant to fill in the time until they came back?

Because they *were* coming back, right?

Right?

After a while, the rescue crew appeared at the top of the staircase. I automatically moved to the side of the step I was sitting on, but then a dreadful thing happened. The woman walked straight *through* me.

It was a sickening sensation. It was like being squished and shoved by a herd of water buffaloes. As her body moved through mine, everything I thought should remain in one place, like my lungs and kidneys and all those other delicate organs that shouldn't, as a rule, be messed about with, shifted to the side to accommodate *her*. I felt like a tube of toothpaste being squeezed.

And worse than all of that was the flavour it left in my mouth. *Urgh, the taste.*

Have you ever tasted human flesh?

Actually, don't answer that. Let's just assume the answer is no. Long story short, it's *nothing like chicken.* It's disgusting. I tasted muscle and fat and blood and also some hastily digested bacon and eggs that were roughly twelve hours old. A mouthful of body.

I tasted other things too. Emotions. Traces of thoughts. Sorrow and grief and fatigue. It was like something wet and cold crawling across my tongue.

She emerged out of me with a small but audible *squelch*. And then, because I hadn't moved from the step, it happened AGAIN.

And then ONCE MORE JUST FOR FUN.

Once they'd all had a go, I wanted to be sick. The sour aftertaste of three humans mingled on my tongue.

The three of them gathered in the hallway. They looked shattered.

Not Mum looked into the faces of the others. 'I'm calling it. Agreed?'

After a pause, the other *Nots* nodded.

She reached for her walkie-talkie. 'This is Rescue, over,' she said.

The device in her hands gave out a blare of static.

Someone said, 'What's the report, over?'

'No survivors found. House checked thoroughly. We presume the family perished down in the harbour. There are no coats or boots in the porch and the house is empty. Over.'

Over.

There was a pause, then the static voice said, 'We'll circle back. Get ready to leave in approximately twelve minutes, over.'

They moved towards our broken front door. Tall Man rubbed his eyes and hung back. *Not Mum* touched his shoulder.

'Ed,' she said gently, 'we've done all we can. There's no one here.'

He sighed. 'I just . . . keep feeling like we've missed something, you know? I have the strongest feeling that someone's still here.'

Is he talking about me? Can he . . . somehow sense me?

'Let me check downstairs again.'

In the sitting room, I gave it my all. I shouted until my throat ached. But although he heard *something* – that much was clear from the way he repeatedly stopped and cocked his head – I couldn't get through. He was plainly a sensitive type – he could *feel* that I was around, but that was all.

Something made him stop. He picked up the newspaper on the floor. The one Dad had been trying to read until I . . .

Until I . . .

What, you want me to tell you *twice*? It was

hard enough the first time.

He rifled through the paper and threw it on the floor again, looking crestfallen.

I hurried over. It had fallen open at a double spread. The headline read:

FREAK EARTHQUAKE ON COAST OF FRANCE KILLS HUNDREDS AND MAY NOT BE DONE YET, EXPERTS WARN.

I peered at it. Next to the headline was a map showing exactly *where* in France the earthquake had struck: a little town called Omonville-la-Petite. Cliffstones was almost directly opposite it. Only a matter of miles, really, across the English Channel. My eyes flicked back to the headline.

MAY NOT BE DONE

Back in the hallway, Tall Man rubbed his eyes. 'It's tragic, really. They had the facts at their fingertips. If only they'd *realised* what that earthquake would do—'

'Stop,' said the other man gently. 'No use thinking

like that. Lots of things should have been done differently. Experts should have issued a warning earlier. It didn't help that there was a power cut just before it struck, and there's so little connection here, I doubt anyone would have seen the alerts on their mobiles in time anyway. It's just horrible bad luck.'

The sound of the helicopter, growling in the sky, grew louder.

Tall Man sighed. 'It's just so desperately sad that this family drowned when they lived in the safest place in the entire village. If they'd stayed, they'd have lived. And then the village wouldn't have been wiped out completely.'

Silently, the woman touched his arm, tilted her head in the direction of the door. The three stepped out of the broken doorway into the roar of the helicopter outside.

I sank on to the hall floor, my thoughts scattering like a flock of seagulls. The full realisation of what he'd said – what I'd *done* – sluiced over me, just as cold, just as deathly, as the wave.

No survivors. Wiped out completely, he said.

But if we'd stayed at home, we'd have lived.

But we didn't get a chance to stay at home, did we?

No.
And whose fault was that?
Yep.

                              Little old me.

- 12 -
NOT VERY PROUD OF MYSELF

THIS IS ALL *my fault*. None of my family had wanted to go out for lunch! They'd wanted to stay at home by the fire! They only came out to *please* me, because they were kind and loving. And I'd repaid that love by leading them right into the mouth of a monster that had swallowed us up as casually as a sweet.

I cupped my head in my hands. My battered fingers explored my new dead face. They discovered the open wound next to my right eyebrow, the cut on my nose, grazes down both cheeks: the result of being dragged along the seabed for a couple of hours.

Oh, do you like my makeover? Yeah, I got it from the universe. Why? Well, I fancied a spot of lunch with my best friend, to stop her becoming best friends with someone else, and basically murdered my entire family. You get the face you deserve, so here's mine, messed up and nasty, just like my HEART.

Guilt, like a million tiny fish hooks, twisted and caught inside me.

A good cry will make you feel better – that was what Mum always said, and I tried to get one going, but proper tears wouldn't come, because: a) I didn't deserve to feel better and b) my tear ducts were dealing with a permanent shutdown, because c) I was *dead*.

The booming helicopters grew quieter, then faded completely. The only sounds in the house were my ragged, dry sobs. I pulled each name out of me with an awful cold sorrow, like counting marbles out of a bag.

Mum.

Dad.

Birdie.

Me.

Ivy, and her family, and my teachers and my classmates, and the woman at the fish-and-chip shop, and the nice man who sang sea shanties on the bench by the boathouse every Saturday afternoon.

Birdie's best friend, little Emma, who always had slightly crusty nostrils, but we all loved her anyway and . . .

The man who dropped the milk off and . . .

Our school hamster.

The white dog who'd tried to warn us.

Everyone. Everyone I'd ever known. My village. My entire life.

When I closed my eyes I saw terrible things, frightened faces and outstretched hands caught for ever like insects in amber.

I was desperate to breathe, to swim to the surface of my grief and take a deep, juddering intake of air, escape the pain. But the sea had stolen my last breath. Instead my mouth opened and shut hopelessly, like a fish that knew its time was up.

Hours passed. I sat in a damp heap on the hallway rug, my clothes still wet, my skin still wrinkly, as the sky darkened.

The gently flickering fairy lights strung on the stairway banisters spluttered until their batteries ran out and then the gloom of the house wrapped its arms around me. And still I sat, and waited for Mum and Dad and Birdie. I was desperate to see them and say sorry. I yearned to hug them, to look into their faces and be scolded, then forgiven. And my brain clung desperately to this flicker of hope, like a raft.

They won't be much longer. They won't. They'll be back. Any minute now.

Any.

Minute.

Now.

- 13 -
LIFE'S TRICKY WHEN YOU'RE DEAD

MOONSHINE HAD BEGUN to struggle through the clouds beyond the door. Still no one came. What were they doing, coming back via the scenic route?

I peeled myself off the floor, leaving a damp patch behind. There was a wet sheen of moisture on my skin and the salt tang was still in my mouth. I had that horrible wet chill you get if you've worn a damp wetsuit too long. Was that normal? Was I *always* going to look and feel as I did at my moment of death? Wet and battered and coated with sea salt? Studded with shells like a trinket box from a seaside gift shop?

Oh, what was taking them so long? Did they need a sign I was here, waiting for them?

I ran to the kitchen. A *torch* was what I wanted. I'd flash out some Morse code from our back garden. If they were in the waves, they'd read my message and come back.

There was just the tiniest problem. I didn't know any Morse code.

Make that two problems.

I couldn't open any of the kitchen drawers to find a torch in the first place. It didn't matter how hard I tried, my fingers slid off their surfaces. I remembered how my attempts to connect with that man's backside had failed – my foot had just darted off at the last minute, like the wrong end of a magnet resisting another.

Yet I was able to touch my own body. I could pull shells out of my rubbery dead skin and run a hand through my matted salty hair, *lucky me*. But I couldn't physically *touch* anyone that was alive.

And, it appeared, the same rule applied to physical stuff – *bits*, glass and wood and metal and other people. Anything outside me, essentially.

I glared at the drawer. Our torch was *inside it*. I tried to hit the handle as hard as I could, scrabbled at it, banged it with frustration, even resorted to growling at it, but no dice. Getting any kind of grip on the handle remained impossible.

So: I could sit on a step but I couldn't open a drawer. I could walk up and down the staircase and move through rooms but I couldn't open a door. I could hear and see people that were alive, but I couldn't make them see and hear *me*. Things could happen to *me*, but I couldn't make *things happen*.

So far, being dead wasn't what I'd call an empowering experience.

Maybe there was one thing. If I was dead, could I . . .

. . . fly?

I did try hard. I gave it a good go. By which I mean, I hopped about a bit, flapped my battered arms and hands around, leant forward and strained, frowning, into space. Nothing.

Flightless as an emu.

There was literally nothing cool about being dead at all.

I slapped a hand to my forehead.

None of this mattered.

Why was I getting distracted? I needed to contact Mum, Dad and Birdie before they spent another night out – I glanced through the study window and shivered involuntarily – *there*. Whether or not I could move through a door or *fly* was totally insignificant compared to that.

Luckily the front door was still open – swinging off

its hinges from being kicked in earlier by the rescue crew. I ran through it and then circled round the house, towards the back garden that faced the sea.

'MUM! DAD! BIRDIE!'

The night swallowed my words up silently.

I cast them out again.

'I'M HERE! FRANKIE! I'M AT HOME! PLEASE – COME BACK!'

In the dark, the sea smiled its treacherous wet smile, replete from its feast.

'I'M SO SORRY WE'RE ALL DEAD! REALLY, REALLY SORRY!'

Out of the silver clouds came a cry. Was it Birdie, calling my name? I held myself still, like a quivering arrow, desperate to hear her again.

But it was just a stupid gull, saying, *EEEE, EEEE*.

What else could I do to find them? Shouting into the darkness wasn't enough.

I had to go to the place where it happened.

To the harbour. Right away. Not a moment to lose.

- 14 -
THIEVING GURNARDS,
SHIPS IN THE NIGHT

FIRST OFF, BETTER get my coat. I turned back to the house, then stopped. I'd never need to think about putting on my parka again, which was probably just as well. I must have lost it in that giant wave. Some fish was probably wearing it; a gurnard, most likely. They always looked like they were after something.

I ran into Alan the bull's field. He looked alarmed, his ears pricked up, and then he reared up on his hind legs and went charging off into the distance. It was sort of gratifying and, on this dreadful day, I would take any comfort I could get. *Not such a big scary boy now, are you?*

I'd just reached the stile at the opposite end when the clouds peeled back, and what remained of Cliffstones was bathed in the moon's merciless light.

Nothing familiar remained – not the playground, or

the half-built village hall, or the little rows of fishermen's cottages. The wave had slithered over it and smashed it in its wake. And as the gleaming light crept over the village's remains, I couldn't help but shiver. *I'd perished down there*. And now I was planning to *go back*?

What are you afraid of, Frankie Ripley – dying?

With a bleak grin, I hopped over the stile.

And then something odd happened. As soon as I reached Legkiller Road, my legs stopped working. Instead of walking, they just jerked back and forwards, like a toy running out of battery.

Confusion filled me on the quiet dark road. Would my body begin to shut down now? Perhaps the last twenty-four hours had been an accidental blip of consciousness on my way to proper deadness. Maybe I was like one of those chickens who ran about a bit after their head was chopped off – and if so, how much longer did I have before I died *properly*?

As these questions ran through me, a large pair of mustard eyes glowed in the darkness, accompanied by a rusty squeaking sound.

I frowned into the shadows. Terror drummed away inside my busted heart. Something was moving up Legkiller Road. Something large. Something crusty and pitted. And it – whatever *it* was – was heading right towards me.

When it was just a few metres away, the clouds parted again and bathed the huge object in a silvery light.

It was a *shipwreck*. Dripping wet, festooned with strings of seaweed, covered with a bumpy skin of molluscs. From its rusting hulk came the briny smell of saltwater and decay.

Oh God.

Had death come for me at last? Had the wave finally realised it was missing a body from its terrible haul and sent this ship to hunt me down and drag me back?

I frowned at the sopping vessel as it came nearer.

Oh.

It *wasn't* a ship.

It was a *bus*.

But it was definitely still a wreck. A double-decker bus wreck. The glass in all its windows had long gone and, despite its creaky yet undeniably *forward* propulsion, all four wheels were flat. It didn't even look like there was anyone at the wheel.

And as it lurched its way towards me, like a tipsy grown-up at one of my parents' parties, I heard, faintly but unmistakably, the sound of children crying and wailing coming from its belly.

Which was obviously, as you can imagine, a really lovely, reassuring sound.

- 15 -
GET ON BOARD, DUCKIE

ALL I COULD do was stand and stare as the bus creaked towards me. The moon picked out every unsavoury detail. Its wheels were flaps of shredded rubber that looked like they'd last been inflated sometime around doomsday. There was a row of crabs clinging to the top of the bus, clacking their claws threateningly like stern Spanish dancers. Most of its side panels were clinging on by a nail. All it would take to blow it apart would be one windy day.

And on each deck, like eggs in a box, was a clutch of faces, all turned in my direction.

The wind howled around us.

I gulped. *Should I shout for help?*

But who would hear me? No one's left.

The sound of slow, determined footsteps rang out from inside the wreck. A few seconds later, the warped front door flew open with a squeak and a bang. And in the doorway, bathed in the ashen January moonlight, stood a middle-aged woman in a shapeless beige suit, carrying a clipboard. She wore the biggest pair of glasses I had *ever seen*.

She glanced at the clipboard in her hands and stared at me.

I straightened my shoulders and returned her gaze.

Somewhere, an owl hooted.

A polite cough. 'Perished in the Cliffstones tsunami of January the third?' she enquired delicately.

'Pardon?'

'Perished in the Cliffstones tsunami of January the third?'

'Was *that* what it was?' I said. 'A tsunami?'

She sighed. 'Did you, or did you not, die in the Cliffstones tsunami of January the third?'

A bat slipped out of the mangled roof and shot into the night.

'I guess?' I said.

This answer seemed to satisfy her and she put a tick on her clipboard. 'Frances Frida Ripley?'

'Yes,' I said. 'How'd you know that? Can you help me find my fam—'

'You're my last pick-up,' she said. 'Time to get on board.'

I stared at her. 'What?'

Through her glasses two leached, drained eyes regarded me.

'On board the bus, duckie. For the Afterlife Club,' she said. Her voice was as flat as the tyres on the bus.

'The Afterlife Club?'

'Yes, dear.' She pointed to the front of the bus. 'Read.'

The faded destination sign said: *The Afterlife Club, for ages twelve and under. Enjoy death with friends, games and endless days out!*

I've always been suspicious of exclamation marks and that one was the most desperate I'd ever seen. I eyed it warily, then glanced at the woman. 'I don't . . . understand . . . What?'

'According to our records, you drowned when you were eleven years old, so this is the bus for you.'

But I had questions, starting with the faces visible through the windows. 'Who else is on that bus?'

'Lots of other children like you, picked up over the years,' the woman said. 'We're quite full now, on account of the tsunami. Had to go down to the seabed for an unscheduled detour. Picked up quite a few new passengers. Bit inconvenient you weren't down there, as a matter of fact,' she added, pursing her lips in a way that reminded me of most of my teachers.

'Um,' I said. 'Sorry?'

'Quite unusual, your corpse wandering away from the site of death. Doesn't happen very often. Only with the most difficult children, I've noticed. Bit of a troublemaker, are you?' She looked at me thoughtfully.

I was only half listening, too busy with my own thoughts. If she'd been down on the seabed, trawling for Cliffstones children under the age of twelve, then . . .

'Is my sister on there?' I yelled.

'What's her name?'

'Birdie. Well, her name's Bridget, but we call her Birdie, because she's constantly whistling. Bridget Ripley?'

My mouth was dry as the woman checked her clipboard.

'I'm afraid not,' she said finally. 'No one of that name on the bus. She must have died *properly*. Younger, was she? Less . . . trouble?'

I nodded, unable to speak.

'I'm sorry for your loss,' she said quite kindly.

I took a deep breath and waited for the pain to subside. My thoughts rattled like an out-of-control slot machine. If we were all dead, then . . .

'Is this . . . heaven?' I asked.

The woman turned and contemplated the barnacled wreck behind her.

From the top deck came the sound of shouting and arguing. Several snotty children in the lower deck had begun to whine.

'Does it look like heaven?' she said finally.

'No,' I admitted. 'Not much.'

She sniffed. 'You've got a funny idea of heaven, Frances, if you think it's carting a disintegrating rust bucket around the world looking after a bunch of kids who never learnt any real manners while they were alive and apparently believe it's too late to start now. *Some* death chaperones get to circumnavigate the globe with Patrick Swayze – now *that* would have been my idea of heaven – but oh no, old Jill from Canvey Island gets lumbered with the under-twelves, which most definitely is not a place of eternal peace, believe you me.'

'But . . . why? If this isn't . . . why am I still around? I can walk, talk, think . . .'

Blinking several times, she fixed me with those tired eyes. 'This all gets covered on the bus. There's a slideshow. I can sit down. Can't you just get on and watch it?'

I jutted my chin out. 'I don't know anything about you. You're *stranger danger.*'

Jill sighed. 'Please?'

'I'm not getting on that bus until I know more.'

She closed her eyes and her shoulders slumped. 'Okay,' she said. '*Fine.*'

- 16 -
A MANUFACTURING SNAG

'WELL THEN?' I said.

Jill pushed her glasses up her nose and they slid back down again.

'Look,' she said. 'There are lots of reasons why people don't properly die. But the most common one is that there's a toodoo.'

I almost laughed. 'Pardon?'

'A toodoo. Hanging over you.'

'Say it one more time.'

'You've got unfinished business,' she said firmly.

'Huh?'

'There's something you haven't done yet that you have to do. Hence, a —'

'Oh!' I said. 'A To Do.'

'That's what I said,' she said.

'Like what?'

'Gordon Bennett, Frances, how am I supposed to

know? It might not be a big thing. You wouldn't believe the number of people who forget to turn their kitchen appliances off. Have you left the gas on?'

'I'm eleven years old.'

'Oh. In that case, any homework you forgot to hand in?'

I thought for a while. From the top deck of the bus, I saw a boy I recognised from Year Ten. We waved at each other.

'Maybe?'

The strange woman in front of me sighed. 'Right, well, you think about that. Because the moment you do it, you can die *properly*.'

'What if I can't think of a To Do? What if there isn't one? What if I'm an All Done?'

'Well, another possible reason you're still around could be that you're a Difficult Button.'

'Difficult Button?'

'The ones that are too stubborn to totally pass over to the other side. Very common in this age group, actually.'

She threw a frustrated glance behind her, barked 'QUIET!' at the fierce row blossoming on the top deck over whose turn it was to sit next to the window, and flicked an eye-roll at me.

'It's all in the slideshow,' she said hopefully.

'Nope.'

Her eyes revealed a great deal of inner suffering. 'Think of yourself as a button.'

'Button?' I said helpfully.

'Now, think of Life as a shirt, and all the buttonholes as Death.'

'Er,' I said.

'Now, normally, when a button – sorry, *human* – dies, they pass through the buttonhole easily enough, slip right through, and they come out the other side, and they're properly dead. Or what we in the trade call "*dead* dead". Everything's gone: consciousness, spirit, soul, the whole shebang. They're buried, there's a funeral, everyone has a cry, then there are sandwiches, right? The normal way. The proper way.'

'Okay.'

'But if you're a Difficult Button, what happens is, you don't quite get *through* the buttonhole. You're stuck in the midway point – one foot in death, one foot in life – causing an administrative headache. Anyway, it's normally the stubborn, hard-headed, *challenging* types . . .' she gave me a loaded look I didn't appreciate, 'who don't die properly. They don't fully surrender to death. In other words . . .'

I remembered, for a moment, how I'd told myself that the wave would turn back, that it wouldn't really break over the harbour wall. Even as the water ripped Mum's hand out of mine, there'd been a tiny part of me insisting, *This isn't happening, this isn't—*

'. . . they *resist*. At the very point it matters most, Difficult Buttons do not accept death, and their consciousness somehow drags them into this sort of halfway house. An existence, without a proper life attached.' The woman shook her head. 'Therefore they're stuck in the buttonhole. Honestly, why they don't cover this in schools is beyond me.'

'So, which one am I? A To Do, or a Difficult Button?'

Jill squinted at her clipboard and then back at me. 'It's not clear yet. You might be both. Between you and me, these files they send from the back office aren't worth the paper they're written on. I'm sure it will all be sorted out eventually. In the meantime, you need to get on the bus. You're an unaccompanied minor, which means you're not permitted to be dead by yourself. You need a guardian, and that is me, and you need a new place of abode, and that is the bus.'

'I can't be dead by myself? Says who?'

'Says the ones in charge.' Her voice was matter of fact yet also firm. 'We've got a strict code of conduct to abide by, rules and re-ghoul-ations. You might be dead, Frances, but there's no need to be reckless.'

I had another disturbing thought. 'Are you . . . *God* then? Or . . .' I swallowed, 'the other one?'

It seemed for a moment that her pupils had grown oddly yellow, like the headlights on the bus. Yet her smile was kind and wise. Or was that just the moonlight rippling over her face?

My thoughts grew electric and wild, as if I'd started flicking through a private diary that I had no business in, and I was afraid. She regarded me a minute, and coughed slightly. Now she just looked like a middle-aged woman in a shapeless suit again, and I was surprised at how much of a relief that was.

'Calm yourself. I'm *Jill*. I'm a death guardian. No one important, just an employee. Thirty-three years of service, thank you very much, ever since lung cancer did for me. Cigarettes . . .' she fixed me with a longing look, '*do* kill you, as it turns out.'

'So . . . where does the bus go?'

'Everywhere,' said Jill simply. 'Well, anywhere

there's a children's attraction, at any rate. This bus will take you around the world – not in style, admittedly.' She shot it a rueful look. 'But it does the job. We make a lot of scheduled stops on the way – lots of chances to get off and stretch your legs, and of course plenty of chances to go on rides completely free of charge. Theme parks, water slides, and of course the Harry Potter studios are very popular—'

'How long's the trip?'

'It can be as little as a couple of months if you meet the obligations of your To Do, or a *lot* longer if you're a Difficult Button and take a while to accept death. Spirits *can* take much longer to decompose than bodies. Whoever came up with the human race *really* didn't think this part through and I'm sure this manufacturing snag is a matter of deep personal regret to them, even now. Now, how about getting on, duckie?'

I glanced at the mangled remains of the bus. Peered past it, towards what was left of the village in the moonlight. If my sister wasn't on the bus, then there was only one other place she could be.

'*No.*'

She looked at me wearily. Glanced down at her clipboard. Pushed her glasses back up her nose and fixed me with her eerie stare.

'Honestly, Frances, I do hope you weren't like this when you were alive. It's *exhausting*.'

- 17 -
LESS AND OTHER PROBLEMS

'COME ON,' SAID Jill. 'Don't make this any more difficult than it has to be. I'm not your enemy, I'm your guardian, and it's my job to make sure you spend your death days in the care of a responsible adult. Now get on the bus.'

'No,' I said again.

A few kids cheered.

Jill's shoulders stiffened. 'Look, no one under the age of twelve is allowed to wander through the afterlife by themselves. I'm doing this for you, Frances. It's for your own good.'

'I can't just *leave* and go wandering around the world in some random bus without seeing my family again,' I said stubbornly. 'They're nearby, I just know they are, and I need to wait for them to come back.'

Jill's face softened slightly, but she shook her head. 'I don't think so, dear. If they haven't made their way back by now, it's highly likely they're gone for good.

Either way, I can't leave you unaccompanied in your house – you'll be all alone.'

'I don't care,' I said loudly. 'I'm not getting on that bus.'

The cheers on the bus got louder.

A few children started to say, 'Miss, *miss*, we don't want to be on the bus any more either.'

'Yeah, let us off too!'

Jill contemplated her nicotine-stained fingers longingly. After a moment, she began to root around in her jacket pocket with a shaking hand. She produced a mouldy packet of chewing gum, unwrapped a piece and began to chew it, all the while muttering to herself.

'You've had a child, they said. You'll *love* this job, they said. You'll be a *natural*. It's so rewarding caring for children . . .'

Part of me was sorry for the trouble I was obviously causing her. Jill seemed okay, underneath it all. But I *had* to stay behind. My family had *died* because of me. I would wait for them at home. It was the least I could do. Besides, what was it Mum and Dad said, anytime we went anywhere crowded? '*If we lose each other, stay right where you are, and we'll come and get you. Don't go wandering off, okay?*'

So that's what I was going to do. Stay in Cliffstones

– or what was left of it. No-brainer.

'Smell you later,' I said resolutely, and turned to walk off.

The children clapped and cheered as I tried to circle the back of the bus so I could resume my walk towards the harbour. Yet, just as they'd done before, my legs refused to work. I gave them a frustrated look. *I am trying to make a dignified exit here, not shuffle about hopelessly. Any chance you could make an effort?*

Jill gave me a sympathetic look. 'Ah, I see you've discovered the Urgent Barrier Enforcement of Juvenile Corpses.'

'Eh?' I said through gritted teeth, straining my muscles as hard as I could.

'Well, it's a safeguarding measure,' she said. 'Put in place to prevent exactly this type of unauthorised wandering by unaccompanied minors. Basically, corpses under the age of twelve aren't allowed to stray more than a few hundred metres from their home if they're alone. It got put in place a few years ago, when management *finally* realised that we couldn't just have wailing dead youngsters wandering all over the country.'

I did some quick experiments. Irritatingly, Jill was

right. My legs *did* feel as if they were being controlled. When I took a step in the direction of home, they moved easily. Any attempt to go forward, however – like, oooh, I don't know, towards the harbour to search for my dead family, for *example* – and they froze completely, as if stuck in cement. I was like one of those supermarket trolleys fitted with an alarm to stop people from taking them further than the car park.

So that was *great*.

Behind us, the bus of dead children began to fill with impatient sounds; someone was doing a very deliberate sigh. The faces at the windows had changed from expectant to exasperated.

Someone began to sing 'Why Are We Waiting?'

'Getting restless,' muttered Jill. 'That will be fun to deal with on the M5.' She did that mouth-pursing thing again. 'Look, Frances, if you stay behind, you won't be able to go *anywhere*, and that will get very boring very quickly, especially when you're alone. Don't bring it on yourself – it's not worth it.'

With a decisive movement, she turned back towards the bus and put one step on the threshold. Its ghostly engine started up again.

'I'M NOT GETTING ON THE BUS,'

I repeated.

She turned from the doorway and regarded me uncertainly.

'Don't you want to go to Disney World?' she said pleadingly. 'See Donald Duck?'

A few children automatically cheered.

'No,' I said firmly. 'I'm too old for that stuff. Anyway, I *won't* be alone. My family's going to come back for me. They'll be here soon. I know it.'

In the doorway, Jill fell silent. The dirty yellow headlights of the bus smouldered in the dark.

I pulled my trump card. 'Besides, if you force me on that bus against my will, I'll spend *years* asking if we're nearly there yet. On repeat. Loudly. In your ear. While I sit next to you.'

She flinched. 'After all, how much harm can you do alone, especially if you can't wander too far from home?'

'*Exactly*,' I said, sensing my advantage. 'That Urgent Barrier thingy for Juvenile Corpses – it's as good as a babysitter. Anyway, it's not like I'm going to be alone for long – they'll be back by the end of the day.'

'Tell you what,' she said eventually. 'I'll come back and check on you, just in case.'

'Pardon?'

'Next time I find myself in your neck of the woods . . .' she glanced at her clipboard, as if checking a timetable, 'I'll swing by, see if you're still around. And if you are – well, I'll save you a seat, in case you fancy joining us. How about that?'

I was oddly touched by this gesture. 'Okay. Thanks. You really won't have to worry though.'

Jill nodded. 'Goodbye, Frances Ripley,' she said. She turned to the bus.

I lifted my hand in farewell.

Just before she disappeared into the innards of the wreck one final time, however, she disembarked and walked back towards me.

To my surprise, she pressed a glass bottle into my hand. 'Drink this when you get home,' she urged. 'It's a sleeping potion for the dead. You'll wake when anyone walks through the front door. In the meantime, the worst of your loneliness will pass you by.' Her face was full of pity and a trace of something softer, as if she was hearing an echo from a time long gone.

She turned away and, a few moments later, the driver's door clanged shut behind her with a laboured groan.

The weirdest bus I'd ever seen resumed its slow,

lurching progress up the road, away from Cliffstones.

I waved goodbye to the children in the windows, and they waved back.

Just before the bus disappeared completely from sight, one of its rusting side panels fell on to the road.

A horrible thought occurred to me.

'Jill!' I shouted. '*Jill!*'

Her sigh was audible. 'What *now?*'

'Jill, will my corpse decompose? Are bits of me going to drop off too? Am I going to . . . rot?'

The bald tyres ground through a few painful-sounding rotations before I finally heard her reply.

'You won't. But your memories might.'

And then

she was

gone.

- 18 -

LATER THAT EVENING

BACK AT HOME, my sense of triumph began to ebb. What if Jill was right? What if my family never showed up? What would I *do*?

Thanks to that corpse barrier, I wasn't going anywhere. And as I'd discovered earlier, my fingers were useless, so turning the pages of a book or navigating the telly with a remote control would be impossible. I'd waved away all the other dead children that could have been my friends; when it came to companionship, I had literally just missed the bus.

Jill's parting shot came back to me. What had she meant by '*your memories might rot*'?

Did she mean I might forget my family? I might forget . . . *us*?

Dizziness engulfed me. I closed my eyes briefly, feeling as if I was standing at the edge of something vast and frightening. But a seedling of indignation unfurled in my brain. *Of course I won't forget them. Jill was talking rubbish.* After all, what did *she* know? She'd spent her entire afterlife squished into a husk of a bus with a bunch of squawking kids, that was her problem. If you wanted to talk about brains failing, let's start with *hers*!

Besides, how could anything fade away in my brain? I was *home*. All I had to do was look around. My family were everywhere.

Well, their things were anyway.

I'd ended up in Mum and Dad's bedroom. The bed was unmade, their chest of drawers was covered in clutter, and there was a heap of unwashed clothes next to their laundry basket, but their room looked like the most beautiful place on Earth. There were only two things missing. I thought of Birdie. Make that three.

Oh, why weren't they here yet? Were they cross? *Is this a punishment?*

My thoughts twisted uneasily. I remembered the way Dad had looked at me when I was shouting about the Crab Pot. Squirming, I remembered how I'd run into Mum's arms to say thanks, and the split second – almost as if she was hesitating – she'd taken before she'd hugged me back. That flash of hurt in Birdie's face when I wouldn't braid her hair.

I'd been awful that morning.

I'd been awful that Christmas.

Perhaps I'd *always* been awful. Had they just decided they were better off without me?

With relief, I remembered weird Jill.

'*Maybe you have a To Do.*'

Let's examine that concept for a moment, I thought. What if there *was* unfinished business hanging over me? That would mean my family weren't staying away to upset me. They were merely waiting for me to do my job. So all I had to do was that one thing, and we'd be reunited, right?

But what was that?

Could it . . . could it be the recycling?

I raced downstairs into the kitchen, found the overflowing box stuffed with bottles and plastic. With desperate, scrabbling fingers, I tried to sort through them, tense with the brittle hope that my family were waiting outside the front door patiently. My hands slid off all the containers. I groaned with frustration. *How can we be reunited if I can't even pick up an empty yoghurt pot?* And the house remained empty.

The hallway clock chimed midnight. I'd been dead

for a full day, and it was exhausting.

I wandered back to Mum and Dad's bedroom and tried to peel back the duvet so I could crawl into their bed – I was *so cold* – but my fingers did their new usual and nothing happened. So instead I just stretched out on top of it, right in the middle of Mum and Dad's pillows.

Mum's pillow smelt of her moisturiser. I turned my head to the side and laid my cheek against it. My eyes closed and I shivered all through the night with yearning and shock.

Dawn had stained the sky a pale prawny pink by the time I felt ready to get up again. The bedside clock read 07:29. All around me was that empty abandoned-beach feeling, and I knew what that meant. Several feelings rushed in at once, all loosely organised around one theme.

Panic – they still hadn't come back?

Anger – they still hadn't come back?

Sadness – they still hadn't come back?

I made a move to get up. Something fell out of my pocket and on to the mattress with a soft thud. It was the glass vial Jill had pressed into my hand.

She'd called it a sleeping potion. '*You'll wake when anyone walks through the front door. In the meantime, the worst of your loneliness will pass you by.*'

On the front was a faded handwritten label.

Sweet Elixir of Unconsciousness for the Not Quite Dead. Reduce painful waiting time, take a break from inertia, and wake up refreshed, revitalised and raring to face the yawning existential void of the afterlife once more!

Underneath that it said: *One drop on the tongue. Spell will be broken in the presence of other people, dead or alive.*

I took another look at the label. *One drop on the tongue.*

What did I have to lose?

I unscrewed the cap, feeling a stab of joy that, on this object at least, my hands worked, held the dropper over my tongue and let go. The liquid was bitter but bearable and within seconds it had dissolved.

I sighed with relief as drowsiness overcame me, welcome as a warm bath.

And when I woke up, surely the faces I'd see would be *theirs*.

My eyes closed. I just had time to wonder, *Can ghosts dream?* before my brain, mercifully, went quiet, and all my questions finally disappeared.

PART 2

- 19 -
SOMETIME LATER

JINGLE. JANGLE.
Mutter. Mumble.

Groggy with confusion, I tried to open my eyes. Hang on. I *couldn't* open my eyes. I was blind! I was dead *and* now blind?

Jill hadn't said anything about *this*.

I touched my eyes with shaking hands. They met with a layer of something cold and velvety. I rubbed it off, shuddering, and it fell away.

Had Mum and Dad's bedroom always been so dark?

I stared in confusion at the soft grime I was lying in.

Oh please, oh please don't say my skin is coming off my body. I don't want to look like one of those medical illustrations in my lift-the-flap What's in Your Body? *book.*

Oh.

It wasn't skin. It was *dust*. All over me, thick as a duvet.

And there was an *alien*, a mass of writhing limbs, climbing in through Mum and Dad's window. It had wrapped itself around the bed and those tentacles were pressing down on my legs. I tried to scream, but my throat felt dry and out of practice.

Stand down.

It wasn't a spidery alien.

It was a bramble.

A massive blackberry bush had sprung up overnight outside the house, pushed its face up to Mum and Dad's window and decided to break in. That would explain the broken glass all over the carpet. It filled the entire window frame and blocked out the sky. Its tendrils had crept across the carpet and grown over the chest of drawers. The bed itself had practically disappeared under the knotty network of its thick vines.

Then I heard that noise again and realised that there was something more important to think about.

I had been startled awake out of my blackout by noises.

Human noises.

Jingle.

Jangle.

Mutter.

Mumble.

'You'll wake when anyone walks through the front door,' Jill had told me.

Which could only mean one glorious thing.

THEY WERE HERE! MY FAMILY HAD RETURNED!

I leapt up off the bed, and my throat worked again, and eventually I managed to force a rusty shout out. 'Hi!'

In return, faint voices.

I stumbled along the top landing – on a grey slippery carpet I'd never noticed before, but I didn't care about that right then and there. I'd just reached the top of the staircase when there was the beautiful sound of a key unlocking a lock.

And the front door opened.

- 20 -
LOOK OUT FOR RATS

MUM AND DAD were in the doorway, gasping and laughing. I joined in. Mostly out of shock at how different they looked. They'd gone completely white-haired, and wore shapeless brown boiler suits, which smelt quite strongly of mushroom soup.

Then they both walked into the hallway properly and my welcoming smile died on my lips.

It wasn't them at all. Just a pair of men I'd never met in my life, standing in my hallway.

They didn't just look and smell weird. They were also *being* weird. This is what they were doing: wincing with pain while smiling joyfully *at the same time*.

One took out an electric lamp from his bag and placed it on the floor. In its dim light, I realised they were blotting beads of blood off their faces. They didn't seem bothered.

'Worth it though,' said the man with the straggly

ponytail as he roughly swiped at his skin with a hankie. 'I'd have fought off a dozen hammerhead sharks just to get in this place.'

'Toadly,' said his companion, a round fellow with a pink face. 'A few nicks and scratches are a small price to pay, really. Tent udder.'

He flicked on the head torch strapped around his forehead and began to dart it around the hallway.

Hammerhead sharks? Tent udder? What were they on about? Then again – what did it matter? That elixir had been next to useless. What was the point of waking up if it wasn't to my family coming back?

What I needed, at this point, was what Mum and Dad in their ongoing attempt to refocus my anger had called 'an alternative thought'. *Break the thought pattern that isn't serving you, Frankie, and try to think in a new way.*

It was as hard and slow as walking up Legkiller on a muggy day, but with an effort I wrenched my thoughts upwards. Maybe they weren't here *yet*, but perhaps my family weren't too far behind. These men might be able to help me find them. Or tell me what I was meant To Do anyway.

'Hi,' I rasped. 'I'm Frankie. I'm dead. Are you dead?'

'Better just check there isn't any gas leakage,' said the man with the white ponytail, fishing a gadget out of his pocket.

Well, that answered that. And I went back to feeling rubbish.

Questions dropped inside me like felled trees. Who *were* these men? Why did I keep seeing unsettling details in the beam from their head torches, like the waist-high drifts of powder piled up against the walls of the hallway? How had they managed to get their hands on our house keys? And why did they smell of mushrooms?

After a few minutes, Ponytail tucked his gadget into his shirt pocket. 'We're just a pair of eyes today, okay? Don't touch anything, don't open anything.'

'No touching, no opening,' said his companion agreeably.

'And look out for rats.'

'Rats?'

'The more established their lairs are, the more territorial they can get, and they've had the run of this place for a while.'

'Toadly. How long again?'

'Well, it's been empty ever since the Cliffstones

tsunami in 2019 . . .'

'And it's 2121 now . . .'

'So a hundred and two years.'

What? A spasm of shock ripped through my body. I tried to steady myself on the top step, slipped on the rotting carpet, and went plummeting down the stairs,

one

step

at

a

time.

- 21 -
SHOES IN THE HALLWAY

TWO YEARS WOULD have been okay. I could have dealt with that. It was just the other hundred I was struggling with. I lay at the men's feet, gasping and trembling like a gill-hooked fish thrown on deck.

The words boomed and banged in my head. *Now* everything made sense. The spiderwebs. That shroud of dust I'd woken up in. The bramble taking over the bedroom. That hadn't happened overnight but year by year. *Decade by decade.*

The only other thing, in my life to date, that had ever lasted for one hundred years – or felt like it had – was double maths on Thursday afternoons. And this was even longer than *that*.

'Start in the kitchen?' said the chubby man.

They moved cautiously, with wonder, as if they'd landed on the moon, their boots leaving track marks on a thick carpet of dust. I staggered in behind them, unsteady and disorientated on weakened corpse muscles, and peered round. Then instantly wished I hadn't.

The last time I'd seen it, before All The Death, the kitchen had looked . . . well, like our kitchen. Like anyone's kitchen. Like yours. Normal. Cheerful.

Birdie's drawings on the fridge. Slightly wilting but valiant houseplants, overdue library books, half-empty jars of strawberry jam on the kitchen counter. You know. The bright sweet tangle of normality you don't realise you love until it's gone.

And now? The kitchen was as brown and mouldy as an unwanted apple left to rot on a branch; collapsed, sunk in on itself, speckled by time. Birdie's drawings had crumbled away from the fridge magnets and fallen to the floor in a heap. There was a disturbing stain on the lino. It must have been caused by all the food in the fridge – those turkey leftovers that could have saved our lives – decomposing, leaking out, and drying to a crust.

And to top it all off, the house had vomited on to the kitchen table.

I took a closer look.

Well, it wasn't vomit, technically. But at some point

over the last century, the kitchen ceiling had ripped open and smothered our kitchen table with dank wood, plaster and what looked like—

'Pigeon droppings,' said the shorter man.

I looked at it in horror.

The men, on the other hand, seemed delighted. Even in the gloom of the kitchen their eyes shone with childlike joy.

'Tent udder,' said the tall man happily. 'Ping fleck.'

The shorter man nodded eagerly. 'Echo that. Verified purchase amazing.'

They were certainly using some interesting words for it. They just happened to be totally the wrong ones.

'What's in there?' said ponytail man, shining his torch through the damp rotting doorway that led to Mum's study.

Off they went.

It looked pretty bad in there too. Black mould covered the walls, carpet and desk in frenzied whorls. It was worst on the corkboard next to Mum's desk. In her lifetime, it had been covered with cheery photos of us.

Well, they weren't cheery any more, not unless you thought people looking like they were being eaten up from the inside by a bubonic plague was cheery.

While most of our old snaps were lost to the creeping mildew, there were some that hadn't succumbed completely. Those were almost worse to look at. Us larking about on the beach as fungus lapped at our feet; Birdie at bath time, grinning at the camera, skin spotted with the first beginnings of rot.

'It would have been better if the ceiling had fallen in here too,' I muttered.

But the two weirdos in my house didn't seem to think so. Instead they went into paroxysms of delight at the sight of Mum's old computer, the crumbling pile of Post-it notes by her keyboard, the framed photos on her desk. As their beams swept over the mildewed motivational posters on the walls and stumps of dead plants on the windowsill, they gushed to each other about how brilliant it all was.

'This home office is so twenty-first century, so *evocative*,' said Ponytail.

The other man nodded vigorously. 'That mountain of old coffee cups,' he said excitedly. 'Great bit of local colour, wonderful insight into the way people worked and the dietary habits of the time.'

I stared at them both. *Seriously?* They were both getting excited by Mum's old coffee mugs? You'd think they'd found the Holy Grail or something. Did they not get out much?

We roamed the bottom half of the house for hours, gasping in delight or horror, depending on whether we were alive or dead.

I couldn't understand it. While all I saw was devastation, they delighted in it. They got excited about the weirdest things. The sofa. Our toilet brushes. Dried-up soap in the bathroom. One of Birdie's school shoes lying on its side under the hallway table, its leather now brittle and cracking with age. They called them 'artefacts', 'snapshots' and 'poignant pieces of a life once lived'.

Eventually, we ended up back in the hallway again.

'Shall we take a look outside? The aerial pictures showed a building out in the back garden, facing towards the sea,' said one.

They walked through the porch. I followed them. There was a snapping, ripping sound. I stared outside and finally understood why, when they'd first appeared, they'd been bleeding all over their faces.

- 22 -
MYSTERIOUS SIGNS, DISTURBED FOXES

IT WAS A jungle out there.

There was no garden any more. Just a century's worth of scrub and gorse wrapped around our house in dense coils. It pressed up and broke through every single window, and poured down the chimney. The house looked as if it was being eaten alive.

But that's not to say it was *all* bad.

The rampaging growth had at least one thing going for it.

It blocked out the sea. I couldn't see it. I couldn't hear it. I couldn't even smell it any more. And that was fine by me.

The men looked at the mass of spiky undergrowth in front of them, took a few stoic breaths, and plunged in.

'Should have brought a machete,' said the chubby

man, as new scratches flowered on his cheeks and thorns tugged at his belly.

'Next time,' said Ponytail, wincing bravely as a stalk jabbed his eye.

I trailed behind them like a reluctant bridesmaid. We may as well have been walking through an overgrown rainforest. Here and there among the undergrowth were reminders of my old life – a few planks on the grass where the picnic table used to be, a toddler-bike skeleton, fragments of the red-brick path my parents had laid.

After what felt like hours of slow bramble-hacking, they came to a stop.

'Here it is,' said Ponytail, in front of a dilapidated, tumbledown shack.

Dad's shed.

It didn't look good. Although, to be fair, it had been on its last legs even when Dad had been alive. Still, time and sea air had left their mark. The felt roof had all but disappeared and when the door was opened, it paused for a minute before falling off completely, startling a small fox inside who ran out indignantly. The wooden floor had given way to grass which towered over our heads. Through its stalks

I saw the remains of Dad's easels.

I hung my head. I could almost smell paint, turps and smoke.

'Well, *don't just stand there,*' I could imagine him saying. '*Ask if they've got any pets! We make our own luck, right? Go on, girl – hustle!*'

The two men walked away, back in the direction of the cottage.

I sniffed the air again, longingly, but the smell had gone.

There was something slower and thoughtful about the chubbier man's movements. All of his earlier exuberance had gone.

'Play again what you know about the Cliffstones tragedy,' he murmured. 'I learnt a bit about it at school, but my download's slightly rusty.'

The older man's face crumpled. 'Oh, it was tent udder sad,' he said, pushing back the brambles as he spoke. 'There'd been a freak earthquake in a French village, which was tragic enough – loads of people there had died. But what no one had anticipated was where the shockwaves of the earthquake might go. It sent ripples along the ocean floor, straight towards Dorset, and Cliffstones bore most of it. The entire village – all three thousand residents – was wiped out completely.'

'Well,' I muttered. 'Not *completely*.'

'Unlike,' said the other man sadly.

'The Ripley house was the only building left standing, because it was so much higher above the village. The family itself wasn't so lucky. They were out at the time, so they drowned too. *That selfish girl Frankie – you wouldn't like her – she was born in a storm—*'

'*All the worst ones are.*'

'*. . . made them all go out for lunch even though they had leftovers to eat and a good film to watch on the telly. Horrible child.*'

'*I heard that. And her hair went frizzy in the rain, didn't it?*'

'*Yeah.*'

'*Makes you think.*'

'*It certainly does.*'

'*Hey, boss?*'

'*Yes?*'

'*Are we having this conversation in real life or in Frankie's guilty conscience?*'

'*Does it matter? It's all true.*'

And that was the second time I heard my death story. Hadn't got any better with age.

*

Ponytail stopped a moment and mopped his forehead with a handkerchief. 'The village was never rebuilt. No one wanted this cottage. Some well-meaning relative boarded up the house. Then, once nature took its course . . .' he jerked his head at the brambles, 'people forgot anyone had ever lived here at all.'

'Until now.'

'Toadly,' said Ponytail. 'The find of the century. Can't wait to get going on it.'

What did *that* mean? And why had they said they'd bring a machete to cut back the brambles *next time*?

And why did Ponytail look so *smug*? Look at him, hacking back at the growth with a triumphant lion-tamer flourish, strutting about like our garden belonged to him. Gazing up at the cottage – *our* cottage – with that calculating expression, like a judge on a talent show deciding whether or not to press a golden buzzer.

And why – seeing as I was in the mood for asking myself difficult questions – *why* was he helping the other man drill a sign on to our front door?

The sign which said:

This property belongs
to Historic Homes.
**OPENING SOON.
TRESPASSERS WILL
BE PROSECUTED.**

And why did they both look so very pleased with themselves?

- 23 -

BATS IN THE DARK

A FEW DAYS after this board went up, the first of many visitors started to arrive at my house. And when I say visitors, I mean total strangers who were uninvited. So, not visitors at all, really. More like unwelcome invaders. Like those bad cannibal ladybirds no one likes, or earwigs.

Anyway, they were there, they had keys to our house, they let themselves in whenever they wanted, and it didn't matter what I called them because none of them could hear me.

They wore purple T-shirts that said *Historic Homes: Cleaning Crew*. They drank a lot of tea. They ate a lot of weird-looking greyish biscuits. They listened to a lot of pop songs, none of which I knew.

Anyway, at first, what they mostly did was clean.

There was an *epic* amount of scrubbing. When you let the housework slide for a century it makes quite a lot of mess, it turns out. But we'll skip over the finer details as you've probably got better things to do than read about eighteen months of house-cleaning. I'll spare you that. I might be dead, but I'm not a monster!

For a time, I kept half an eye on the front door. For Mum and Dad and Birdie. In case. *'You didn't think we'd just leave you* behind, *did you?'* they'd say.

But once six months had passed, and still no sign – that was when I knew.

Dad could be pretty slapdash with time management, but even he would have managed to get back up the hill within that time without getting distracted. It was time to face facts. If they hadn't come back in one hundred and two years plus six months, then they were never coming back.

After the Cleaning Crew did their thing, they sent in the Restoration and Rebuild Gang.

That's when I would have given anything to go back to the cleaning phase. Because when you're dead and a bunch of people you don't know rebuild your house, it's confusing and sad. You never know where to go. There aren't any spaces to call your own. There's always someone, somewhere, talking about joists.

Sometimes I'd be able to hang out in my bedroom all by myself, but there were months when that too was full of builders and restorers, and my only option was to hide myself away in dank, uncomfortable places. Even that came with considerable risk. I got stuck inside the airing cupboard for a *month*. It was like a nightmarish version of hide-and-seek.

For ages, I racked my brain to understand *why* they were doing it at all. Why clean and rebuild a cottage that wasn't theirs? Why not concentrate on their own homes? How could it possibly benefit them? The answer I came up with eventually was pure kindness. That was who they *were*. The ones who do noble things because of the richness within their hearts. When they weren't doing up dead people's houses, they were probably rescuing kittens.

And do you want to know something crazy? They did everything *in the dark*. They installed these special shutters behind the curtains to keep out all but the weakest light, and they worked in the gloom, like bats. Perhaps that was just how they did things.

Or maybe the past needs to be dimly lit to be seen at all.

The worst bit about the Great Clean-up was when

they threw things away. They did try to restore as much as they could, I'll give them that. But a lot of our stuff was beyond saving.

Duvet covers, the rug I'd got for my bedroom, my favourite stripy blanket, most of our books and *all* of Birdie's teddies went. Mum and Dad's clothes that hadn't been put away. Even the homemade Christmas decorations, abandoned on the tree for a century, were shoved unceremoniously into bags and thrown out of the door. The tree, now nothing more than a bald twig the height of an ice-cream stick, also ended up in the skip.

Once or twice I tried to stop them. I'd stand in the doorway, try to block their way, hold my hands out and beg to be allowed to keep them. I'd even make a grab for the bags myself.

But – at best – my fingers would slide off them. At worst, whoever was trying to get past me would walk straight through me, and I'd stand there and shudder for a while, trying to get the taste of *them* out of my mouth. In the end I just waved them on.

My only consolation during these bleak moments was that it wouldn't last for ever. One day they would all leave, and my home would be mine again, and in the peace and quiet I could finally work out what I was *for*. Why I was still around, and what I needed to do so I could be reunited with Mum and Dad and Birdie.

And if anyone's thinking how lovely that sounds – a spot of soul-searching, and wondering about existence, and our place in it, before we finally pass on through to the great death gateway in the sky – then why not come and have a go yourself, then tell me how lovely it is, all right?

- 24 -

SOMETHING FISHY THIS WAY COMES

ONE MORNING, THEY all seemed even more excited than usual. And not in that weird way that sometimes went on, when they found crusty old possessions of ours and went into inexplicable raptures that veered on the embarrassing.

This glee was more understandable. The whole house was full of happiness, like the night before Christmas. And while before they'd looked very much like they were in the middle of *doing*, now their faces shone with the satisfaction of having *done*. Instead of bringing *out* their tools, they were *putting them away*. Everything they did had an air of finality about it, a sense of a job being wound up.

Perhaps they were . . .

. . . leaving?

The joy hit me all at once. I wandered around

the cottage to check. Yes, they were very definitely *packing up*.

Happiness seeped into me, the kind you get when those boring relatives you think will never leave say, over breakfast, 'Better get back and water the hydrangeas, I suppose.'

My bliss intensified when I realised just how nice they'd made the place. The cottage felt more watertight and cleaner than it had ever been during my lifetime. There was even a brand-new *welcome* mat on the front step. Perhaps it wouldn't be so bad, staying here by myself, for a while.

Why, the restoration crew had even cleaned up that photograph of us, the one of us on the hay bales at the wedding. But there was something not quite right about it. It was in the wrong spot.

Instead of being in its usual place on the mantelpiece, also known as *where it belongs*, it was now hanging up in the hallway. And underneath it was a sign.

THE RIPLEY FAMILY, 2019.

Hmmmm.

I went around again, my good mood deflating. Things were a little off. The whole place had that skew-whiff feeling like when someone tidies up your bedroom without your permission and puts everything back wrong.

Mum's study had been stripped of all its paperwork. Her desk was still there, and so was a laptop, but it wasn't *her* laptop – this one was black and didn't have stickers on it – plus the tower of coffee mugs had disappeared and so had all her potted plants on the windowsill. Instead there was a row of cactuses, and they were okay, but they weren't *right*.

In the sitting room, where there had once hung a lovely seascape by Dad, with greys and pinks of an early-morning sunrise, was now . . .

. . . a framed print of one of Dad's pet portraits. It was a pug dog, with a laminated sign underneath:
PERCY THE PUG BY DOUGLAS RIPLEY.

But Dad *never* hung his pet pictures up inside our house. He did his pet portraits for money and sent them away. At home, we'd had his seascapes. Did we *look* like a family that liked having pictures of *other people's pugs* over our head while we watched telly?

The list of Things Not Right About Our House got longer. The walls had been painted the Wrong Colours. There were Strange Things wherever I looked. In my bedroom, next to a photo of me, someone had framed my *school uniform* and hung it on the wall. My bed was on the wrong side of the room – and it wasn't *even my bed.*

Downstairs in the hallway in the spot where we'd always kept an old crate for our flip-flops was a round table instead. Why was *that* there? And what was that red hardback book on top of the table? That was new too.

I went to take a look.

On the front of the book were these words, embossed in gold:

VISITORS' COMMENTS.

Underneath *that* was the most mystifying sentence of all:

Please rate your experience of Sea View today, so we can make your next visit here even better!

I stared at that for a while, but for all the sense it made, it might as well have been written in hieroglyphics.

My eyes kept going back to the same five words.

Visitors? Your experience? Next visit?

- 25 -
MAKE YOURSELF AT HOME

THE SOUND OF violins snapped me out of my reverie.

Someone had left the front door open. I stared at it, the mysterious book temporarily forgotten. Tinkly laughter floated through the air. There was rapid chatter.

'You *mumble* so proud of what's been *mumble*,' somebody said.

There were people outside. And for the first time in ages, they weren't using chainsaws, hammers or drills. They were clinking glasses. I could feel the air of celebration even from the hallway. The last time I'd been in the garden, it had been an almost impenetrable mass of brambles. Now there was bright green lawn, glowing in the sunshine.

There was the sound of laughter. Something was very definitely Happening Outside. But what?

Only one way to find out.

I walked through the porch and stepped outside the front door.

The air felt quite lovely on my corpse. I squinted in the light. For a few moments, all I could see were dazzling diamonds of bright whiteness. And then my vision adjusted.

The old cherry tree near where we used to park our van was in blossom. *It must be spring,* I thought dazedly, as three waiters in red jackets walked past me, carrying trays of crystal glasses. *Spring is still a thing.*

I followed the waiters to the back garden, to the source of the noise.

It was a *party.*

Someone had strung up bunting and brightly coloured lanterns. People I vaguely recognised as the restoration crew were there. They'd all got dressed up for the occasion, although their clothes were odd: silky dressing gowns, long nighties. It was as if they were all off to a grown-up sleepover. One or two had eye masks perched on the top of their head like sunglasses, and here and there jewelled slippers in bright colours shone like slices of tropical fruit.

Still, at least they looked smart.

I looked down at myself, horribly aware of my

rotting Christmas jumper and bruised body. For once I was grateful for my invisibility.

All the bramble had been hacked away, revealing the sea again. I gave it my best dirty look. Then my attention was caught by something. In the spot where Dad's painting shed used to be was now a one-storey building. But it looked nothing like his shed. It didn't slope dangerously like the Leaning Tower of Pisa, for one thing, and it wasn't made of old planks. This was a proper modern building, with right angles and windows and a sign:

DOUG'S STUDIO CAFÉ: WHERE EVERY MEAL IS A MASTERPIECE!

Over the 'é' in 'café' someone had painted a teeny-tiny paintbrush, as if that made up for anything, as if that made up for pulling down his shed.

As well as the café, there were patio tables and shrubs and deckchairs, and manicured flower beds so tidy they looked fake.

In the oak tree was a brand-new tree house. That made me feel wistful. Building a tree house for Birdie and me had been fairly near the top of Dad's Things I'll Do One Day list. And now it was too late.

An hour or so later, when the sun had risen higher in the sky and several bottles of that golden bubbly liquid had been drunk, a slender woman in red pyjamas, hair glinting in the light like silver thread, strode through the crowd. People clapped as she moved past. She gazed out with a proud smile. On her lapel was a badge:

```
OLIVINE OBLONG,
SEA VIEW MANAGER.
```

When the applause died down, she began to speak.

'Thank you,' she said. 'It's been eleven-udder to care for this historically significant family home.'

There was another smattering of applause. I felt an odd mixture of pride and confusion. *Thanks for restoring it. And tidying up. That was very kind. But don't any of you have homes to go to?*

'Yet I'm not going to lie,' she said. 'There have been challenges. We went over budget, blah blah blahbiddy blah . . . but we got there, in the end. And here is the result: a living slice of the early twenty-first century, ping fleck solid, authentic, completely non-virtual, off-screen. Sea View brings us right up close to family life from another time.'

Somebody said, 'Bravo.'

Everyone clapped. This lot *loved* to clap.

'And now there's only one thing left to do,' said the woman called Olivine. 'Follow me!'

The crowd surged forward, wound itself around the cottage, and ended up in front of the front door. That was when I saw the red ribbon which had been tied around its middle. Like the house was a present.

'I am thrilled to declare Sea View Cottage officially open,' said the silver-haired woman, cutting the ribbon with a pair of oversized golden scissors, and everyone clapped yet again, because they were obviously quite easily pleased.

I did not like those words. Especially 'officially' and 'open'.

This was what the last year and a half had been all about. Why they'd painstakingly restored our home. They'd never had any intention of *leaving*. They'd claimed ownership of it the day they walked in.

'Now if you'll all come inside, I'd like to introduce you to some *very* special people,' Olivine said.

And everybody walked in through what used to be my front door.

- 26 -
YOU'RE HERE!

IT WAS A tight squeeze. The strangers crammed themselves into the porch and hallway. As they grew silent, I heard something just out of earshot, something that pulled at my heart before I'd even registered what it was.

Then I heard it again, properly this time, and a grin began to tug my mouth upwards. It felt as if my skin might crack from the novelty of it. Because I'd heard someone whistling a tune: a made-up, dreamy melody that only . . . It sounded like . . .

'*Birdie?*' I gasped.

'Frankie?' said Birdie.

She was upstairs. I wanted to cry and laugh at the same time.

I pushed through the crowd, retching repeatedly and not even caring – none of that mattered now – and I raced up the staircase. I'd just reached the middle step when—

'Mum? Dad?'

They were *there*. All three of them. Standing at the top of the stairs, beaming down at me. They'd come back. They'd come back for me.

'You're here,' I sobbed, leaping up the final steps.

I reached for Birdie and pulled her in for a hug, yearning for that sweet warm feel of her and . . .

. . . I felt nothing.

I opened my eyes.

My arms had wrapped themselves around *me*, not Birdie.

I looked at my sister anxiously. She must have stepped away. And now she was acting as if I didn't even exist. Oh, I got it. She was *sulking*.

'Birdie?' I said. 'Birdie, I'm sorry—'

I tried for another hug, but my arms went straight through her.

Bewildered, I looked at my parents, who, like Birdie, were also staring straight ahead.

'Please – please forgive me,' I begged. 'I've missed you *so much*—'

Birdie giggled again, but now it was clear she was giggling *at the crowd*. And they were lapping it up, staring at her with delight like they'd seen a baby lamb in a party dress.

Downstairs, Olivine cleared her throat, and began to speak. 'Ladies and gentlemen, meet Bridget Ripley.'

'Hello, everyone,' said Birdie in a curiously artificial voice.

She sounded weird, as if someone had—

'Welcome to our home.'

. . . *Stapled* her words together.

I turned perplexed eyes to Mum and Dad. They too were looking at the assorted crowd, smiling and nodding. But we were dead, weren't we? So why . . . why was all this smiling going on? Could the crowd see *them*, somehow, and not me?

'Please, *talk to me. Tell me what's going on!*'

Dad, acting as if I hadn't spoken, not even blinking in my direction, merely grinned at Mum and then looked at Birdie. 'Where's Frankie?'

Dad's words also had that weird staccato rhythm, as if the words were being punched out by a machine.

'Has anyone seen her? Frances Frida Ripley?'

I stared at him. 'Dad,' I said. 'I'm literally right in front of you?

Then I heard the most baffling thing of all.

My voice. My *actual voice*. But someone else was using it.

'Just coming.'

The person coming out of my bedroom wore *my* denim cut-offs, *my* favourite T-shirt and *my* friendship bracelet that Ivy had made me.

And this impostor walked up to Mum and Dad, put her arm around both of them, grinned at Birdie, and then faced the crowd as well, smiling.

'And here's the entire family. Everyone, meet Rachel, Douglas, Frances and Bridget Ripley,' said Olivine. 'Our new holograms.'

And everybody clapped again. Of course.

The replica Ripleys walked down the stairs, smiling beatifically at the crowd below.

As they wandered around the hallway, saying 'hello' in a friendly, blank way, like well-trained pop stars on a meet-and-greet, Olivine explained.

'Thanks to our digital archive restorers, we were able to download the Ripley family home videos from their computers, mobiles and tablets. And we've copied and cloned their voices with the help of found footage. So this twenty-first-century family can welcome twenty-second-century guests to their home.'

But basically, what she might as well have said was:

'WELCOME TO HELL.'

I stared in numb horror as our holograms roamed the crowd.

'They'll change clothes depending on the season, play games with the kids and interact with the adults. They can give painting classes, play hide-and-seek, demonstrate how they used the house and answer almost any question posed to them about their life here.'

'Oooooh,' said the crowd.

'Go ahead. Ask them something.'

'I'd be delighted,' said a man. 'Mrs Ripley, what do you think about the restoration of your house?'

Mum instantly turned and faced the man head on, like a servant who'd been called to attention. After dropping to her knees in a sweeping curtsy, she said, 'I think it's *amazing*. We're so excited to welcome you to our home. Have you got any other questions?'

While I watched, stunned – *since when had Mum curtsied?* – the crowd roared their approval.

Someone shouted, 'What's your favourite breakfast, Birdie?'

Birdie cocked her head to the side, as if thinking.

'We're very proud of that gesture,' Olivine said. 'She

- 145 -

does that while the tech scans for the right answer. Makes her look so lifelike.'

'I like my daddy's pancakes,' said Birdie's hologram finally, in a sweet voice. 'Have you got any other questions?'

I watched her glumly.

She *looked* like Birdie, with her heart-shaped face and those two wonky front teeth, but she didn't *glow*, not like Birdie did. Birdie's face had practically shone, like a garden after a rainfall. This flickering thing in front of us was just a collection of sound bites put together by some nerd in a lab.

But no one else downstairs seemed to care. In fact, they got a little bit overexcited, asking Birdie's hologram lots of baffling questions at once and shouting out over one another.

'What was your ping fleck subject at school?'

'What did you want to be when you were fully loaded?'

'Did you have a boss minister?'

Eventually, she just looked overwhelmed and ran to Mum's hologram and buried her head in her clothes.

'Aaaaaah,' went the crowd.

'She's rebooting,' said the woman. 'Let's give her a break. Does anyone have any questions for Frankie instead?'

There was a pause. A few people turned in the direction of my hologram, who unfortunately, at that moment, had chosen to pick her nose. (Thanks, Dad, for capturing that magical moment on camera.)

Someone murmured, 'Think I'll swipe, thanks.'

And everyone looked a bit embarrassed.

The woman in charge nodded decisively, as if to round things up. 'We've seen enough to get a sense of the experience. Thank you all so much for coming.'

There was more clapping.

They said: 'What an achievement! It's just like going back in a time machine and walking through their home!'

But they were wrong. It wasn't like home at all. It was like someone had taken the skin off my original home and sewn it on to another house. It was basically Frankenstein. I was abandoned in a stitched-up monster-house, my family were never coming back for me, and no one wanted to talk to my hologram.

- 27 -
YOUR INFORMATION PACK

SEA VIEW COTTAGE: AN ORDINARY HOME MADE EXTRAORDINARY BY TRAGEDY.

HELLO THERE, CHERISHED VISITOR. WE HOPE YOU HAVE AN AWESOME DAY DISCOVERING THE RIPLEY FAMILY HOME.

IS IT YOUR FIRST TIME VISITING US TODAY? HERE ARE SOME FREQUENTLY ASKED QUESTIONS YOU MIGHT FIND USEFUL!

1. Why is it so dark in here?

The furnishings inside the cottage are now extremely old, and the wallpaper, curtains and fabrics are deteriorating by the day. Any natural light will cause further damage. By keeping the curtains shut and the lights dim, the house will live on a bit longer.

If you do find yourself longing for natural light, feel free to wander into the back garden, where, as well as traditional twenty-first-century family meals, you can also enjoy the finest synth meat and veg plate-ups, and enjoy a delicious fresh CuppaGrubba (ExoGrinds are also available) made from the finest coffee-grubs in the cosy garden café at the back.

2. Where are the flushers?

Public flushers can be found in the café. There is also a small flusher next to Mrs Ripley's study, but this is not for use as it is part of the house and for exhibition only.

3. Why can I hear weird sighing noises from time to time?

Unlike our modern, digitally-run houses, older houses will always 'talk'. The 'sighing' noises you may hear, which also occasionally sound like exasperated 'tuts', are caused by nothing more than the bricks and the pipes shifting and moving as they get used to changes in temperature.

That's all it is.

4.   Why is there always a smell of damp somewhere in the house? And why do some of the rooms suddenly become freezing?

We agree – there is often an inexplicable smell of seawater that curiously moves from room to room. Sometimes you can even smell it in the garden! We're still looking into why, but a likely explanation is plumbing. That's all it is. Just a harmless bit of plumbing! Nothing to worry about. Nothing at all!

As for the temperature dropping – just the plumbing again. We're reluctant to modernise the heating inside Sea View as we think it will compromise the integrity – and authenticity – of its structure. If you are cold, please help yourself to the scarves and hats that we have hung up in the rooms.

We would be grateful if you could obey the 'two questions per paying customer' rule with the holograms, as too many can overrule their systems and lead to all sorts of glitches.

Don't forget to leave your comments in the visitors' book in the hallway as you leave.

Thank you for supporting Historic Homes: bringing the stories of the past into the present. And ask us about the benefits of membership!

- 28 -
THE CALM BEFORE THE STORM

AND SO MY house became a tourist attraction.

In the first few mad days after the opening ceremony, I did try, at first, to remember my manners. It was easy to guess what Mum and Dad would have said, if they'd been there. '*Stop glaring at them like that, Frankie, and remember that they're our guests.*' I kept myself out of the way and did not make a fuss.

In fact, I developed a simple rule: ghosts *inside* the ropes, tourists *outside*.

The ropes were the thick red room dividers, looped between two bronze stands, placed across every doorway in the cottage. They kept the tourists on the other side, just beyond, looking in from the doorway. Even though occasionally I felt like an invisible animal in a zoo, at least it meant I had rooms to myself.

More or less. There were the Room Sentries to

share with now.

These were the members of staff stationed in each part of the house. They were there for two reasons: if the holograms were elsewhere, the Room Sentries could be asked questions about the house or our lives. I also think they were there to make sure that nothing got stolen or damaged.

There were eight sentries in total. Four downstairs: Chrix (sitting room, liked to eat boiled eggs), Brae (kitchen, huge tattoo on neck, sometimes helped out in the café if they were short on staff), Medow (Mum's study and utility room, wore experimental necklaces) and Ada (hallway, *very* warty). Upstairs there was: Poe (my bedroom, liked to write in notebooks), Yos (Mum and Dad's bedroom, huge shoulders, looked quite intimidating), Turl (Birdie's bedroom, hummed a lot) and Skiffler (hallway and the bathroom, bit smelly).

For all of June and most of July, my days fell into this rough routine:

8.45 a.m.: Jingle of keys in front door. My cue to get out of bed, scrape hair back, roughly swipe at my face and tug at the rotting rags on my corpse in attempt to smarten up.

8.50 a.m.: Historic Homes lot arrive, make their weird purple tea, talk through the day and switch on the holograms.

9 a.m.: Sea View Cottage open to the public – mostly middle-aged people and well-behaved people from different countries. They're quiet and relatively docile and murmur a lot.

9–12 p.m.: I stay upstairs for the morning.

12–1 p.m.: Tourists drift to the café for those weird drinks they make from ground-up insects and some lunch. This is my 'safe time' to go down the stairs without anyone walking through me.

1–5 p.m.: Depending on weather, I either stay in the sitting room behind the ropes or wander into the back garden.

5 p.m.: Sea View closes for the day. The holograms are finally switched off.

5–6 p.m.: Derk and Debs, the cleaners, arrive to hoover, dust, empty bins.

6 p.m.: Derk and Debs leave.

6.30 p.m.: Olivine the manager leaves.

The last thing I do is:

6.45 p.m.: Read the latest entries in the visitors' book – that book on the table in the hallway, which was always left open at the latest page.

It wasn't really out of choice – it was the only thing I could read, thanks to my fingers, which were now useless at opening paperbacks. Unfortunately, it was never going to win any Nobel Prizes in Literature, because it was pretty repetitive.

Most entries fitted into one of three categories:

1) Those with enthusiastic, sweeping statements about how wonderful everything was. (Lots of exclamation marks.) For example:
   GREAT SLICE OF TWENTY-FIRST-CENTURY LIFE!!!!!!!!
   – BILLY AND JENAX from UTAH!!!!
2) A sniffy comment about the catering, like:
   Shame the CuppaGrubba isn't as delectable as the views.
   – Colin, Leamington Spa
3) Someone using the word 'thought-provoking'.

So that was my routine.

It wasn't *great*, but I coped.

And then the summer holidays started, and everything changed.

- 29 -
WHEN THEY TOOK
THE ROPES AWAY

Small ones.

Tall ones.

Big smelly ruffians.

Shy ones.

Loud ones.

Weird snotty whining ones.

And that was just the parents.

After the first day of the summer holidays, when the door had finally been shut, Olivine turned to the rest of the staff with a stunned look on her face, and said, 'We're going to have to get rid of the room ropes. It's the only way we'll be able to fit them all in.'

'But the ropes are there to protect the rooms,' protested Ada. 'The carpets, the floorboards – they won't survive the crowds.'

I gave Ada a grateful glance.

But Olivine was shaking her head. 'That roof isn't going to fix itself. Those holograms are expensive to run. The ropes must go. Let's pack them in! Fill this house to the rafters! You have to make hay while the sun shines!'

She got her way. The ropes went. My safe spaces shrank overnight. I no longer had rooms to stretch out in. Now I just had tiny divisions. Like the top of my bed. Or squished next to the fridge, while family after family filed past me and complained about the cost of the parking. There was nowhere to call my own.

Even though I knew no one could *see* me, it was still horrible to become trapped there, hour after hour, while hordes of adults and their children tramped around my life, circling me, glancing my way without properly noticing me. It was like standing naked in the middle of your school's playground, waiting for someone to start laughing, any second. It was *that* feeling, except all day, Monday to Sunday. (Actually, they closed at midday on Sunday. But that's not the point here.)

Any time I fancied some fresh air and a break, I'd have to brave the crowds, walk through at least twenty humans, then collapse on the grass outside, retching. Then, when it was time to go back in again, I'd have to do the same thing in reverse.

As if that wasn't enough, I became a *magnet* for dog wee, because I was dead and dogs like to wee on dead things. Oh, and flies. Flies *loved* me.

After a few weeks, my existence felt like it had become an endless game of Monopoly, with the cottage as the board, and me a reluctant player. I could already tell I'd lost, and had no property to call my own, but I was forced to keep playing. All I could do was race around and around the board, knowing that wherever I landed, I'd have to pay.

If I wasn't tasting human flesh, waving flies away or getting weed on by guide dogs, I was trying to extricate myself from crowds of snotty toddlers, wincing as huge bulky handbags churned through my torso, listening to people ask our holograms the same stupid questions, or watching people smirk at the pug picture.

There was nowhere safe to land, it all belonged to someone else, it had stopped being fun a long time ago, and no one would let me leave the game.

And if this metaphor has bamboozled you, let me

put it another way by simply saying:

EVERYTHING WAS AWFUL.

And those emotions inside me that I thought had faded away began to whirl and stretch.

A month into the summer holidays and the carpets upstairs were threadbare and the holograms had started crashing from repeated overuse and the visitors' book was filled with crayon scribbles and comments like:

MY BIG BROTHER IS A SMELLY POO BUM, HA HA HA HA HA!!

And still they kept coming. And coming. And coming.

My standards dropped. I slouched, I lay on top of my bed all day, sighing and singing rude songs, shouting at babies.

But here was the weird thing. Even though they came in their hordes, and queued patiently, and handed over their money – even though it was clear they'd all gone to some effort to get to our cottage and have a good look around – most of the grown-ups didn't seem to enjoy it much. They were always so preoccupied. They liked to tell their kids off a lot, and seemed obsessed with whether anyone needed a wee.

They spent a lot of time taking photos on their phones and then sending those photos to everyone they knew. This gave us one thing in common, I suppose: we were both used to letting other people stare at our lives. Maybe they were worried about being forgotten too.

Even the rare ones who *did* seem interested, who booked themselves into the Paint Your Pets sessions with Dad's hologram, engaged with all the interactive exhibits and willingly sat through the documentary on the Cliffstones tsunami – even *they* ended up with what I came to call The Look on their faces.

A shell-shocked expression. Like they'd realised somebody else's life was pouring into them, and they didn't like it.

Their smiles would become strained. Their eyes would dart to the windows and they'd gasp: 'Outside?' Where they'd all breathe a sigh of relief as if they were filling up with themselves again.

And they'd whisk themselves off in the direction of the car park without so much as a backward glance. Then they'd fold themselves up into their flying cars and disappear off into the smog of the twenty-second century. And I'd never see them again.

Because no one ever returned.

Apart from one boy, that is.

A funny-looking boy in a funny-looking top.

Who didn't seem able to stay away.

- 30 -
THE BOY

HE FIRST APPEARED at the beginning of August, in the early gasps of the school holiday madness. Even among the crowds he was hard to miss, in his oversized pink T-shirt covered in lurid lime squiggles.

His skinny body floundered around in that T-shirt like it was quicksand. And his face was as pale as his top was colourful.

He came to my house about three times a week and even shelled out for a Repeat Visitor card, drawing surprised looks from almost all the staff although they tried to hide them. But he never gave the impression that he actually wanted to be there.

In fact, he seemed more interested in his shoes than anything else.

But once or twice – if he had to navigate a particularly busy crowd out in the hallways, for example, and if our paths were crossing – his narrowed green eyes would land almost directly on me.

He can see me! I'd think, with panicky delight.

But then almost immediately his face would glaze over, and it would become clear he hadn't spotted me at all. At times like this I'd feel both disappointed and relieved. If you've been invisible for a while, you get used to it. The idea of being seen for the first time in over a century made me nervous. Plus he looked like *hard work*.

The man he was with though seemed much nicer.

Unlike the boy, he had an interested, polite manner. He was always careful not to push in queues, and went to great lengths to smile at all the Room Sentries. His chubby pink cheeks and soft caramel-coloured hair made him look as meek as the boy seemed sharp. The man wore clothes that soothed me just to look at them – velvety corduroy, faded denim, things in calming colours. He had a habit of blinking a lot, quite rapidly, as if he found crowds alarming, which made him look so harmless and shy I thought he must do something very mild and sweet for a living. Like breeding hamsters, or knitting things.

And he carried a big, stained, black leather bag with him at all times, as if he wanted to be prepared for anything. Perhaps he was a Scout leader, or a teacher of something practical, like geography.

Although, if he *was* a geography teacher, he can't have been a very good one. He had a dreadful sense of direction for one thing. It didn't matter how many times he came to the cottage, he never seemed to remember which room was which. If all the crowds were wandering in one direction, he'd go in the opposite. He opened doors marked *Private* and once he went straight into the staff room and interrupted Chrix's sacred hard-boiled-egg-eating.

The man and the boy spent hours at the cottage when they visited, but I never saw them buy anything at the café, although the boy would occasionally throw longing glances in its direction. And whenever they left, the man would lay an arm casually across the boy's shoulders, making him jump slightly, and say, 'Seen anything interesting today?' And the boy would shake his head firmly, which endeared him to me even less.

If you ever want to forget something completely or make it utterly invisible, here's a piece of advice. Put it somewhere you'll see it every day. Ideally in a frame, and at eye level, somewhere you're likely to walk past a few hundred times a week.

As August drew to a close, as the grass out on the lawn began to die, so did my memories. It was hard for me to even *see* the framed photographs, copies of Birdie's drawings, the replica motivational posters in Mum's study. Even the holograms became harder to notice. (Every cloud . . .) The more I saw them, the less I saw them. We had turned into the past; a faded snapshot on a wall.

The only thing that felt vivid, unavoidable and impossible to ignore, was the crowds.

Clogging up the narrow corridors and staircase, standing in line for the loo, shuffling around the kitchen and sitting room. Tired grown-ups with their thousand-yard stares, like wounded soldiers waiting to be told where to go next, occasionally rolling their eyes at each other when their children weren't looking.

They didn't just take over the house. They stuffed themselves up my ears, into my brain. I heard *everything*. Conversations about the shocking cost of the car park, how their children were driving them up the wall and they still had four more weeks of holiday to go. I heard about family feuds and nasty divorces, got stuck in the middle of endless sibling squabbles. Children my age saying, 'Remind me why we're here again', and 'What is that horrible damp smell?' and 'I don't *want* to learn local history. I want to eat my crisps instead'.

When I closed my eyes, I saw them, and no one else. When they left the house, I still heard their voices inside my head.

Had Mum and Dad *also* counted down the days till we returned to school, just like these parents did? Had they rolled their eyes at each other over our heads too?

I started to see things through the eyes of the tourists, not mine. Our rooms *were* crooked. Mum did have a bit of a potbelly. Dad hadn't been a brilliant artist. Perhaps he'd been a . . . failure? Perhaps we'd been a joke?

I remembered what Jill had said. '*You won't rot. But your memories might.*'

I wanted to take back control.

So I think what happened next was totally and completely understandable.

BUZZ

BUZZ

- 31 -
THERE'S ONLY SO MUCH A DEAD GIRL CAN TAKE

WHEN IT CAME to crowds inside the house, rainy days made them ten times worse. At the slightest drizzle, people would cram into the cottage, filling the rooms with the smell of wet clothes and disappointment. They made the house feel even smaller, even darker. On days like that, Sea View felt like an unexploded water balloon, quivering with unspilt energy.

I'd spent most of the morning in what used to be my bedroom, curled up on top of a flowery duvet cover I'd *never* have chosen for myself, while children said pitying things like 'Did they *really* not have multiplayer console VR micro-box pixel lagoon skins in their rooms?' before asking 'Where next?'

I could have gone anywhere else in the house. Could have sat on top of Birdie's bed. Taken refuge under the kitchen table for a few hours. I could have sat, undisturbed, in a flower bed outside. If I had, maybe things would have been different.

But I went to Mum's study instead, and it had happened there.

It was crowded. Medow, the shyest and most timid of the Room Sentries, was there, nervously fiddling with one of her experimental necklaces.

Inside the room were also two giggling teenagers, an older man holding a steaming cup of CuppaGrubba and a woman whose twin boys were climbing on to Mum's desk.

To top it all off, Mum's hologram was also crammed inside, saying repeatedly, 'Have you got any questions about working mothers in the twenty-first century and how I balanced work and parenting?'

Whenever she said this, however, the man would just roll his eyes and take another gulp of his foul-smelling bug drink and the teenagers would giggle and say things like: 'Thanks, but no thanks.'

And suddenly, out of nowhere, an old pulse began to beat inside me. Not a heartbeat, obviously, but a familiar buzzing feeling, something I'd not felt for a while. I glared at my unwelcome companions and that pulse got stronger. They were literally using Mum's study as a *waiting room* until the rain eased off. Her life – her career – was nothing more than a jokey stopgap where they could pass the time and drink nasty grub coffee until lunch. Not one of them was doing what Olivine called 'engaging and learning from the stories of our past'.

Well, maybe the two young boys were. If running through Mum's hologram and shrieking with laughter as if she was a *garden sprinkler* was 'learning from the stories of the past'. But, with that feeling of immense generosity that often accompanies blinding flashes of wisdom, I suddenly knew there was no point in blaming these idiots. It wasn't their fault they couldn't see how special that study was. Because it was *wrong*.

For starters, it was way too orderly. Back when Mum had been alive, this room had been an absolute mess, only a couple of months away from a guest appearance on one of those *How Clean Is Your House?* programmes. There would always be at least fifteen cups of half-drunk coffee on the go, teetering mounds of paperwork, plates with half-eaten snacks on, loads of half-used coral lipsticks lying around – she wasn't a 'tidy-as-you-go' kind of person at all.

Now though there was none of that. No wonder the

tourists didn't feel anything in there. It was nothing like her. It wasn't true to life. It was *devoid* of life. All it had now was a laminated sign on her desk which said: *Like typical working mothers in the early twenty-first century, Rachel Ripley attempted to hold down a job as she worked from home. In this cramped spot, Rachel had a desk, laptop, filing cabinet and phone, which would have met all her working needs at the time, primitive though these basic tools may seem to us now.*

I didn't understand what all of that meant, but I knew one thing. I did not like Mum being called primitive. Or typical. She wasn't typical. She was *brilliant*. And she'd been *mine*.

'Mummy? Time to swipe. There's nothing good to see here,' said one of the boys, who had now tired of running through Mum's hologram.

'I'll give you something to see.' My voice sounded rusty and tangled, like a bunch of broken Christmas lights stuck in an attic for too long.

No one paid me any attention.

I tried again.

BUZZ

BUZZ

'I *said,*

"I'll give

you

SOMETHING

to see.'"

BUZZ

BUZZ

BUZZ

This time, the words came out more easily. It felt good, to speak aloud in my own home. *When did I last do that?*

I'd forgotten how easily I could raise my voice when I was in the mood. How nice it was to speak aloud and hear the crackle and snap in my voice.

I stepped into the study. It felt like a beige sterile box. No wonder the boys were bored. No wonder they all were. The place just needed some atmosphere, that was all. It needed to be *messed up a bit*.

The thought blew into my brain as easily as a leaf through a door. My hands curled into fists.

This is usually the time, I thought, flexing my fingers experimentally, *that Mum or Dad would tell me to stop and go away and work on my feelings until I'd calmed down.*

But they're not here, are they?

- 32 -

THE FACE IN THE DOORWAY

My LIMBS ACHED and fizzed, as if I'd been sitting on them for a long time and they wanted to come back to life.

Okay, time to concentrate, Frankie. First things first. What's this room missing? What were Mum's little touches?

Well, that's easy. Paper. Mum always had loads, everywhere. Remember? Piles and piles of it. All in a mess.

A slight movement in the corner caught my eye. It was Medow, shifting from one foot to the other. Clutched to her chest was a bundle of those Treasure Trail fun sheets in her arms, the ones she always tried to give away to the younger children so they could 'engage with the stories of the past' and not 'just rush around the cottage saying it was bor-ing'.

They'll do.

Without thinking too much about it, I reached out and made a grab for them with my fingers. And then something incredible happened.

I *touched them*.

Even more miraculously, I *pulled* them out of her hands.

I didn't know who was more surprised – me, for having picked up something successfully for the first time since the twenty-first century, or Medow, who gasped in confusion.

I felt a pang of remorse – I didn't want to frighten her – but at the same time, these people needed to see what Mum's room – what our *life* – had really been like. I snatched another handful from her trembling arms. To my delight, the second attempt was even easier than the first, and the paper came cleanly out of her embrace. She practically offered them up, in fact, with a small whimper, which I took to mean '*Please, help yourself!*'

What's happening? I can do things again!

Elated, I shook the Treasure Trails about, like a raffle winner holding up her winning ticket. As the trail leaflets danced about in the air, Medow staggered backwards, one of the teenagers fainted and the other was sick on the floor. The two little boys whimpered.

'Not so bored *now*, are you?' I said, throwing the

paper around the room, clapping and whooping as it landed in heaps on the desk and carpet. Mum's study looked better already.

The old man looked concerned, coffee cup slack in his hand. 'What's happening?' he said.

'I'll tell you what's happening,' I said, throwing the paper up in the air as giddily as an aunt throwing confetti at a wedding. 'A historical re-enaction. Never mind those holograms, this is the *real* authentic Ripley experience. You lucky people!'

And I chucked another bundle of Treasure Trails into the air to celebrate. Unfortunately they hit the ceiling light, which made the lampshade swing violently about and throw eerie shadows around the room.

The teenager who hadn't fainted fled the room.

Shakily, Medow began to punch some buttons on her walkie-talkie.

The two boys and their mother were moving, very slowly, in a huddle towards the door.

'Don't go!' I yelled. 'I'm just getting started!'

I ran to the door and grabbed its handle, shrieking with joy at the *actual feel of it* in my hand. Then I slammed the door shut with a satisfying bang, pulled the key out of the lock and threw it to the ground.

'There – now you *have* to stay. I've got so much more to show you!'

Everyone in the room shrieked too, although they didn't sound quite as joyful as me, and it looked as if one of the boys might have had an accident in his trousers, and I was sorry about that, but in all fairness, I was doing them a favour. If they left now, they'd miss the best bit.

Both boys started to cry.

I rolled my eyes. Talk about gratitude. This was going to be the learning experience of a lifetime, and they didn't even know how to enjoy it? Why, only a few seconds ago, one of them had been complaining there hadn't been enough to see!

'You're *welcome*,' I said, then I went back to work.

A short while later, I surveyed the room, panting but elated. *Everything looks so much better now.*

This is what I'd done:

a.   Yanked the curtains back. They should never have been closed in the first place – Mum had always liked to look out at the garden.

b.   Ripped the blinds away from the window frame.

I felt bad when I realised I'd broken them, but if you asked me it was a price worth paying – the study was *lighter*, which was how it had always been, back when we were alive.

c. Opened the window to let in some fresh air. Well, I say 'opened'. When I'd realised it was bolted shut, I'd solved that problem creatively by throwing the laptop *through* the window, which had smashed almost all of the window completely. This was admittedly unfortunate. Still, now there was a nice summer breeze drifting in past the jagged stumps of glass. Mum would have liked that – she loved working with the window open. Said she could hear the blackbirds better that way.

d. But the icing on the cake was the coffee. I'd borrowed the old man's cup of CuppaGrubba by easing it gently out of his hands. Then I'd flung it all around the paperwork and desk for that authentic coffee-stained vibe Mum always went for. I might have accidentally thrown some on the tourists as well, but you can't make an omelette without breaking a few eggs.

After regarding the room appraisingly, I gave a satisfied sigh. It wasn't perfect, and maybe it could do with slightly less broken glass, vomit on the carpet and coffee dripping down the walls, but it was so much closer to what home had been like. Fresh air, a *view*, some of that healthy scruffiness you only find in proper family homes . . . I was quite proud of it, actually.

And I felt amazing too. Happier and less freezing, for one thing. Excitement ran through me, warming and thrilling my corpse. It had been so brilliant to be able to touch stuff again, to make things *happen*. Honestly, although I was dead, I'd never felt so *alive*.

If only the same could be said for the others. They were taking the restoration quite badly. Instead of clapping in admiration, they were either wailing softly or cowering in a corner.

Medow, who had been silently pressing an emergency button on the wall for a while, sobbed with relief as Chrix forced the door open. The tourists ran out, sobbing too.

Like an athlete at the end of a marathon, I started to shake and tremble all over. I sank to the floor, exhausted and spent.

As Chrix ushered a stumbling Medow out of the room, saying, 'It's all right – you're safe now' soothingly, my head fell back against the wall.

There was a subtle movement by the door. Through a fog of tiredness, I thought I saw a glimpse of someone, pale and solemn, shaking their head at me from just beyond the doorway. But when I squinted into the shadows to check, there was no one there.

- 33 -
'POLTERGEIST'

A FEW MOMENTS later, Chrix, Olivine and Skiffler came bustling into the study. They carried mops and buckets and cleaning products. No sign of Medow – she was probably breathing into a paper bag somewhere.

Instead of clapping their hands with delight at my handiwork, turning to each other and saying, 'What a wonderful display of *truth* this is. Let's leave it untouched forever,' Chrix and his colleagues swept up the glass, mopped up the coffee, sponged at the puke, and taped cardboard over the broken window. *Philistines*.

And as they tidied, I heard the same word whispered over and over.

'Poltergeist.'

Poltergeist.

I glared at them, whispering and sweeping so fussily, and my jaw clenched. I'd gone to all that effort to show them proper authenticity, and now they were scrubbing it away?

'Stop it,' I snapped from the carpet, not tired all of a sudden. 'Don't touch it. Leave it exactly like that, please.'

But they didn't hear me, and carried on. So I decided to use the only language that worked. I went and rearranged the study again.

And this time, my reasons seemed to flex and change shape. It was more out of anger, if I was honest, less about authenticity. I did it because I was – *ah*, finally, the relief of feeling something properly again! – *furious*. Furious at being contained and trapped and ignored and labelled and dismissed and pitied and misunderstood. I was sick of being alone and abandoned. I was mad I'd never got on that stupid bus, and angry they'd never come back, and cross that some weird death guardian in huge glasses had told me I might have to do something in order to ever see my family again, but hadn't said anything useful about what that *was*.

As I smashed and threw and ripped, somewhere inside me a delighted little voice said: *There's no one telling me not to. For the first time ever.* No disappointed faces. No one yanking me back on a leash or talking about energy fields. It was almost a blessing. Finally, I'd found something *good* about being dead! I could lose my temper and no one could stop me! I was angry and it felt *amazing* and I was going to properly explore it, for *once*, without being told to stop just as I was getting going.

Once I'd done the study again, I didn't feel quite as exhausted as I had the last time. In fact, I even had a bit of energy left over, so I trashed the kitchen too. Then my bedroom. And Birdie's. And the upstairs bathroom.

Every now and again, I'd stop, panting, and stare at my hands wonderingly. Now I knew what made them work again. I'd worked it out. Anger made me powerful.

And really, I had quite a lot to be angry about. All that time of being ignored, mocked, and crowded out of what used to be our home, watching helplessly as my safe spaces got smaller and smaller. Hearing our real stories get distorted by holograms, and listening to people feeling sorry for us just because we didn't have lagoon-tech banana skins or whatever gadgets *they* had that they thought were indispensable. Listen, sunshine, you stick around for a century, then we'll talk about *indispensable*, all right?

Oh, I can't tell you how incredibly fantastic it was to *finally* lose my temper, all of it, all at once! It was like tipping an entire bag of sweets into my mouth in one go, after only ever being allowed to eat them one by one before. It felt *delicious*, and a little bit dangerous, and way too much fun to stop. So I did it all afternoon.

Occasionally, when I was in the middle of a particularly laborious bit of healthy emotional expression – ripping a blanket in half, say, or throwing a chair down the staircase – I'd hesitate suddenly, worried about the extent of my new-found abilities.

What if I ran out halfway through? Would I wind down, like a clock without a battery? Would everything go back to how it had been before: me not being able to do *anything*?

But then, in a moment of dazzling clarity, I realised that there was no need for my fury to run out. *All I had to do was look around.* I could keep my anger going as long as I wanted to. It was like a rechargeable battery.

I may have gone over the top by the end. I took a sudden dislike to the sink in the upstairs bathroom. I know it sounds weird now but trust me. It was *maddening*. It was the wrong colour, for a start. And – oh, who cares what the reason was.

It was *there*. And so was I. And I had a new-found superpower, and I was going to use it.

With the help of the emergency hammer conveniently hanging nearby, and with some gratifyingly loud smashing sounds, I managed to make the entire sink come completely away from the wall. As the torrent of water began to stream out of the bathroom and down the staircase, I watched it happen with a shiver of delighted satisfaction. It had been *fun*.

I contemplated my work. The water cascaded down the staircase, the lightshades hung broken from their fixtures, and there were piles of torn bed linen lying in strips on the floor next to broken wardrobe doors and dented walls. And do you know the best bit of all?

I'd played and played, and no one would be able to get me to tidy up.

Later, with all the tourists fled or evacuated, I swaggered around the empty rooms, enjoying my new sensations of power and strength. I felt brilliant. Like a crisp duvet pulled tight across a bed, all fresh and wholesome. Washed clean.

At the end of my victory lap, I found myself standing in front of the framed photo in the hallway.

For a split second I couldn't remember who any of the people in the picture were.

Who is this suntanned quartet sitting on a hay bale, and why am I standing in front of them?

Was this my favourite pop band or something?

Then something clicked, the words poured into me in a relieved rush, and I gasped them out loud. 'Mum, Dad and Birdie.'

Of course it is. Of course. I'm just a little tired, that's all!

To distract myself, I glanced down at the visitors' book.

The comments were grumpier than usual.

Not coming back ever again; chaotic, horrible vibe downstairs.

Staff seem plus plus terrified – must be tripleshifted.

Had quite a decent cup of ExoGrind in the café, but as we tried to leave there was a noisy outburst in the study. When we tried to find out what was going on, the door was slammed in our face. Unforgivably rude. NEVER COMING BACK.

House falling to bits. There was a flood upstairs and a child must have broken something. We tried to explore, but we'd only just arrived and then we were told to leave! And we'd only just got here! Next time we'll save our money for the World of Data in Worth Matravers, thank you very much, as you always know what you're getting there (and the parking's cheaper).

I grinned at that.

The last entry on the page was so small I nearly didn't see it. The handwriting was cramped and jerky, like it had been scribbled down in a rush.

It was just one word.

It said:

STOP.

- 34 -
THE CHAT

A FEW DAYS later, once everything had been fixed and repaired, Sea View opened to the public again. The tourists I'd terrified were given discount vouchers for the café as compensation. The general public was fed the official line that the damage I'd done had been caused by bad plumbing.

I wasn't looking for the limelight, particularly, so I didn't mind the lie. All I'd wanted was for things to change. For my family's history to be treated with a bit more *respect*. But . . .

. . . everything remained the same. The comments, gasps for air, the endless chats about when to treat themselves to a CuppaGrubba. Oh, and I was still completely alone. I could smash the world to bits and I would still be completely alone. Nothing had changed at all.

And that just made me even angrier than ever.

Outside, in the garden, I glared at the crowds queuing up for lunch. I was in the kind of mood where I only had to *glance* at something to feel furious about it. That stupid café, for instance, where Dad's shed should have been.

I walked in through its open door. It was the café's busiest time of day. Long queues. Harassed grown-ups bearing trays overloaded with bowls and plates and cups and mugs.

Very overloaded trays. Brimming with stuff, they were.

I mean, that was just asking for trouble.

Sometime later, panting and covered in food, I finally stopped.

I wasn't sure at which point the café had emptied completely. Had *I* broken the coffee machine which now lay in a pathetic heap on the floor, burping out jets of steam and making a worrying hissing noise, or had it fallen over by accident? I could dimly remember screaming, but wasn't sure if it had been mine or someone else's.

I couldn't recall *exactly* if I'd opened the ice-cream counter and scooped out all the flavours and thrown them at the walls, but judging by my slippery multicoloured hands, I had to admit it was likely.

Just as I was admiring how pretty the mustard and ketchup looked smeared on the windows, a stern voice behind me said: 'You really need to stop doing this, you know.'

I whipped around and found myself face to face with the skinny boy in the bright top.

'Are you talking to *me*?' I said, an incredulous smile tugging at my lips.

He looked around the empty café and raised an eyebrow.

'Who else would I be talking to?' he said.

'But . . . but . . . you're . . .'

'Alive?' He spoke as if he was in a library and didn't want to get told off – quietly, barely moving his lips.

'And I'm . . .'

'*Dead*,' he volunteered.

'Yeah.' I felt all sorts of things: confusion, relief and panic, and underneath it all, like a golden precious egg, hope.

'Have you . . . have you always been able . . .' I gulped, 'to see me?'

He flushed.

I held his gaze.

Finally he gave a tiny nod.

'Why haven't you said anything till now? You've been coming here for *weeks*.'

He shrugged. 'Waiting for the right time.'

I looked around the shattered café, at the toddlers screaming on the lawn, the grown-ups shouting at each other in confusion as they attempted to gather themselves and flee.

'And this is it? This seems like the perfect time to introduce yourself?'

A sharp row of yellow teeth appeared before he clamped down on them with his lips. Had that been a *smile*?

All of a sudden the chaos outside felt a little quieter. As the mustard and ketchup slowly dripped off the glass and pooled on the floor, we stared at each other.

Then the boy broke eye contact. He turned his head and scanned the thinning crowds outside. I occupied myself by contemplating the most complicated face I had ever seen.

Looking at it was like stumbling into a prairie town just before a shoot-out. It was all angles and shadows and wide empty plains, taut with secrets. Sallow, almost waxy skin stretched tight over sharp cheekbones. A pair of narrow lips, as thin as if they'd been slashed into his face with a stub of crayon. His beaky nose looked like someone had half-heartedly grabbed a bit of flesh between his cheeks, given it a sharp pinch, then said: 'That'll do.'

Nothing was soft or curved; there were no kind gradations. No wonder his face had that waxy unwashed look. If I had a face like that, I'd probably give it a wide berth too. Those cheekbones alone could give you a nasty paper cut.

How old was he anyway? It was hard to tell. He was shorter than me, but he had a brutal crew cut and there was no puppy fat in his face. Then there was the way he held himself, the tense wiriness of his body, the way he stared out at the crowds with a weariness that hinted at a boy older than his years. From a distance, he could have been a fifty-year-old war veteran who'd seen terrible things on a battlefield that he could never talk about. On the other hand, he was still wearing that revolting pink and lime top, which any sensible child over the age of ten would refuse to wear, so that confused things.

The only lovely thing about him at all, in fact, was the colour of his eyes. They were soft and palely green, like lichen on sea stones. But even *those* weren't given gracefully, shrouded as they were by his lowered eyelids. As if the inside of his brain was like my cottage – full of vulnerable furnishings – and he didn't want to let the daylight in.

I tried to gather my thoughts. 'So . . . if you're alive, and if I'm dead . . .' My voice tailed off helplessly. It had been so long since I'd talked to anyone, I'd forgotten how it worked.

'How can I see you?' he prompted.

'Yeah.'

A shrug. 'I just can. See ghosts, I mean. Talk to them. It's . . . something I've always been able to do.' His lips darted to the side. 'And you're . . . well, you've become impossible to ignore, haven't you?'

'What do you mean?'

He raised a meaningful eyebrow at the dripping windows. 'Not many ghosts can do that, you know. I've met a few in my life, but you're the only poltergeist I've ever seen.'

'*How* do you see me?' I was curious. 'Am I sort of washed out?'

'Nah,' he said. 'Most ghosts are quite flickery and faint. You're not. You've got the strongest lines I've ever seen. It's like you're alive, to me.'

My proud, astonished smile faded at the bleak look on his face.

I glanced outside. Approaching swiftly across the garden were that nice-looking geography teacher and Olivine.

'I have to go,' muttered the boy in that ventriloquist way, staring at his shoes. 'But . . . Listen, you can't keep throwing things around, drawing attention to yourself. Just stop it.'

I realised who'd been behind that entry in the visitors' book. STOP.

'Why?' I said, puzzled.

He was still talking hurriedly. 'Take it from me, okay? It's better if you quit.'

'What are you *on* about?'

'Just trust me on this. It's—'

The door flew open and the boy pressed his lips together so tightly they went white.

'Scanlon, my boy, we've located you. I heard there was a disturbance – I was so *worried*.' The man rushed in and pulled the boy into a tight hug.

So *that* was the boy's name. Scanlon.

Funny name.

Funny boy.

Behind him, Olivine smiled uncertainly. 'Well, I'm just glad we were able to find him, Mr . . .'

'Lane,' said the man smoothly, pulling back at last so Scanlon was at arm's length, but still holding on firmly. 'Crawler Lane. Call me Crawler.'

While Crawler certainly looked pleased to be reunited with his son – his grip on Scanlon's shoulders was so tight Scanlon was practically wincing – I couldn't help noticing that Crawler wasn't *looking* at the boy he was so overjoyed to find safe. Instead he was more interested in what was around us. And the broken plates, overturned tables and steaming coffee machine seemed to have an effect on the shabby slight man in the soft faded clothes. It was as if some of that gentle absent-mindedness just peeled right off him, to be replaced by a bright-eyed alertness.

'I do hope this won't put you off returning to Sea View,' said Olivine. She contemplated the wrecked café unhappily. 'It can be easy to become a little, er, frightened of the, er . . .' she glanced up at the ceiling, not quite meeting anyone's eye, '*draughts* around the property, which can occasionally cause . . . disruptions.'

'Draughts,' said Crawler soothingly. 'Of course.'

They shared a conspiratorial smile.

'We don't mind a *draught*, Olivine. If anything, it's *draughts* like this that just make us love Sea View all the more. There's nothing like a historical house with a bit of *life* in it, eh? Stay away? We'll be back tomorrow! You just try and stop us!'

And, placing a hand on the back of Scanlon's neck, Crawler guided the three of them out of the café, throwing one last look over his shoulder.

- 35 -
DID I GET IT ALL WRONG?

ONCE THEY'D GONE, the kitchen staff tiptoed back into the café and began to sweep up the mess timidly, shooting glances around the room as if on the look-out for another flare-up from old Freaky Frankie Ripley.

But they needn't have worried. I was far too pleased to smash anything else up, for the time being at least. His name drifted into my mind and hung there, all sparkling, like someone had carried in a birthday cake with candles.

Scanlon Lane. I rolled the words around in my mouth with delight.

My new friend, Scanlon Lane.

Well. I frowned. The candles spluttered. Perhaps *friend* might be too strong a word. I picked thoughtfully at one of the shells in my legs.

He hadn't said much. There had been just as many awkward silences between us as words spoken. All I really knew about the boy was that he had no sense of style. And saw ghosts. But even *that* he hadn't told me with any real enthusiasm; he'd just muttered it reluctantly out of the corner of his mouth.

In fact, the only thing Scanlon had shown *any* passion for was in telling me what *not* to do.

'Listen, you can't keep throwing things around, drawing attention to yourself.'

Mmmm. Perhaps 'friend' was a stretch. Maybe he was more like an . . . *acquaintance*. Still, you had to start somewhere. It wasn't a promising beginning, but it *was* a beginning at least.

Anyway, I thought, stepping over the broken coffee machine and out into the garden, perhaps Scanlon had a point. As much as I enjoyed scaring the tourists and smashing stuff, it had its drawbacks too.

All that destruction requires so much *work* – you really have to see things through to the end once you decide to trash a room. You can't just throw a chair on the ground and leave it at that. No – that would look very slapdash. You need a concept. You need to commit to this concept, and give all your time and energy to it too. Like any other creative pursuit, being a poltergeist can take over your life. Also, it was quite alarming making so many people wet their pants all at once.

So I could certainly think about stopping, as he'd suggested. If not wrecking the house meant I'd have someone to *talk* to, then I could stop.

I might not know much about Scanlon, but I knew one thing: he was *wise*. Plus he was the only person who knew I existed. I couldn't wait to see him again.

Unfortunately, Scanlon didn't seem to feel the same way about me. Even though he came back the very next day, with Crawler in tow, he acted as if our chat in the café had never happened. Worse than that – he acted as if I'd never happened.

I'd gone to such an effort as well. Arranged my rotting rags as tidily as possible. Made a firm resolution to keep a grip on my temper, as requested. And then I'd curled up under the table in the hallway, and watched the front door like a hawk. When he appeared with the first lot of tourists at 9.01 a.m., I'd jumped up and shouted as welcomingly as possible, 'Hello!'

But Scanlon didn't even bother to look in my direction. He *blanked* me. It was a brush-off, plain and simple.

'H-hello?' I stammered. 'Remember me? Frankie? The, er, poltergeist? We met yesterday, in the café?'

Nope. Not so much as the tiniest of flickers in my direction. Instead he bit his bottom lip and stared at the carpet. Just like every other time I'd seen him.

Our friendship seemed to be regressing.

For a second, I thought I saw him shake his head quickly. Left, right. Like he was saying *no*. Or *stop* again, knowing him.

I rolled my eyes.

'I *understand*,' I said. 'No breaking stuff. I get it. I won't, I promise.'

But instead of replying, Scanlon's behaviour went from rude to weird. He began to walk around the house, staring into the nooks and crannies of the rooms, in a noticeably artificial way, using exaggerated glances and weird, staged neck movements. It was like watching a very bad pantomime.

Each time, Scanlon would shake his head in a disappointed way and say, 'Definitely not here.' His dad would sigh and say, 'Very well. Swipe to the next room.' And the whole peculiar routine would begin again.

I had no idea what they were searching for, but

they obviously wanted it pretty badly. Maybe they could visit the staff room and check Lost Property, and while they were at it, ask if anyone had handed in Scanlon's *manners*.

Back in the hallway, I lingered, half expecting Scanlon to at least write an explanatory note in the visitors' book, but even that he neglected to do.

'*Bye then*,' I said sarcastically to his retreating back.

I spent the rest of the afternoon puzzling over what had happened. Had I done something wrong? Had he changed his mind?

Shame and embarrassment twisted through my cold body. Could I have handled our meeting in the café better? Maybe I should have promised straight away to do what he'd asked? Or should I have played it cooler? Maybe I'd laid it on too thick. Had I come across as . . . *desperate?*

They returned twice more that week, and Scanlon ignored me each time. By the end, I'd given up. I was sick of the sight of him, sick of trying to work him out. Why had he talked to me in the café if he was going to ignore me afterwards? In fact, why come at all? He never cracked a smile, never seemed pleased to return.

Even Crawler's permanently amiable manner seemed to crack slightly, became a touch more strained with each repeat appearance.

Why did they keep visiting if it made them so flipping miserable? I mean, did they not have anything better to do with their summer holidays than repeatedly trudge around a badly lit cottage with a tragic past? I was there because I *had* to be. The staff were there because they were *paid* to be. But nobody was forcing *them* to come back. Why not just take their cue from all the other tourists, who only ever came once?

As for their increasingly long faces, those puzzling terse exchanges between the two of them about finding 'it', the way Crawler stood with his arms folded while Scanlon peered into every corner of the cottage? Random! Weird!

What *were* they trying to find? If it was that important, why wasn't Crawler helping out occasionally, instead of letting his son do all the work? Just how special could one item of lost property be? What was it, another hideous top? Big deal. Who cares?

YOU'VE **LOST**
SOMETHING?
SO WHAT?
I'VE LOST
MY ENTIRE
FAMILY.

Why couldn't they just go away? Then I could begin the process of forgetting him – like I was forgetting *them*. And then everything would be simpler and less confusing all round.

- 36 -
AN UNDERSTANDING, OF SORTS

It was late on Friday afternoon, in the first week of September. With just an hour to go before closing time, the house was quiet. Only a few stragglers remained. I was sitting in my room when I heard someone pounding up the stairs.

'No running,' shouted warty Ada.

'Sorry,' said a voice.

A moment later, Scanlon appeared in the doorway, panting.

'Welcome,' said Poe from the corner of the room, not looking up from his poetry notebook.

'Hi,' said Scanlon.

Then he looked at me, widened his green eyes, and jerked his head in the direction of the corridor.

For a moment, I nearly got up to follow him. Then I remembered how he'd ignored me for an entire week, and how much it had hurt.

He stared at me again. Bunched up his lips in what looked like an apologetic grimace.

Too little, too late.

'Can I help you?' I said. 'If you're seeking another dead child to irritate, may I recommend you try elsewhere? I hear the local cemetery is very good at this time of year. I'm *busy*.'

He raised an eyebrow.

'Busy *thinking*. You wouldn't understand,' I said.

Please, he mouthed silently.

I took a deep sigh.

'Oh *all right*,' I said. 'This had better be good.'

And I slowly and deliberately got up from the bed, enjoying his look of barely concealed impatience. I followed him down the stairs and out into the hot quiet garden.

From the side of his mouth, he mumbled, 'I thought we could . . .'

Surprised, I noted the tinge of pink creeping up his neck towards his face.

'I thought we could brain gage IRL together.'

'*What?*' I said.

'Brain gage IRL. You and me. This afternoon?'

'What are you talking about?'

He blinked. 'Sorry. Sometimes I forget you're from the past.'

I tried not to look insulted. 'How would you say it the old-fashioned way?'

'Erm . . .' He creased his forehead in concentration. 'Hang out?'

'And you all say *brain gage IRL* now?'

'Yeah?' He looked at me as if that made total sense. 'Right.'

'I haven't got long,' he prompted me again. 'Only an hour or so.'

But he wasn't getting off the hook that easily. 'Why have you ignored me for the last week?'

His face didn't move a muscle. 'I don't want my father to know I can see you.'

'*Why?*'

He flicked those eyes at me, and then I realised. How had I been so dense?

'Oh, because I'm *dead*? Would he think you'd lost your marbles?'

Now it was his turn to look stumped. '*What?*'

'Gone crackers? Mad? Er, mental data glitch?'

He rubbed the back of his neck. 'Something like that.'

I gave an airless sigh of relief.

Of course. Scanlon didn't want to get a reputation for seeing ghosts. Well, that made total sense. I could understand why you'd want to keep a thing like that to yourself. At the start of Year Five, Melissa Troutbag went through a period of insisting she could see her dead grandmother's face in our school canteen's baked potatoes. No one sat next to her at lunch for a *whole term.*

Scanlon checked his watch. 'I haven't got long. Is there anywhere we can go without those flipping Historic Homes people staring at me all the time? Somewhere quiet?'

Small shadows leapt across his face. I glanced up at the leaves rustling over us and had a brilliant idea.

'I know just the place,' I said. 'Brain rage ABC coming right up.'

'It's . . . Never mind.'

- 37 -
FRIENDSHIP AND RIDDLES

FOR TWO BLISSFUL weeks, I had a buddy. Our friendship didn't, admittedly, look good on paper. It wasn't what you'd call conventional. My friend never stayed long, never invited me back to his house, wasn't much of a conversationalist, rarely smiled . . . and he smelt quite bad.

So yeah, it wasn't standard. We weren't giving each other *Bestie For Ever!* necklaces, put it that way. But there were four or five wonderful afternoons when Scanlon managed to give his dad the slip and come alone. He'd race to the house on an old bike, looking and smelling so peculiarly pungent that the other tourists in the queue would draw their children closer and mutter about raising the price of the admission to keep the place *special*.

I hated to admit it, but they had a point. Scanlon was no oil painting. He'd turn up in stained clothes, reeking of sweat and paint and other odd industrial smells I couldn't place. Sometimes I'd detect another smell too, a sickly-sweet stench like a plate of fruit that had gone bad in the sun, but that would come and go.

And he was often sunburnt all over, with cuts and grazes on his hands. But he wouldn't be drawn on how he got them. The one time I asked if he was all right, he'd muttered something about doing some DIY for his dad, he was *fine* and couldn't I just drop it? Then he'd given a meaningful look at my threadbare Christmas jumper, shell-studded legs and battered face, and I hadn't asked again.

Our favourite hide-out was the tree house. Apart from being the only place without a Room Sentry, in the drowsy late-summer afternoons there was something lovely about lying on its rough boards while the leaves danced over us. It was also surprisingly easy to evacuate. Scanlon would simply sit on the wooden planks, with his particular *aroma*, and stare at the other children in that unnerving way of his, while I shook a tree branch or two to get the message across.

On the rare occasions that didn't work, he'd tell the kids that the café was giving out free ice creams. Once all the children had scrambled eagerly down the rope ladder, he'd draw it up quickly, so none of them could come up again, then turn deaf when they begged him to let them up. And he'd keep ignoring them until they drifted off.

'Ignoring children is something you're *really* good at,' I'd tease him, and for a second, he'd stare at me warily, then flash those ratty teeth, and give a short, sharp laugh of surprise.

Like Sea View on a rainy day, conversations with Scanlon needed to be navigated extremely carefully. I quickly learnt which topics of conversation he preferred, and which to steer away from.

Talking about his home, or where he lived, wasn't an area he seemed that comfortable with. ('We move around a lot, depending on Dad's work,' he'd explained curtly.)

What did his dad do? ('Collector,' he'd said, then abruptly announced it was time for him to leave.)

Once he *did* tell me how old he was. ('I turned twelve a month ago.') But when I'd replied excitedly, 'Me too! Well, nearly. We're practically the same age! We should have a joint birthday party!', he'd just stared at me impassively. Then he said: 'Your concept has flaws.'

He was closed up about his mum. ('She died when I was six. No, I don't have any brothers or sisters.')

He wouldn't be drawn on what Crawler wanted him to find at Sea View Cottage. ('I don't want to talk about it. Anyway, he's not going to find it. Not if I have anything to do with it.')

He wasn't much good at small talk either. If I asked if he'd had a good day, he'd shrug and mutter something unhelpful like: 'Define "*good*".'

When I asked if he had any hobbies, he'd snorted and said witheringly, '*Oh, absolutely*, I sail in the summer and ski in the winter.' And that had been that.

So yeah, not asking him anything too personal was a good rule of thumb. But I'm not saying he was bad company. Not at all. Some things he was much happier to chat about. He was obsessed with schools. He couldn't get over the fact that when I'd been alive, every child in Great Britain had been able to go to school for free. 'Education has changed completely since you were alive, Frankie. There *aren't* any state schools any more. They've all been closed since the government decided to spend the money on World War Three instead.'

'*What?*'

'Sorry. World War Four. Now, most kids, unless they're *mega-rich*, just use Skool Tools at home – it's like a plug-in? And if there's anything we want insta-cog for, we ask Coddle and then you normally get an instant load. If you have the tech credits, of course, which I usually *don't*.'

He loved sharing what he'd been able to learn from his plug-in schooling, whatever that was.

That was how I *finally* learnt what tent udders meant.

'People don't say things are "good" or "bad" much these days. Most adjectives have been replaced by . . . numerical grading,' Scanlon explained. 'In your century – or what *we* call the User Experience Age – people got asked so often to rate their experiences on the internet that it changed language permanently. That's what Skool Tool Module Twelve says anyway.'

After puzzling over this for some time, I worked out that words like 'brilliant' became, over time, replaced by the phrase 'ten out of ten'. Which, over time, changed into 'ten outer'. Which changed to 'tent udder' and sometimes just 'tent'.

And he said that people smelt of mushroom soup because loads of clothes were made out of mushrooms in the twenty-second century. Something to do with cotton not being sustainable, or something. The last thing he shed light on was the whole pyjamas-during-the-day trend. He said that people in *his* century wore sleepwear fashion in the same way that people in *my* century wore sportswear fashion: 'As a bit of a lie. Like, a lot of people in your century wore sportswear and never did any sports at all, right? But they did it to look healthier than they actually were.'

Basically, people in the future didn't get much sleep but tried to pretend they did through wearing pyjamas during the day to give the illusion they were more well rested than they really were. And then, looking more enthusiastic than usual, Scanlon started using words he'd learnt from Skool Tools. Words like 'status indicators' and 'sartorial power statements', until I asked him to stop because my brain ached. At which point he'd laughed shyly, and asked, 'Is this how brothers and sisters talk to each other?'

But above and beyond all of those topics, there was one thing he loved to talk about the most: my family. Although, really, it was me that did the talking. He just liked to listen.

- 38 -
A LULLABY

USUALLY, HE'D TURN up with *very* specific questions about the life we'd had at home, and then settle back against the trunk of the tree with a satisfied sigh, like I was his favourite box set. Questions like: 'What does "tuck you in" mean and is it fun?' or 'Did anyone ever make you a cake for your birthday, and what was it like?'

At first, it was hard to answer him. Not only was it painful, but my memories had grown rusty.

'There are holograms down in the garden for that sort of thing,' I snapped, the first time he asked me about the past, one afternoon in the tree house. 'Why don't you ask *them*?'

Warm, fat raindrops began to fall. The edge of the boards shone in the light.

'I'd rather hear it from you,' he said simply. 'So, *did* you ever go camping?'

My throat grew thick. Panic filled me when I

skimmed my thoughts. *I can't remember!*

But Scanlon looked so eager, so encouraging, that my fears melted away.

'I'm not sure,' I said slowly, experimentally. 'I think so. Maybe.'

Like tiny flowers, images began to open up softly in my mind. 'There was one place we used to go near here, called . . . Blue Cove, I think? You could only reach it if you knew the secret way through the woods . . .'

It was like opening an old toy chest and finding all my faded favourites waiting inside for me. As I sifted through my half-remembered life, pain and love approached each other, gently.

'We'd go there on Friday afternoons, after school, as soon as it was warm enough. We'd string up four hammocks on these trees we always used . . .'

Scanlon made himself more comfortable by lying down on the boards with his arms behind his head. 'What would you do then?' he murmured.

'Well . . .' I drew my knees up to my chest. 'We'd light a fire and have crisps and squash, and then we'd rest some baking potatoes on the grill for later, and then we'd swim in the . . .' my voice stumbled, '. . . sea.'

The pain turned sharp. I bit my lip.

Scanlon gave me one of his gentlest close-lipped smiles and it helped.

'Birdie always went in the water first – she was like that – and Dad would always go last, doing a big showy-offy dive, making a noise like a whale with a blowhole . . .' I laughed then, out loud. 'Then we'd go back to the hammocks and the baked potatoes would be ready, which we'd have with baked beans and sour cream, cos you have to have sour cream with baked potatoes – that is a *fact*.'

'I'll take your word for it,' said a soft voice.

'Then me and Birdie would drink too much lemonade and have a burping competition, and Mum and Dad would drink rum, and we'd play cards, and when the moon was high they'd tuck us into our hammocks and . . .'

There was a soft, repetitive sound from Scanlon, like deep breathing.

I stared at the wet boards. '. . . there were always loads of shooting stars.'

I closed my eyes. For a moment I saw the orange flames dancing in the night's velvet, heard the snap of the logs and the sound of my parents talking quietly, while the waves moved gently on the beach as if they would never, ever hurt us.

I tilted my head back and listened to the rain fall on the leaves overhead, as my eyes widened with realisation. I'd been lucky. I'd been happy. I'd had everything a human being could need: adventure, love, a rickety-rackety house at the top of the world, parents who cared more about spending time with us than loading the dishwasher.

Yet ever since I'd died, I'd been *pitied*. Tourists had marvelled at how little we'd had, how simple and unlucky we'd been, and I'd believed them. Well, we *had* been unlucky – at the end. But the rest of the time we'd lived life the way it was meant to be lived.

But that sort of joy – quiet and private – is hard to imagine, unless you have it too. True happiness is the biggest secret in the world. It's as impossible to capture as mist. You might as well try to put the solar system in a jam jar. It can't be contained or explained; it's beyond words.

So if the tourists didn't understand – so be it. If all they saw was what we *didn't* have, that said more about them, not us, and I'd just have to make peace with that. Besides, who could blame them for not really getting it? They did their best with the relics we left behind.

If they thought we'd had a picture of someone else's pug over our sofa, what did it matter? After all, when someone shows you their life, what are you expected to notice?

And it would happen to them too. One day, *their* descendants would look back at *their* time on Earth, and misunderstand them as well. It was just the way it was. But at least *I* knew what we'd had. I saw it properly, for the first time, and that was enough.

I looked over, feeling as if something inside me had loosened, and wanting to say thank you somehow, but Scanlon was fast asleep and snoring gently.

- 39 -

SHINING EYES, SMASHING GLASS

ONE AFTERNOON HE turned up with vivid bruising down his arms.

'What happened to *you*?' I asked.

'I was building for my dad,' he muttered in that sideways manner, flashing his Repeat Visitor card at Chrix and slipping into the dark hall. 'Slipped. Fell into some scaffolding. Nothing to worry about.'

I eyed him uncertainly. I wanted to ask him what he'd been building that could have been so dangerous – he was *twelve*, after all, so it could barely have been anything more challenging than Lego – but something about the way he glared at me defiantly made me hold back.

Once we'd navigated the hall and kitchen and made our way into the garden, we fell into an uneasy silence. I waited for Scanlon to climb up the rope ladder of the tree house, as usual, but he seemed distracted.

He took a deep breath and glanced around. Something in the skin of his face seemed to sag. That smell came back too, the one of rotting fruit, and I was unexpectedly filled with dread.

'Frankie, this is my last visit. I've come to say log off,' he said.

'What?'

'Log off. Er . . . goodbye? We're leaving today. Packing up. We're going somewhere else. Dad wants us to go to the Republic of Scotterland – he's got a tip-off he'd like to investigate for his collection.'

'D-do *you* have to go?' I stammered.

He nodded grimly. 'Yeah,' he said softly. 'I have to go. I always have to go.' He straightened his back and met my eyes. 'But honestly, Frankie, this trip here has been the *best* I've ever had.' He blinked rapidly, looked up at the sky. 'I've had an okay time. I've . . . well, you know – you.'

I stared at him, stung by how final he sounded.

'And you've only just thought to tell me this *now*? You've had an *okay* time?'

He flinched. 'Please don't get angry,' he said through lips gone white and bloodless. 'Please. You promised you wouldn't.'

'Why? What difference does it make? You're not even going to be here. Look at you, dishing out instructions as you abandon me. Wow, whatta pal—'

As my voice tiptoed steadily closer to fury, Scanlon began to look around the garden with horrid jerky movements, like a frightened bird.

'Frankie, I'm begging you. Don't do this. Just . . . let's say goodbye calmly, okay? I know you're upset—'

'*You could say that.*'

He squirmed, then looked me in the eyes with a dreadful sincerity. 'Look, Frankie, don't take this the wrong way, but this is a *good* thing. I'm *glad* I won't be seeing you again.'

At the sight of my face he had the grace to look sheepish and said, 'No, sorry, that came out all wrong.'

But it was too late by then. Things inside me were flapping their jagged wings.

'I thought we were friends, Scanlon,' I said. And then the full reality of what this meant sunk in. 'If you leave, I won't have anyone – *anyone*. You can't go. I . . . need you.'

You're the only person in my life – death, whatever – now. You're the only one who can see me.

'You *don't* need me,' he muttered. 'In fact, you're better off without me.' And he gave me a searching look before saying, 'Log off, Frankie.'

Then he turned and walked back into the house through the kitchen.

I followed him, stumbling and inadvertently walking through tourists, light-headed with anguish, trying and failing to work out how to persuade him to stay, to not abandon me too – not like . . .

We'd just reached the hall when a figure seemed to materialise out of the dark.

'Hello, son,' said the shadow.

'Dad,' said Scanlon in a curiously guilty voice, like he'd been caught with his hand in the sweetie jar. 'I . . . was just—'

'Saying your goodbyes?' Crawler said.

Something about the way his eyes raked around the hallway set my teeth on edge.

'When I couldn't find you at home I had a hunch you'd be here.'

Scanlon's whole body seemed to shrink as he walked towards his father.

'Got any souvenirs you'd like to hand over?' asked Crawler.

Scanlon shook his head. 'No,' he said tonelessly. 'I'd tell you if I had.'

'Would you now?' Crawler said. 'Would you?'

It was Scanlon who looked away first.

After a moment, Crawler said in a light voice, 'I suppose you can't win them all.' And, clapping a heavy hand on Scanlon's shoulder, he pushed him towards the front door.

If Scanlon walks out of that door, I may never have a conversation with another person ever again.

I stumbled after them both, past a father trying to strap his baby into a pram.

'Scanlon! I overtook him and held my hands out pleadingly, looking him in the eyes. 'P-please let's talk about this . . .'

With a chilling look of foreboding, Scanlon looked to the right and left, but his father kept steering him straight towards me, and a second later he'd pushed Scanlon right through me.

Well, that's torn it.

I stood there, gasping, spluttering at the taste of sweat and stale doughnuts all sour and stringent, and underneath *that* I tasted something else too, like cold ashes, the remains of a dead fire. And I should have paid more attention to that, really, but by then my temper was up and dancing about with gusto, and caution didn't stand a chance.

'SCANLON LANE,'

I screamed, so loud that the air around us seemed to flex and change and the baby in the pram began to cry. 'Scanlon Lane, don't you *dare* walk through me.'

In a daze, I became aware that all the bulbs in the murky hallway around us were spluttering, as if an electric charge was messing with their filaments. Warty Ada looked up at them, bemused.

Scanlon's face drained of colour, and Crawler slowly bent and started fiddling around with his old, stained, black leather bag.

I barely glanced at the odd contraption – a cross between a laptop and a Dustbuster – that Crawler had brought out.

I didn't even care that Crawler had started muttering to Scanlon, 'Whatever it is you're doing, keep doing it, cos it seems to be working.'

All I could do was stand and shout at Scanlon, while he shook his head and plucked at his father's arm and said something that sounded like: 'Please, Dad, not this one.

Please.

Please.'

Crawler was ignoring Scanlon's pleas and Warty Ada's attempts at asking him to pack up because it was closing time. Instead he seemed intent at jabbing, with determination and shining eyes, at the buttons on his gadget. I glanced at it distractedly. There were metal tin cans sticking out of it. *Weird.* But my attention snagged on something else: Crawler's face and how much it had changed. I forgot about the gadget.

Because he no longer looked like an affable geography teacher, not any more – how could I ever have thought he was mild and meek? His eyes were full of dark purpose and there was something sinister about the way his smile got wider the more Scanlon plucked, ineffectually, at his jacket.

Then Scanlon kicked the gadget with an awful angry cry, at which Crawler, without even looking, landed a hard flat blow on Scanlon's cheek. Although I could see a bright red smudge appear where his father had hit him, Scanlon made no sound at all.

I stared with fury at the man who had hit my friend, and then out at the world I could just about glimpse through the doorway. Furious, I grabbed the nearest thing I could find, which happened to be the pram with the crying baby strapped in.

'Oh, shut *up*,' I yelled, and threw it as far as I could down the hallway.

The bottom step of the staircase halted its progress and when it landed on its side, both wheels spinning madly, the father ran over and lifted the baby out, his face ashen.

'I'm so sorry,' began Warty Ada, as the man and baby fled from the house.

I picked up the pram again and, marvelling with a white-hot surprise at how strong I'd become, threw it against the wall. All the light bulbs above us seemed to explode at the same time and then the hallway filled with a loud droning noise, like a hoover had been switched on.

Scanlon sobbed. 'Dad, when is enough going to be enough?'

The world around me whirled and spun, and I felt something pulling and tugging at me, sucking and squishing me through a narrow tube, before I landed with a *thump* in what felt like a cramped metal box.

One which smelt suspiciously like *tuna*.

'What's happening?' I shouted. 'Scanlon? Are you there? Help!'

After a few moments, I heard the muffled sound of an engine starting, and a low continual throb as if from a vehicle.

Later – I lost track of when – there was a rusty squeak, the sound of a door opening then slamming, and Scanlon was asking, in a strange, flat voice, 'Where should I put this one?'

'Usual place,' said Crawler. 'Usual place.'

PART 3

- 40 -
WHERE AM I?

I WAS SWUNG upwards through the air. There was a clanging sound of metal meeting metal. Another door; the sound of it shutting. Then everything went still, as if time had stopped, as if the planet had grown tired of turning.

'Scanlon?' I said, my voice weak in the dark.

I stretched my arms out in the gloom as far as they could go. My hands met cold, ridged walls. I pressed my fingers against them, mystified.

Where *was* I?

One minute I'd been screaming at Scanlon and throwing that baby – I felt a flush of shame at the memory – and the next – *whoosh!* – I'd been jerked through the air like a trout on a line. And now I was trapped in a snug tin box. With no windows. Which would have been great if I'd been *dead* dead and looking for a coffin, but was not so great because I was dead-ish and liked being able to see and move.

How had any of this happened?

Had my rage somehow taken me into another dimension of the afterlife? Was death essentially a series of containers getting increasingly smaller, like Russian dolls? And if so, what next? A matchbox?

Or was something else going on?

Uneasily, I remembered the bizarre computer-hoover Crawler had been fiddling with during my hallway meltdown. Almost immediately after Crawler had pressed a couple of buttons on its display panel, my whole world had gone dark. I couldn't have been – had I been? – forced up inside the pipes and into the cans? Had those pipes *slurped* me in? Was I somehow *inside* his computer-hoover? More specifically, inside one of those cans that had dangled off the end?

I shook my head at myself. I'd seen a few odd things since dying, admittedly, like buses full of dead children and reluctant death guardians, clothes made of mushrooms, holograms, and people drinking crushed-up and insect skeletons, but that would be taking it way, way too far. Of *course* Crawler hadn't sucked me up like a dustball and squished me into a tuna can. Adults could be weird, but not *that* weird.

What I needed to do, clearly, was find someone who could tell me what was really going on.

'Scanlon?'

My ears strained for a response. There were muffled sounds of life – music blaring out of a radio, a noise like the pop of a cork exploding from a bottle – yet Scanlon did not reply. The only person I heard was Crawler, whooping and cheering as if he was having a party. You'd think he'd just won the lottery or something. And he was saying the same puzzling phrase over and over: 'Caught a whopper! Caught a whopper!'

In the few seconds of silence before he said it again, I became aware of another, much softer sound, coming from beneath me.

Someone was crying.

'Scanlon?' I shouted.

For a brief moment the crying stopped.

'Scanlon?'

No reply. I'd had enough of his ignoring me. I smacked my hands ineffectually on the metal around me. This gave me a brilliant idea.

I went back over the day, starting with the moment Scanlon told me he was saying goodbye. I deliberately focused on all the things that had gone wrong, and spoke them aloud to make them more effective.

'Not sticking around . . . *glad* he'd never see me again . . . trapped in a . . . no one telling me where I am . . . how DARE . . . I deserve better . . .'

As the fury kindled, my arms and legs grew warmer and agile. I pushed against the walls around me once more, and this time my container wobbled slightly.

Yes!

I pushed harder, muttering to myself, 'Reeks of tuna . . . worse than cat sick . . . absolute *joke* . . .'

A second later, like a beer barrel flung into a cellar, I flew through the air and landed on something hard with a clatter. There was a sharp intake of breath. After a moment, I felt a lifting motion, as if I was being picked up softly by hand.

Then everything went quiet again.

'Scanlon, I *know* you're there,' I said. 'Please can you get me out of this thing?' I tried to keep my voice steady – the darkness was beginning to get to me.

'I can't,' he said finally.

'What do you mean you *can't*?'

'Crawler put you in there, and only Crawler is allowed to get you out.'

'What are you talking about, Scanlon?'

A low but audible moan came from outside my box. Scanlon was crying again. I listened to it for a while, helpless, not knowing what to say.

'Look, things can't be that bad, Scanlon,' I said as gently as I could. 'Now, how about you help me get a bit of fresh air and some light in here? It's *so* dark, and it stinks of tuna. If you can't get me out, can you at least punch some holes in the walls?'

There was a deep sigh. 'I'd prefer it if you couldn't see out,' he said finally.

'That's *not very nice.*'

'I didn't mean it like that. But . . . if you want an explanation, I'd rather I couldn't see your face when I'm giving it.'

'*Why?*'

'Because once you know the truth, you'll look at me like you hate me.'

'Scanlon, don't be daft. You're my friend. There's *nothing* you can tell me that will make me hate you,' I said firmly.

When he spoke next, his voice was bitter and cold. 'We'll see.'

- 41 -
IT'S WHERE WE LIVE

HIS WORDS HUNG over me. Memories from the summer
scuttled through my mind.

'*Seen anything interesting, son?*'

'*Please, Dad, not this one.*

Please.

Please.'

An icy clamminess broke out on my corpse. What
had I got myself tangled up with? Who *was* this boy?
Desperately, I poked at the fading embers of my anger.

'I *demand* to be able to see out. Scanlon. *Please.*'

For an awful second, there was no reply and my mind
shimmered with dark doubt. How well did I know him,
after all? What if he left me in the dark for ever?

Then he said, 'Oh *all right*. Wait a sec', and I nearly
fainted from relief.

There was the sound of rattling. Moments later,
something began to tap on the panel in front of me.

After a few attempts, the tin buckled and flexed. Then a silver pointed tip appeared.

'Screwdriver,' explained Scanlon.

He pulled it out of the hole, and a tiny yellow dot of light broke in. When he'd made three peepholes, I pressed my face up to the nearest one, before gasping with fright.

'What *is* that?'

In front of me was a huge dirty white ball, with pulsating red lines running through it.

'Sorry,' said Scanlon, moving me further away from his eyes. 'Better?'

'Yes,' I lied. 'Much.'

His face was haggard and miserable, with puffy eyelids from crying and a long line of snot hanging from his right nostril. Crawler's blow on his cheek had come up as a painful-looking red weal.

'I need some answers, Scanlon. Am I in a tin can?'

'Yes.'

'Was I sucked up by that computer-hoover?'

'Yes.'

'Am I absolutely tiny?'

'Yes.'

'How did that happen?'

'My dad compressed your ghost. He uses a hydraulic press for spirits – he invented it himself.'

There was silence as I tried to absorb the news. I failed.

'Where am I?'

'Our caravan.'

'Is this your home?'

A bleak look crossed over his face. 'It's where we live.'

'Where are we?'

'About five miles south of the remains of Cliffstones.'

'No, I meant – where are we *in your caravan?*'

'Oh,' said Scanlon. 'Storage room.' His voice sounded taut, and my senses pricked up.

'Show me,' I said.

He hesitated.

'*Show me.*'

He spun the can around. I caught a dizzying blur of what looked like old books and a map. 'There you go.'

'Can I see a bit more than that? I want to, um, get my bearings.'

This was only partly true. Because despite the weird situation, his obvious despair and all the confusion in my head, I yearned to have a look around. *This is the future.*

Plus I was in Scanlon's house! All this time, we'd only ever met at *mine*. Here was my chance to have a nose around *his* life, and perhaps all those blank spaces in his life could get filled in.

'Can you walk around? So I can see it properly?'

'Fancy a tour, do you?' said Scanlon, curling his lips. And something inside him seemed to snap into life, and he quivered with a reckless, confessional energy. 'Here you go.'

As he lifted me up and moved around the room, he slipped into a high, adult voice, which I soon realised was an uncannily accurate impression of the Historic Home sentries.

'Ladies and gentlemen, boys and girls, welcome to the Lane caravan, a mobile *hole* totally unsuitable for modern living,' he said. 'We are currently standing in the East Wing, also known as the Box Room, also referred to, by those in the know, as the most hateful, rankest place in the world.'

I gasped. He didn't seem to care, and just went on spitting out his words.

'Take a moment to appreciate the filthy carpets, heaps of mouse droppings in the corner . . .'

The room was very small, and barely lit by the

solitary bulb hanging from the ceiling. Its light was so meagre that the yellow gleam it cast was almost greasy, an effect not helped by the squalor around us.

Meanwhile, Scanlon was getting into his stride.

'May I point out the authentic damp stains on the walls, and those dead flies, boys and girls, which date all the way back to the Minging Dynasty . . .'

I stared at the shelves which were piled with dizzying jumbles of things: loops of wires, mildewed clothes, crates of beer. A row of cans, like mine, lined up on a top shelf, above old hunting traps, wide open, like jaws waiting to snap. Dusty bottles with labels that said:

POISON.

'Inhale, if you will, the distinct aroma of the place, a mixture of stale air, unwashed humans and things going bad. Is there anything more atmospheric, more distinctly *Lane*, than the smell of their dirt?'

Even through the can, I caught that awful stench of rotting. It was very strong just then, and I gagged on it, then pretended to cough.

In the dim light, his eyes were black and desperate.

'It's not *that* bad,' I said eventually. 'It just needs a

bit of a clean-up – could be quite nice . . . I like what you've done with the . . . erm . . .'

My voice tailed off under his scornful look.

I was about to turn away, having seen enough, when I caught a glimpse of a photo taped to one of the bottom shelves. The light was too murky to see all the details, but it looked like a young woman holding something little and baby shaped in her arms. There was also a dirty mattress on the floor, next to a bundle of crumpled clothing.

Sticking out of the pile was a lurid stripy top. Pink and lime. My mind whirred.

'*What* room did you say this was again?'

'Storeroom,' he said quickly.

'What's that mattress for then?'

He said nothing.

'Is this where you sleep?' I said, as softly as I could.

My response was a fierce glare from his mossy eyes.

'Scanlon,' I said. 'What's going on?'

His throat worked a few times and finally he said, through lips as sharp as a paper cut, 'It wasn't always like this. When Mum was alive, it was much nicer. I had curtains, clean clothes, toys . . . She'd tuck me in. She *loved* me.' He shot me an anguished look.

I nodded. 'I believe you.'

'But she died. A long illness, something to do with her heart. I was six.'

'I'm sorry.'

'Then she came *back*.'

'What do you mean?'

He took a deep breath. 'Her ghost came back. To the caravan. We talked to each other for ages – she played games with me.' He nearly smiled. 'She came for seven days in a row. She always waited till Dad had gone before she appeared though.'

He stared into the shadows. 'I wish she'd never come back at all.'

'Why?'

'One day Dad came home early from the Alcohole. He was so quiet, neither of us noticed him. He saw me chatting away, laughing and singing along with Mum.' His jaw clenched. 'I should have just *lied* and said I was playing a game, that she wasn't really there, but . . . I was stupid. Me and my big mouth. "*Guess what, Daddy? Mummy's been visiting me. I can see her so clearly!*"' His mouth twisted into a grotesque leer as his voice changed into a mocking little boy's voice. His hate towards himself was so thick the air around us thrummed with it.

'What happened then?' I whispered.

'He *made* me ask her loads of questions. Things only she would know the answers to – like what my first word had been, when I started walking, things like that. Things I couldn't possibly know. She kept trying to leave, but I thought it was just another fun game, and I begged her to stay and tell me.'

Scanlon seemed wrapped up in his desperate recounting.

'After an hour of that, he believed me. He knew I could see her ghost. I *started it all off*.'

My can began to shake. Scanlon was trembling all over, from head to foot, a startling look in his eyes.

'What do you mean, Scanlon? Started what off?'

He lifted his face to mine. 'Oh, Frankie, do I have to spell it out? Once Dad realised I could see ghosts, he made me hunt them. That's why you're here. You're our latest catch.'

- 42 -

SCANLON'S SECRET

HE MADE A quick, angry gesture at the room. I stared at the map I'd seen, the mildewed books haphazardly piled up on the shelves.

'Guides to Britain,' he said quietly. 'A map showing places of *historical interest.*'

He spoke as if the words were thorns in his mouth. 'Anywhere ghosts might roam. Castles, ancient battle sites, old mines . . . seaside villages where everyone tragically drowned at the same time . . .' He shot me a look. 'You name it, we've raked it.'

Despite what he was telling me, I couldn't help but feel a flare of pity for Scanlon. Had he really been dragged to those spooky places looking for dead people? As a six-year-old? When I was six, the only things I'd hunted were Easter eggs.

Scanlon was on a roll now. His face was lit up in a horrible way, like a lump of radioactive waste inside him had started to glow.

'Oh, you wouldn't believe the excitement when Crawler found out about Sea View.' His mouth split open in the gloom and it was the abysmal smile of a boy who hadn't smiled for a lifetime. 'I was surprised the caravan didn't catch fire, the speed he tore down the motorway.'

He flapped another arm at the shelves. 'At the beginning, he tried hunting traps. Muzzles. Not very effective. Too slow. Slid off them. Then he built his machine. The Suck 'Em and Press 'Em. Works every time. Been doing it for years. Perfecting our *technique*.' His lips curled around the last word.

'I'm the bait,' he said finally. 'I lure them. That's what that stupid colourful top is for. It's *meant* to draw attention to me. Works with young children . . .' he closed his eyes for a moment, 'really well. They love the colours. It reassures them. There's a little girl in one of the cans up there . . .' His voice faltered. 'She loved it the most.'

He swiped roughly at his nose. 'And Crawler – well, you saw his clothes, that nervous blink? It's fake. Those pink cheeks? He uses blusher. It's all calculated, all part of the trap.'

I wanted to pull his vile story out of my ears and throw it away like a tapeworm, but there was nothing to do except listen.

'He's the mastermind,' he went on. 'He does the research, locates the sites. *He* can't see ghosts, so he uses me to make friends with them and reel them in. Then – well, you know the rest.' Scanlon closed his eyes for a moment. 'Mum never came back. Not once she saw what we were doing.'

'You . . . hunted me?' I said, after a while.

Scanlon hung his head.

'You have to understand,' he muttered, sounding younger. 'I didn't want to. It's *his* idea. It's always been his thing, not mine. I just do what I'm told.'

'Oh, well, that makes it all better, Scanlon. If you just do as you're told. You're off the hook there then.'

He flinched. 'I *tried* to warn you. I didn't want you to be caught. Don't you remember?'

Dimly, I did. The warning in the visitors' book. *Stop.* That afternoon in the café. '*You really need to stop doing this, you know. Take it from me, okay? It's better if you quit.*'

'That was why I ignored you when we first turned up. You have to believe me, Frankie. I pretended I couldn't see you. *To protect you.*'

'Well, you did a pretty bad job of it then.'

And then the scale of what he'd said rushed at me all at once.

'You've trapped other ghosts. They're in here, aren't they? Around us. On the shelves. *That's* why it's called the storage room.'

He hung his head and I knew I was right.

'Do *they* know? Like I do?'

'No. I haven't spoken to them since they got caught. I couldn't bear it. They all . . .' He gulped. 'They all went quiet eventually. They've been in there for years. *He* says they're in a state of stasis – like, when they're conscious, but barely. A sort of hibernation?' He almost looked hopeful.

My thoughts scrambled over each other, writhing like rats. 'How does he make you do it, Scanlon? What happens if you *don't* hunt? Does he starve you? Chain you up outside? Are you forced into it every time?'

Please say yes, I thought desperately. *We can still be friends if you say yes.*

'No,' he said eventually, in a small voice. 'He does none of those things.'

Little by little, it clicked into place. I felt my throat

tighten. 'He doesn't have to force you, does he? You don't ever say no. You . . . go along with it. Out of your own free will. Because . . .'

After months of not seeing things for what they were, now it was all I could do. The unbearable truth was everywhere, all at once.

'Because you *want* to hunt us. Because . . . you're *lonely*. And once we've seen you, and trusted you, and called you a friend – that's the best part of it all for you, isn't it?'

Scanlon looked like a cowering dog, waiting to be kicked.

'And even though you know what will happen, you always go along with Crawler's plans. Oh, you might try to fight it, at first,' I said quickly, not fooled by that flash of protest on his face, 'but not for long. That was why you didn't *keep* ignoring me. Why you came without Crawler. Why . . .' my voice broke, 'we went to the tree house all those times. You *like* it when we trust you. You want us to. You love being needed.'

As soon as I said it, I knew I was right. Scanlon had told me he'd never been to school. So he had no chance of making friends – not ones that were alive anyway. Even if, by sheer fluke, he *did* come across anyone who wanted to be his buddy, I couldn't see him inviting anyone back to this dump. Plus – let's call a spade a spade – he was dirty, he smelt, he wasn't much of a talker, had yellow teeth and weird clothes and . . . that *face*. So different, I thought, with a complicated mix of disgust and pity, to the glossily confident children who'd trampled through my house all summer. Those kids weren't the type to give him a second look, unless it was to double-check he wasn't standing too close to them.

'Dead kids are the only friends you'll ever have,' I said.

'You've got it,' he said tonelessly. 'Well done. Full marks to you.'

Scanlon peered carefully through the holes in my can and stared for a moment at my face.

He gave a grim nod. 'Told you,' he said.

There was the heavy thud of footsteps somewhere.

'But *why*, Scanlon? Why hunt ghosts at all? Why trap them in cans and stick them on a shelf for years on end? What's the point?'

The door to the awful room slammed open. I plummeted through the air in one dizzying quick motion, as if Scanlon was trying to hide me behind his back.

'You're not *talking to it*, are you, Scanlon?' Crawler sounded as smeared and lurching as the light bulb overhead. 'We've talked about this. Don't chat to it, don't sympathise. You can dismantle the friendship now. You've done your job.'

'I was j-just—' Scanlon stammered.

'Scanlon, what have I always told you?'

Scanlon muttered something.

'Louder, please,' said Crawler.

'Don't mistake them for humans,' said Scanlon.

'Exactly. Put it away.'

My can wobbled, then went still.

He's put me on the top shelf, I thought. Like a dirty secret. Next to all the others.

I pressed my eyes up to my peephole and saw Scanlon curl up on the mattress, still fully dressed in his filthy jeans and T-shirt. *No wonder he smelt*. No wonder he always moved so stiffly during the day, if that was his bed.

Then Crawler flicked the switch, and everything went dark.

- 43 -
THE THING IN THE WOODS

TIME LIMPED ON. While I sat in my tuna can, staring at the walls, Scanlon was kept busy all day and long into the night, running errands for Crawler. Although it was hard to tell one hour from the next, there seemed to be a rough pattern to our days.

When Scanlon got up, bleary-eyed, and stumbled out of the room in response to Crawler shouting his name from elsewhere, that was morning. When he limped in hours later, yawning, and crashed out on the mattress, that was evening. The intervals between, when he'd run in and fetch a bottle of poison or dusty book from the shelves, those were daytime.

Occasionally, and only if Crawler wasn't shouting for him, Scanlon would reach tiredly for a battered old laptop he kept next to his mattress. I guessed this was Skool Tools time.

And apart from the odd, shamefaced glance in my

direction, Scanlon largely acted as if I wasn't there at all. It was as if his terrible confession had never happened. Or rather, as if it *had* happened and he'd rather bury himself in busyness than make eye contact with the latest dead person he'd betrayed.

My feelings about it all were complicated. I knew he expected me to hate him. But I couldn't. He was too pitiful for that. You can't hate a rat for scavenging through a bin for scraps. Neither could I blame a motherless, lonely boy for conning ghosts into friendship, even though he knew what would happen to them if he did. No. I couldn't hate him.

At times I wished I did, because that would have been a good, honest, strong feeling. A sign he still *mattered*. But the truth was, most of the time I didn't feel anything about him at all. I certainly didn't feel happier when he came into the room, not like before. Something had died between us, and I don't just mean me. He wasn't the person I'd wanted him to be. He wasn't brave, or special, or wise. He was just . . . ordinary. An ordinary wretched coward. I hadn't lost a friendship, because it had never been a friendship to begin with.

In fact, nothing much went on in my brain at

all during those lightless days.

I wasn't plotting my revenge on Scanlon. I wasn't even working out how I could escape back home. What would have been the point in that? Home is a place where people miss you if you're not there. But nobody would be missing me. Seriously, who would care that Frankie Ripley, long-deceased resident of Sea View, was now nothing more than a canned ghost? I mean, would they be putting out a Missing Poltergeist alert? Crying into their pillows at night, longing for my return?

My guess was no.

If anything, Historic Homes were probably breathing massive sighs of relief that doors weren't being constantly slammed and prams weren't being thrown and windows weren't being smashed and Chrix's hard-boiled eggs were safe from harm. Sea View belonged to them now, not me.

And another thing. Crawler had found it as easy as anything to kidnap me from Sea View. All it had taken had been that handmade ghost squisher of his. That Juvenile Corpse Barrier thing that had meant to *protect me* had been broken as easily as if it was made of butter.

No one had turned up, asking Crawler what his

intentions were. No checks, no passport control, no 'Mind *if we take a look in your bag, sir? Anything to declare?*' He'd helped himself and smuggled me out and no one had done a thing to stop him. If Jill – or anyone else in the afterlife, for that matter – really cared about keeping dead children safe, they had a funny way of showing it.

It was time to wake up. I was completely alone. My friendship with Scanlon had been fake. And I had no one to blame but myself and those destructive feelings of mine. Let's face it: every time I felt anything, it usually led to death or disaster.

Maybe the answer was just to feel nothing instead?

So that's what I decided to do. I sat in the darkness, and let it drain me of myself.

After a while, it was as if my brain had been scraped out by a spoon, leaving just a big blank space where Frankie Ripley had once been, and very nice that was too. I felt light-headed at the beautiful emptiness inside me, like a terrible stomach ache had finally gone.

'Right then, my trophies. Moving day. Up and at 'em. Time to stretch your legs.'

It was Crawler.

My can shook, was lifted through the air, and a few seconds later there was the sound of a lock snapping in place. Sluggishly, I peered around. Had Crawler just said we were on the *move*? But where to? Were we going to be *released*? Plopped back into freedom, like a crab returned to sea by day-trippers? And where on Earth would I go then?

An engine started. Things around me went *whoosh* and *zoom*. Everything shook, as if we were driving along a long dirt track. I was jolted around like popcorn in a pan.

Footsteps, a door opening. Lifting again.

Through my punched holes, I caught glimpses of fir trees, dancing in the wind. Birds sang.

I felt incredulous. Perhaps we really were about to be let loose? Maybe Crawler wasn't that bad, after all. Who knew *what* went on behind that deceptively bland face of his? Maybe this was all part of some extremely complicated ghost rescue mission or something?

Then there were glimpses of something else. Man-made and dirty-bright. *What is that?* I pressed my face against the can and stared. In front of us was an ugly mishmash, a strange castle – a sprawling perspective-defying construction. It had turrets sticking out at mad angles and slanting windows in places that made no sense. It appeared to have been cobbled together from old bits and pieces: a jumble of wooden pallets, garden sheds, corrugated iron panels, splintered fence posts. It looked like it had been designed by a toddler and nailed together by a madman. Its overall lunatic design was enhanced by very rough brushstrokes of red and yellow and green paint.

I stared at it in confusion, not convinced. *I thought maybe I was about to be released into the woods like an endangered rare panda? Unless the castle was to be my night shelter, or something?* I eyed it warily. It didn't look like something you'd want to sleep in at night – or even during the day, for that matter. It didn't look like something that you'd want to close your eyes in at all. It would give a migraine to a blind man. It didn't look like a haven.

It looked like a nightmare.

'Isn't it beautiful?' Crawler sounded as if he was contemplating a glittering cathedral, not the garish mess I saw.

There was no reply from Scanlon.

On the move again. The crunch of boots on gravel.

A door squeaking open. A low downward motion and, seconds later, I was still.

'Come on then, Scanlon,' said Crawler. 'Bring out your dead.'

- 44 -
THERE ARE OTHERS

MY CAN SPUN quickly, like a weird carousel ride. There was a sawing sound, the grind of ripping metal, and then the top was lifted off. I blinked upwards, into the grey light above – and at a pair of sallow cheeks that could have been Scanlon's, until I realised it was Crawler eyeing me. He'd skipped the blusher. Now I could see how pasty his skin *really* was. It was like looking at a human crossed with an albino rat. Or a creature from the deep you only saw on nature documentaries. The ones that were disgusting.

'Wow, your blusher must have been *really* good—'

'Out,' said Crawler.

Gingerly, like a mole, I crawled out of the can, blinking, cautious. As my eyes adjusted, I saw we were in a large shadowy room.

Once I'd struggled free of the can I saw the red letters on its label.

FIDDLER'S TUNA: IT'S GREY AND SMELLS BAD, BUT IT'S CHEAP AND FILLING!

Just as I'd suspected. Tuna. The devil's own food.

I looked at my body in shock, held up my minuscule fingers to my face with horrified wonder. Would I ever get back to my usual size again?

'Who are *you*?' said a voice next to me.

I wheeled around in surprise.

Next to me, a pale face was peeking out of *MILLER MUSHY PEAS: HEAVY ON THE MUSH, LIGHT ON PEAS!*

The face gave a friendly nod.

Too taken aback to do anything else, I raised my tiny matchstick fingers in a stunned wave.

The face looked back into its can and said excitedly: 'Obediah, there's a girl here!'

'Well, stop lollygagging and get a move on so I can get out!' came the muffled reply.

A few minutes later, two young boys had crawled out of the pea can. They stood shivering in faded cotton trousers and threadbare shirts. Both had the same shiny new-conker hair, the same alert, interested way of lifting their chins attentively, as if ready for anything that should come their way. In fact, if it hadn't been for the stained red patch on the taller boy's shirt, the obvious lack of limb where his right arm should have been and the vivid bruising on the shorter boy's forehead and his bashed-in temple, I'd have found it hard to believe they were dead at all.

'What's your name?' asked the boy in the bloody shirt.

'I'm . . .'

'She's forgotten!' he guffawed, nudging the other boy with his remaining arm.

'I haven't.'

But I had, for a second.

- 45 -
PEOPLE iN CANS

TRYING TO KEEP the uncertainty out of my voice, I said:
'I'm *Frankie*. Who are you?'

'Obediah,' said the one-armed boy. 'And this is my
baby brother, Theo.' He indicated the boy with the
bruised head, who was staring around the dark room in
a sort of trance.

'From the Camberwell spike.'

'The *what?*'

'Spike,' said Obediah. He widened his eyes. 'Don't
tell me you don't know what a *spike* is. Ain't you never
met a workhouse boy before?' He eyed my shredded
clothes uncertainly. 'You don't look like a toff. What
are you, soft in the head?'

'Have you seen a boy, about our age?' said Theo
eagerly. 'He gave us much merriment. I have often
wondered where he went.'

'You mean Scanlon,' I said grimly. 'He's over there.'

The boys both fell silent as they caught sight of him, shuffling his feet a few metres away.

While the boys stared at Scanlon in confusion, Crawler occupied himself with inspecting the room around us, tapping walls and flicking switches as excitedly as a kid with a new toy at Christmas.

'*Him?*' said Theo, sounding disappointed as he took in Scanlon. 'Never! He's taller, for a start. Our friend was our height. And that person's face drops like a dead man from the gallows. *Our* friend was a proper gigglemug.'

'And yet that sharp nose is certainly his. I feel that *is* him, but grown like a tree,' said Obediah.

'Our friend has greatly changed,' said Theo.

'No,' I said heavily. 'He hasn't. He's been doing the same thing for years.'

Obediah looked at me with interest. 'Are you from Camberwell, Frankie? You do not seem familiar.'

I stared at him. 'No, Cliffstones.'

They looked at each other, then back to me. 'What parish is that?'

'P-parish?' I stammered.

Theo muttered to the older boy, 'Where are her *clogs*? She is practically barefoot. What spike doesn't give out clogs?'

Half-remembered facts and bits of lessons ran through my mind. 'I don't belong to a spike,' I explained, 'if you mean a poorhouse? They don't exist any more.'

'Oh,' said Theo and Obediah together, and a peculiar happiness stole over their features.

We were interrupted by a whining sound, the cry of something very young, nearby. I felt it pluck at my ankles and felt an immediate desire to kick it as far away as possible. I'd only given it a little tap with my one trainer when—

'You'll *murther* the lamb,' said Theo, giving me a filthy look, as he swooped in and picked up the snotty mess at my feet.

The child could only have been two, at a push. She had a dirty red bow dangling loosely from her curly hair. She threw me a baleful look and then turned her eyes towards Theo.

'Ma,' said the toddler. She looked as if she wanted to say something else, and for a second her face crumpled up in anguish, and then her emotions seemed to pass, and she simply stuck her thumb in her mouth and stared at him with vacant, almost unseeing eyes.

'Ma? Oh, bless you, duck. Where is your mother today? Is she in your can?' And he reached out and tickled the girl under her chin until she giggled softly.

But it was clear the can was empty.

Obediah, watching this exchange, said to me: 'Theo's always been like that. He'd befriend a mouse rather than kill it. He's only here because he ran in after me and got caught too. Heart like butter.'

I threw him a distracted smile, as the cogs of my brain worked slowly.

'Boys,' I said quietly, 'when were you born?'

Theo stopped tickling the little girl under her chin. 'I dunno,' he said simply. 'No one ever told us that.'

Obediah grinned. 'What are you, a *beak*?'

They both fell about laughing as if this was the wittiest joke on Earth. I eyed them uncertainly. It was like talking to a dictionary that kept opening at random words.

'Erm, well, who was your queen, or king, when you were alive?'

Now they seemed more certain.

'Queen Victoria, of course,' said Obediah.

Queen *Victoria*? That meant they'd been alive . . . I counted back on my fingers. *Back in the nineteenth century*. If there had ever been any remaining doubt about Scanlon's story, it disappeared then and there.

He *had* collected ghosts – and not just from my time either. Obediah and Theo had died more than two hundred years ago.

I eyed their wounds uneasily.

Obediah saw me staring and gave me a level look.

'Cotton press,' he said simply. 'She got me in the end. Theo crawled in to pull me out, and she got 'im too.'

For a moment, I could say nothing.

Obediah gave me a small smile. ''S all right, Frankie. It's just what happens at the spike. All the time. We got off lightly. We've seen bodies pulled out of there with no skin left. Theo's bash in the head is nothing to complain about – and I'm practically armless.' He grinned. 'You?'

'Drowned.'

They winced. 'In the bath? I always thought they were *wicked* things,' gasped Theo, eyes wide.

'No, in the sea.'

What a relief it was, to meet others like me! I was no longer the only dead child around. There were four of us now: the boys, the little girl in Theo's arms, gripping on tightly to his thumb, and me.

There were also other ghosts climbing out of their

cans. Beyond us, from a *TINNED SCRAMBLED EGG – NO SHELL, NO MESS, NO PROBLEM!* can, a mud-smeared and broad-shouldered woman was beginning to emerge, her matted blonde plaits just visible beneath her crumbling bronze helmet.

'Look at that driggle-draggle!' said Theo in wonder.

At the sound of human voices, she looked over and immediately raised her spear.

We all took a step back.

The last in the line to emerge, apologising profusely as she did so, was a slender young woman in a black dress. As she pulled herself out of *COCKROACH BROTH: JUST LIKE MUM USED TO MAKE*, a rectangular dent on her body became visible, starting just below her throat and ending around her belly button. She was practically flat around her tummy, as if something huge had landed on her once.

She saw us looking and said politely: 'I'm Vanessa. Have I missed anything important? I'm sorry if I held anything up!'

She caught me and the boys staring at the bruising on her neck and gave a sweet smile.

'My fault,' she said. 'Should have taken my purse.' Then she looked into the shadows. 'Where's that lovely boy? He said I could look after him.' She touched the tightly braided cornrows on her hair gently with shining red nails. 'He was the same age as my . . . as my . . .' Her voice tailed off.

'Oh dear,' she said simply. 'I've forgotten again. Mind like a sieve! Never mind! Ignore me!'

Just as I was trying to work out where *she* came from, with her shoulder pads and vivid blue eye shadow, Crawler cleared his throat loudly.

'All right then,' he said. 'Let's get started.'

- 46 -
CRAWLER LANE

CRAWLER STARED IN our direction with a fixed, blank look. 'First thing to know is very simple: I'm in charge here. If you remember nothing else, remember that, and we'll get along just fine.'

'Oh, I *love* having a boss,' said Vanessa. 'I hope I do a good job.' She paused. Looked around worriedly. 'What *is* the job? Do you know, duck?'

I gave her an uncertain smile and shrugged. 'Your guess is as good as—'

'Second thing: congratulations! You've won the afterlife lottery!' said Crawler. 'I'm offering you bed, board, work, an adoring audience. And the best bit of all is: you'll never have to deal with the outside world ever again.'

I looked down the line of ghosts. It was clear none of us had any idea what he was talking about. '*An adoring audience?*' What did *that* mean?

Even Scanlon looked confused.

'Ma,' the little girl with no name said uncertainly.

'Third thing,' said Crawler. 'I know you can see me, but it's not mutual. You're invisible to me. The only ghost-seer in this family is *him*.' He jerked his head in Scanlon's direction. 'But I can't. Never could. Never will. So even if you don't like what I have to say, don't bother whingeing, because I won't notice. All right?'

The little girl in Theo's arms gave a faint whimper, and was promptly soothed by Theo rocking her gently.

Crawler smiled. 'But I don't think there'll be much complaining. Because you're going to have a worry-free existence. You're going to have *purpose*. You're going to be useful, and I know how much you like to be useful. And once you've got used to how I like things to be done,' said Crawler, 'why, then we'll all be one big happy, money-spinning, showbiz family, and that's a Crawler guarantee!'

He spread his arms with a flourish and looked to the shadowy thing to his right again. I peered into the gloom, intrigued, to see what kept drawing his eye. I saw several rows of plastic chairs, in pairs.

'And because a business – and its employees – works best when it knows how it started, I'm going to tell you how it all began.'

And as we all slowly inflated back to our usual sizes, Crawler finally revealed the truth.

'Once upon a time, I had a wife and a baby boy. We lived in an old caravan, held down insignificant jobs, and plodded on through life. Although Scanlon's mother—'

'Her name was Nina,' muttered Scanlon.

'. . . always maintained that if we had each other, we had everything, I disagreed. I spent hours asking myself: how could I give myself a better life? How could I eat fine food, wear fine clothes, and travel the world in style? The answer boiled down to one thing, and one thing only: *money*. And we had none of it. But this was solved when my wife died of heart failure, leaving me with a healthy sum of money from her life insurance—'

'That was *meant* to go towards paying for me to go to school and a *house*, which you agreed to when she was in hospital,' muttered Scanlon.

Crawler made a flicking gesture with his hand, as if these words were pests to be swatted away.

'Now, not long after she died, she did something most surprising. She *returned*. Not to me.' Crawler glanced at Scanlon. 'To him. And this was fascinating, granted, but also completely useless. *What use are ghosts? I thought to myself. Ghosts don't put crystal glasses on the table.* Until one day, when I saw something that helped me realise how Scanlon's skill could be used.' His face shone with an eerie, passionate zeal. 'I saw a queue.'

I choked back a snort. Big *whoop.*

'Made up of at least a hundred people, jostling each other impatiently, desperate to be first in line. And it wasn't for the CuppaGrubba Drive-thru. It wasn't even for the toilets, although that queue was also pretty long. *It was for a fairground ghost train.*'

I looked again at that snake-like construction coiled next to Crawler in the gloom. Saw the mechanical levers at the front.

'In that queue,' Crawler went on, his voice getting faster and more animated, 'I saw excitement. I saw potential. I saw *money.*'

Crawler looked into the shadows with glittering eyes.

'I said to myself: if people are paying to be scared, that means there's money in it. And if there's money in *fake* ghosts, *just think how much money you could get with real ghosts.* And that's when I had my idea. One that would change our life.'

Crawler's voice grew gentle and his entire body relaxed. I realised that he wasn't really talking to us at all. He was recounting his plans and schemes just for the pleasure of hearing them aloud. Perhaps it was the first time he'd done so. Either way, he was practically floating with satisfaction.

'The two pauper boys were our first catch. Scanlon spotted them wandering around a block of residential flats in Camberwell, on the site of the old workhouse they died in. He was only seven back then, which was quite an advantage, in fact, as he was able to capture their sympathy and earn their trust in a way a grown man may not have done. Back then, of course, he didn't know what I had planned, so their friendship grew very strong, quite organically. He had no guilty conscience, you see. Proper pals they were, weren't you, son?'

Scanlon hung his head.

'The woman came next. Er . . . Vanity? Valerie?'

'Vanessa,' said Scanlon.

'Hello, poppet,' said Vanessa with a delighted wave. 'Where did *you* get to?'

'*That* ghost we found roaming the lobby of the bank where she'd worked. It took a bit of a shine to my boy, as it missed its own daughter, apparently.

Scanlon was nine then. It confided in him about how it died – a vending machine landed on its chest, back in the 1980s.'

'It swallowed up my only coin,' sighed Vanessa, 'and I'd promised to get a Twix for Giles the accountant. But I didn't want to return to him empty-handed. So I gave it a shake, hoping to dislodge some chocolate anyway – and it landed on me. Silly me.'

'Bad luck,' I whispered.

'Thanks.' She smiled. 'Although Giles sent some lovely flowers for the funeral, so that's nice.'

'Scanlon found the toddler up in Glasgow, all by itself, crawling out of an empty tenement somewhere near Pollok. We're not sure about its origins at all. Apparently it can't speak properly, and let me tell you, that's a blessing. Blank spaces are wonderful opportunities for audiences to imagine their own stories, put their *own* imaginations to work, and that's gold dust in this trade. Can you imagine all the tragic harrowing backstories punters are going to dream up for it? Plus there's the fact that it's a baby crying for its mother. People are going to go *wild* for it.'

As if on cue, the little girl with the grubby red

bow said, 'Ma . . . Ma . . .' again, and Theo looked at her adoringly.

That was when it really sank in.

We weren't just prisoners. We were *entertainment*.

- 47 -
THE ICING ON THE CAKE

CRAWLER CHECKED HIS watch and looked at us again. 'Isolde, the Iron Age hag, came all the way from Swaffingham in Norfolk. A local man had written to the local news churn saying he'd heard the sound of thundering wheels driving through a playground. I consulted my books and realised that playground was all that remained of an ancient wood – one that had, twenty centuries ago, been home to an Iceni tribe. Well, you can imagine how exciting that was.'

We all turned to look at the woman with the plaits, and she scowled at us and made a threatening motion with her spear. We looked away.

'Capturing it took a few months, but Scanlon was able, eventually, to gain its confidence by building a fire and roasting a squirrel to eat. It couldn't resist abandoning its chariot and wandering over to tell him he was doing it all wrong. Now, Isolde's quite hard to understand, on account of it speaking the Moronic language—'

'Brythonic,' muttered Scanlon.

'But, frankly, I think its non-verbal aggression will go down *very well*. So, after six painstaking years of hunting, I had the workhouse boys, Valerie—'

'Vanessa,' said Scanlon.

'. . . the Scottish baby and Isolde. But I knew I needed someone very, very special to complete the display. I wanted someone unlike the others. I wanted a ghost with *oomph*. Oh, I looked long and hard for someone like you, Frances Ripley. In fact, I'd almost given up on ever finding a *poltergeist*. Until one of my sources . . .' he tapped the side of his nose, 'tipped me off about you. Reports of supernatural disturbances, he said, down in Dorset. Unexplained wreckages. Old house. It was textbook. And then – well, you know the rest.' He threw a proud look in my general direction. 'We caught a poltergeist. Exceptionally rare, almost impossible to find, let alone *trap*. You're the icing on the cake, Frances. Top-drawer stuff.'

I saw the other ghosts look at Scanlon then. Saw it dawning on them, as it had dawned on me, the lie that their friendship had been. And I almost felt sorry for them all, until I gave myself a shake. *It didn't matter any more*. I was done with all of that.

'So there you have it,' gloated Crawler. 'Now you know. My search is over. I have what I need. I'll be opening a ghost train with *actual* ghosts. It's going to be an absolute smash.'

He clicked a button on the slender gadget in his hand, and on the large screen opposite us, a rippling image appeared.

'Had these made up specially,' he said. 'They're going out tonight.'

I squinted at the screen. My reading skills weren't the best any more, what with only having a visitors' book to practise on, but I managed to make the following words out on the brightly coloured poster:

LANE AND SON SPECTRE-CALS
PROUDLY PRESENT:
THE ONLY
GHOST
TRAIN
WITH 100 PER CENT
AUTHENTIC GHOSTS
MARVEL AT THE EXHIBITS,
FROM PREHISTORIC SAVAGES, TRAGIC TOTS AND
LEGGY LOVELIES CUT DOWN IN THEIR PRIME!
PLUS OUR VERY SPECIAL GUEST: FRANCES
RIPLEY, LOCAL TSUNAMI VICTIM TURNED
POLTERGEIST EXTRAORDINAIRE!

Obediah painfully attempted to spell out the words for his brother, stumbling at every other letter. 'We didn't have much schooling at the spike,' he said eventually, blushing. 'What does it say?'

But before I could help, Crawler was off again. 'You are standing in the ground floor of the Crawler Lane Haunted House and Ghost Train™,' he said cheerfully. 'Painstakingly and lovingly hand-built by us.'

Scanlon looked as if he was going to say something, then shrugged and went back to staring at a spot just above my shoulder.

Something clicked into place. All those cuts and grazes he'd turned up with over the summer, his bruised knuckles and the paint splatters . . .

'It's a labour of love,' smirked Crawler. 'It's a masterpiece. It's right in the middle of a very large private wood, so we're *very* remote. And people will travel for millions of miles and pay *whatever we tell them to pay* for a half-hour ride,' Crawler boasted, rocking on his feet and looking up at the ceiling, as if contemplating just how high his money would reach.

'D-dad,' stammered Scanlon, 'you never said we were going to put *them* in here. You said we were going to go into entertainment, and leave the ghost-hunting behind!'

'I lied,' said Crawler impatiently. 'It was for your own good.'

'Oh, you were *lied* to, were you, Scanlon?' I said. 'By someone you trusted? That must hurt.'

- 48 -
SOMEONE AT THE DOOR

CRAWLER FLICKED ON a few light switches and told us to board the ghost train. 'I'm going to show you your rooms,' he said.

With a groan and a clang, the train roared to life, before taking us down murky passages and claustrophobically small tunnels. The entire Haunted House was built around a winding, almost never-ending rail track, which, Crawler explained, was *meant* to disorientate the passengers, so they never knew exactly where they were.

'Heightens the experience,' he said knowledgeably. 'Make people feel lost, and you're frightening them already.'

As we flew through dank spaces, staring into the darkness around us, Crawler shouted instructions over his shoulder.

'You never ask for help. You never address the

customers directly, unless it is in character and agreed beforehand. You do not mention the ghost train at all – you maintain the illusion that *they* are visiting *you* in your own authentic time and place of origin.'

One of the rooms we sped past contained a working replica of a cotton loom, a massive, noisy, clattering beast made of wood with a heavy barrel in the middle which shunted from one side of the room to the other quickly.

'I want the workhouse brats to run in and out of the loom, trying to dodge it, as they attempt to rethread the needle and clean the dust from the machinery,' said Crawler. 'At various intervals throughout the day, I want them both to die all over again, screaming in pain. But – make it *funny*. Throw a little slapstick in there. You know, a few pratfalls here and there, before they get mangled.'

'We're being asked to just scream and run for a few hours a day?' Theo looked as if he couldn't believe his luck.

Obediah nodded. 'That's not *labour*. That's a holiday.'

The toddler, the Girl With No Name, meanwhile, was to have her own room, a replica nursery, with one cot, one faded blanket and one dirty old teddy bear.

'The room's been rigged so that whenever the ghost train enters it, creepy lullaby music will play through the speakers. The punters are going to love it,' Crawler told Scanlon.

The girl began to cry.

The train made an abrupt turn and led us down a few more corridors, before slamming through a pair of saloon-bar doors, which swung behind us. The room we were

in was very bare, with an elevated plinth and a bucket with silver spears inside.

'This is Isolde's room, a special place for a bit of role play,' said Crawler. 'The spears will be for the customers to throw at it. It has to stand on that plinth and dodge them, while growling and getting angry. If any spears actually *hit* it, it must pretend to die.'

He'd turned Isolde into a dartboard.

'How am I going to explain any of that to her?' said Scanlon, anxiously glancing at the exhibit in question, who was busy picking fleas out of her braids and flicking them away.

Crawler shrugged. 'It will get the idea eventually, I expect.'

Vanessa's room was what looked like one big meeting room, with a large desk in the middle. Around the desk sat three male dummies, wearing grey suits and red ties.

'Oh, I feel right at home,' said Vanessa.

'I want the squashed woman to sit here for a while, staring at the pie charts and profit graphs on the wall with a confused look on her face, like she can't understand it,' said Crawler.

Vanessa stared at the pie chart. 'I think the calculations on the graphs are ever so slightly *off*,' she whispered to Scanlon. 'I may be wrong, of course, but—'

'Then it will ask if anyone wants something from the vending machine. Then it excuses itself and walks to this . . .' he gestured at the snack dispenser by the wall, 'and tries to get something out of it. I've rigged the machine up so it will collapse on her sixty seconds after the ghost train comes in. And then I want proper death throes, right? Nice and loud. Give it some welly.'

I looked around the room. And then a delighted gasp began to ripple out of me.

'I've just realised,' I shouted gleefully, 'the flaw to all of this.' And I began to laugh.

Within a minute or two, the other ghosts around me were giggling too, uncertain of the joke but swept up in my bleak amusement.

Isolde's mud-smeared face broke into a smile and she clapped her hand on my back so hard that I nearly slipped out of the ghost train, which made us all laugh even more.

'Ha ha,' I gasped. 'Heeee hee.'

'Ho ho,' went the others. 'Teee hee.'

Even the little Girl With No Name stopped crying and began to gurgle happily.

From the front, Scanlon watched the six of us laughing with a look of yearning and loneliness. Once or twice his lips even stretched away from his teeth, before snapping back into place.

'What's happening?' snapped Crawler, as if aware we had become distracted.

'The ghosts – well, they're laughing.'

'*Laughing?*' said Crawler. 'Why?'

Theo and Obediah and Vanessa shrugged and promptly fell about in hysterics again.

I crowed, spluttering through my laughter: 'Because he's got worms for brains.'

Scanlon hesitated. 'Frankie says you haven't thought this through.'

'And why's that?' Crawler said very softly.

'Because *no one will be able to see us*. Who's going to pay money to visit a haunted house if they can't *see* the *ghosts?*' I jumped up and down on the spot again, thrilled to have got one over on the odious Crawler at last.

After a moment, Isolde began to jump on the spot too, shouting unintelligible words, giving me respectful glances as if she thought I was enacting some kind of war dance.

'All of this . . .' I swept my arms around, 'has been a colossal waste of time. His plan is flawed. It's cracked. It's doomed to fail.'

Scanlon turned to his father, and repeated what I'd said.

'Ah,' said Crawler, but to my surprise, he grinned. 'Yes. There is that.' He smiled approvingly. 'Well spotted.'

Everyone's chuckles died down, and they shot confused looks between me and Crawler.

From somewhere within the deep caverns of the ramshackle building, there came a loud, booming thud.

KNOCK.
KNOCK.
KNOCK.

'Right on time,' Crawler said conspiratorially, checking his watch. 'You're going to love this bit.'

He raised his voice. 'Door's open,' he shouted out into the corridor. 'Do come in.'

- 49 -
CRAWLER'S SPECIAL COCKTAIL

THE MAN THAT put his head round the door had bloodshot eyes and greasy stubble. 'Found you,' he said fondly to Crawler. 'What *is* this place?'

He weaved towards us as uncertainly as if he was an apprentice sailor.

'*He's* been at the Geneva,' whispered Obediah, miming putting something to his lips and gulping from it.

Crawler unfolded himself from the front seat and walked over to the stranger, who stood in the gloom swaying, with a sleepy smile on his face. With a smooth, practised movement, Crawler reached into his jacket pocket and pulled out a small glass bottle.

'Taxi drive comfortable for you, Will?' Crawler asked, as he began to shake the phial in his hands.

'Tenty tenty,' said the man. 'Why am I here again?'

Crawler clamped his arm around the man's shoulder as if to steady him, although his grip was so tight the man almost winced. 'You agreed to take part in a demonstration for me.'

'Did I?' asked the man.

Crawler nodded.

'What's that then?'

'All I want you to do, dear man, is some counting. I want you to count, then take a sip of something, then count again. Think you can handle that?'

The man's rubbery face contorted with silent laughter as if Crawler had said the funniest thing in the world.

'Well, I reckon I'll be pretty good at the middle part,' he said eventually. 'And as long as the numbers aren't too high, I 'spect I can manage the counting as well.'

Holding him firmly by the shoulders, Crawler spun the man slowly around the room.

'Look carefully,' he said. 'Don't rush it. How many people can you see?'

The man called Will laughed again, then made a great show of counting on his fingers. 'Well, there's me. *One*. Then you. *Two*. Plus your son on a funny little train over there – all right, lad – *three*.' Will beamed stupidly up into Crawler's face. 'Three people.'

'*Very* good,' said Crawler. 'Clever chap.'

'Is it the drinking part now?' asked Will eagerly.

'Of course,' said Crawler lightly, almost as if he'd forgotten. 'No flies on you, are there?' And he casually dropped the glass bottle into the man's outstretched hand. 'There it is.'

Will held the bottle up to his face with shaking fingers. His voice stumbled as he read the words aloud. '*Proparanol, hemlock, ricin.* What's all that then, mate? Some type of special brew?' he said, licking his lips.

'Just a little cocktail I've dreamt up,' replied Crawler lightly.

'Moonshine, eh?' said Will, unscrewing the top with deftly hands.

'I call it Ghoul Aid,' said Crawler. 'It allows you to see all sorts of fascinating things. Tailor-made. Years of research. Down the hatch now, there's a good man.'

'It would be an honour.' With a practised flick of his wrist, Will took a huge gulp in one swift movement.

Me and the other ghosts gave each other a look.

'Whoo-hooo!' Will shrieked, gasping for air and panting quickly. 'Yeee-*hah*! That will put hairs on your chest, and no mistake! Wow, Crawler, what on earth is in that?'

'Three types of poison.'

'Tent udder!' shouted Will, slapping his thighs. 'I should say so! Only the best! Poison!' He laughed again, then tipped the rest of the bottle down his mouth before going through the whole gasping and panting thing again.

All the while, Crawler watched him very intently, like a cat observing a wounded bird. Soon, Will began to rub his chest, before hitting it gently with his hand, as if to dislodge a pain that had started there.

His foolish grin became less sure, and a furrow of worry appeared between his eyebrows. 'Seriously, Crawler, what *was* in that cocktail? I don't . . . feel so good. My heart's gone funny.'

'I told you,' said Crawler. 'Three types of poison. One to slow your heart rate right down, to the brink of it stopping, and two to slow your organs down, to bring you to the point of certain death.'

Will frowned. 'You've . . . poisoned me?'

Crawler nodded. 'Indeed.'

'You're . . .' Will's lips trembled, 'killing me?'

'That's *murther*,' said Obediah, shocked.

'Murder,' I murmured. 'That's what we call it now.'

- 50 -
WiLL DOES SOME COUNTING

IN THE DARK, cold room, Crawler cocked his head to one side and regarded the dying man.

'I'm not killing you. I'm bringing you to the *brink* of death, in order to enhance your viewing pleasure. Now, let's go back to the counting. Last bit of the experiment. I think you'll find it very interesting.'

'No, no,' shouted Will, lunging towards the door. 'I'm not going to do any counting. I must get help. I'm *dying*! Got to call the ambulance – my heart . . .'

'You'll do no such thing,' snapped Crawler. 'I won't let you die, I assure you. I have an antidote right here . . .' he patted his other coat pocket, 'which will render the poisons useless and pull you back from fundamentally expiring. Once I decide it's time. But now you're going to do your last bit of counting, as *agreed*.'

Will slumped in the doorway, looking yearningly

out towards the corridor. He allowed Crawler to guide him back into the room, walking with small, shuffling movements. His skin had turned a horrible greyish, purple colour. He looked like a dying jellyfish.

'Now, count again. Tell me how many people are in this room,' demanded Crawler.

With a bleary, confused face, Will counted aloud with slurred words. 'Me – *one*. You – *two*. Your son . . .' There was a pause, while he struggled with the calculations. '*Three*.' And then his eyes widened. 'Wait. Wait. *What? Who are you?*'

'What can you see?' Crawler's voice was taut. 'Tell me.'

Will's face swelled with fear. 'A girl . . . in ripped clothes – it looks like she's wet herself. *Four*. A big woman – *tall* – with plaits. *Five*. Two little bo—' He gasped again and rubbed his chest. 'Two little *boys*, all – wrong an' . . . blood. An' a tiny dirty toddler . . . er, *eight*.'

The looks he gave us were full of fear. 'And a woman – funny dent in her chest – *nine*.'

'*Yes!*' shouted Crawler, dancing around the room in triumph. 'Bingo! Jackpot! All those years of experiments have paid off!'

'But who *are* they?' whispered Will, as his body trembled like a cold dog. 'What are they doing here? Where did they come from?'

'I will explain everything to you another time,' said Crawler, giving Will a blister pack containing two pills. 'For a price. Come back when you're better and you can see the whole show. Now, take your medicine – on me. You're *welcome*. You'll vomit for a few days, but that will go, and I expect you'll be raring to come back and see this lot properly. Off you go now. Taxi waiting right outside to take you back to the caravan park.'

Will limped out, casting a fascinated glance over his shoulder at us.

There was a stunned silence once he'd gone, then Crawler smirked triumphantly in my general direction. 'Hopefully that deals with your, er, concern.'

Scanlon swallowed. 'But,' he said slowly, 'do you seriously think that people – ordinary people – are going to *willingly* take poison so they nearly *die* just so they can see a couple of ghosts?'

'Yes,' said Crawler matter-of-factly. 'I do. I know people. Look at Will. He did.'

'But he's one of the most stupid people at the

caravan park,' Scanlon said. 'And you *made* him. Not everyone is like that.'

Crawler looked at his son. 'Never underestimate mankind's desire,' he said, with eyes that seemed suddenly hollow, 'for escape. Most of humanity poisons itself every day with all sorts of rubbish. Some people will take absolutely *anything* if it promises them even ten minutes of entertainment or comfort. Most people really are happiest when they just have something to stare at. My stuff will allow them to do that.'

'B-but . . . even if you're right and they do all take it, won't they get bored? All they'll see will be some sad-looking dead people,' Scanlon said.

'No they won't. They'll see the *only ghost ride in the world with real ghosts*. And they'll see *proof of eternal life*. Bored? Not a chance. Once word gets out, they'll be *fighting* each other to be the first in line. They'll open their wallets and tell me to help myself. And they won't be able to get that poison down their throats quick enough. Because . . .' Crawler smirked, 'they'll see a show they'll never forget.

Scanlon fell silent.

Crawler's gaze settled somewhere a few centimetres short of my face.

'Now then, Frances,' he said. 'Time to see your room, I think.'

- 51 -
TEMPTATION

THE GHOST TRAIN resumed its slow chug along the track, through a windowless tunnel that got colder the higher we climbed. Everyone had gone quiet; the shock of Will's poisoning and the reality of our situation were sinking in. Behind me, Obediah and Theo clutched each other as we clattered through the darkness; the little girl's eyes grew wide in the gloom, and she whimpered slightly.

It dawned on me then how upside down this whole thing was. As far as I could remember, humans were meant to be frightened of haunted houses. But here, it was the ghosts who were scared, and Crawler seemed completely at home. The whole place seemed to fit him like a second skin.

The train groaned and squeaked on its hinges, and an eerie, discordant organ tune filled the building.

After a while, the train slammed its way with a

clatter through a set of double doors, and I found myself in a bedroom that looked eerily familiar.

'How'd you like it, Frances?' shouted Crawler from the front. 'I tried to make it as much as possible like your old room.'

I remembered how much Crawler had stared whenever he'd visited the cottage, how his eyes had seemed to scrape every corner. Now I knew why. He'd been *taking notes*. It had everything. Same type of bed, same duvet cover, same rug. The bookshelf and desk and curtains were the same. One thing was different though.

On every single wall, hung in different types of frames, were pictures of the sea.

'Just in case,' Crawler said, 'you wanted any motivation.'

I looked around. I felt a fluttering in my chest I couldn't recognise.

'Ask your father . . .' I tried to keep my voice steady, 'what he expects me to *do* in here.'

Scanlon repeated my question to Crawler, who laughed.

'I want you to wreck it. Over and over. That's your job. You're a poltergeist, aren't you? So act like one.'

*

Crawler got out of the ghost train and began to open drawers and things.

'I've got it fully stocked for you,' he explained. 'There's linen to rip, pictures to destroy. Feel free to tear the doors off the wardrobe and bash these walls. That mirror there is made of especially brittle Venetian glass that makes a delightful tinkling noise when it breaks, so do try to throw something at that a few times a day.'

I blinked.

'This is all mine . . .' I tried, but failed, to keep the unsettling emotion out of my voice, 'to smash?'

Scanlon looked at me oddly, and then repeated my question to Crawler, who smiled.

'All of it. As much as you like. You'll never run out of things to destroy. Because at the end of every ride, we'll clear it all away and replace it with a whole new kit. Endless fun, won't cost you a penny, and the best thing of all: you'll have a supportive audience cheering on your every move.'

My thoughts pushed and pulled against each other. I didn't like Crawler, or what he'd done to me and the others and to Scanlon, but . . . I had to admit, he'd certainly gone to a lot of effort. And it did look . . . strangely tempting.

Besides, Crawler had a point. I *was* a poltergeist, wasn't I? Over the last few weeks, I'd never felt quite as alive as when I was losing my temper. Also, I was good at it. And let's face it – what else was I going to do? Back at Sea View, no one *welcomed* my anger. But Crawler did. Crawler wanted it to walk in through the front door, sit in the best chair, and put its feet up on the coffee table.

Why not just do what he asked? It almost seemed... beautiful. Like easing into a warm bath.

On the other hand, I remembered how he'd trapped me, the sneaky stalking around the cottage. A flame of resistance glowed inside me for a second.

Half-formed words of protest rose and died.

'I don't . . . You can't make me. I could just walk out of—' But my voice got feebler every time.

Because, suddenly, there seemed no point in fighting back. Abruptly, I had a clear, matter-of-fact realisation about what my options were. I wasn't somebody's daughter. I wasn't somebody's sister. I wasn't Frankie any more. Hadn't I scraped myself empty, back in that can? Here was my replacement – a simple, straightforward role – and all I had to do to make it permanent was say yes. And then I could throw that old life away, like a snake shedding its skin. A clean start. A fresh slate. Who was I to refuse?

As if he could sense my confusion, Crawler threw a confident smile in my direction. 'Come on, girl,' he said. 'Face it. If you left now, where would you go? Back to smashing light bulbs in a place you've grown too big for? You're better than that, and you know it. Don't you want to play with your considerable skills? Show off what you can *do*?'

My limbs twitched then – a small but perceptible movement, like a puppetmaster had pulled my strings.

And then, with an eerily confident glance, Crawler seemed to stare straight at me, and for a fleeting second, I felt as if his shadowy eyes had looked right into my churning heart and picked out the one thing I was trying to hide.

'Don't you want to be *seen*?'

Crawler turned to Scanlon. 'Well?' he demanded.

Scanlon's eyes raked my face and I gave one tiny, brief nod.

'She'll do it,' said Scanlon in a flat voice.

Crawler's face blazed in triumph. 'Rehearsals start tomorrow.'

- 52 -

SWITCH iT ON, SWITCH iT OFF

WHAT FOLLOWED NEXT was a month of gruelling drills. While Scanlon was put, reluctantly, in charge of rehearsing the others, Crawler appointed himself my coach.

This consisted mostly of him urging me to smash up my room in increasingly inventive ways. He pushed me to my limits. If I merely tore the duvet or pulled down the framed pictures, I'd be rewarded with a sneer. 'Don't be so *pedestrian*, Poltergeist. You can do better than that.'

He liked it when I pulled all the pictures off the wall, crying, and then made them fly across the room at his head. He liked it when I ripped all the linen and emptied the pillow of feathers and made the wardrobe fall over. 'Rip into it, Ripley,' he'd urge. 'Unleash the beast.'

He pushed me to work on my stamina. 'You're

going to be doing this for eight hours a day, every day,' he said. 'You've got to learn to pace yourself, and keep the rage going as long as you need.'

Sometimes he'd take Ghoul Aid himself, so he could speak to me directly. If I got tired, he'd tell me that ghosts didn't get tired. If I felt wobbly or weak, he'd shake his head in derision.

'You have to do it without thinking,' he said. 'Without feeling. Like a machine. It's just who you are. Empty your mind of everything. Get rid of your frailties. Forget your memories. Stay in the moment.' Then he'd check the timer. 'Five hours and thirty-three minutes. It's not *bad*. But it's not great either. One more time, from the top. Scanlon, new stock please!'

After four weeks – when I was able to wreck and kick and scratch and break for exactly nine hours without a break – he even broke into a smile.

'Bring in the mannequins,' he said one morning.

'Mannequins?' I stammered, pushing some matted hair out of my face.

Scanlon silently wheeled in a trolley full of stuffed dummies, some child sized, some adult sized.

'Of course,' said Crawler, panting slightly from the poison in his system. 'You didn't think you'd just be chucking plates about, did you? People are paying for some *fun* here. You'll be throwing punters across the room at least twenty times a day. Now, try to pick one up.'

Heaving and grunting, I tried to pick up the nearest one. 'What's it stuffed with, *lead?*'

'Sand. Should make you feel right at home.' He gave me an evil grin. 'Try again.'

This time, I succeeded in picking up the smallest dummy by half a centimetre.

'Oh dear,' he sighed. What a weakling you are, Frances. Totally puny. Call yourself a poltergeist? Think anyone's going to be applauding *that?* You've got star billing here, so try not to embarrass yourself.' He looked closely into my face.

'I can't do it,' I said, feeling beaten. 'I just can't.'

'What a defeatist you are. Do you want to leave? Is that it? Well then, go. The exit's that way. If you can't be bothered, I'd rather you went, so I can go and find a poltergeist who really *wants* this.'

'No,' I stammered. 'Y-you don't have to do that—'

'Were you this much of a deadbeat when you were

alive? No wonder your parents didn't bother coming back for you – if they would've been welcomed by an attitude like that . . .'

'Shut *up*,' I snarled.

'Try again,' said Crawler, smirking.

This time, I picked up that tiny child-size dummy and managed to hurl it as far as his feet.

'Take it back,' I muttered. 'Take it back.'

'No,' he said. 'It works. Look at you. You're trembling all over with rage. You needed that.'

After a few more days, I could throw the biggest dummies across the room with ease. The most surprising thing of all was that I didn't even need to make an effort any more. I was doing it automatically.

'It's better when you don't feel anything,' Crawler told me, and I believed him. 'Too much emotion can make you hysterical, and renders you useless. You need to learn to make it happen without even thinking about it.'

One day, Crawler said, 'Frances? Can you throw your bed across the room?'

I stared at him blankly.

Then he said, 'Throw that bed across the room,

Poltergeist', and I did it immediately, without question, without thinking.

He gave me a satisfied smirk.

'I think we're ready to open.'

- 53 -
GO AND DO YOUR THING

'Er, WHAT IS this?'

The guest list had been drawn up, the invites had been sent out, the bookings had been taken. Every centimetre of the ghost train had been decorated with fake cobwebs and fresh splatters of artificial blood. From outside the Haunted House came a human mumbling sound and it was growing louder by the second.

Tonight was the *premiere*. I'd been primed and trained till I was destroying my bedroom with my eyes closed. And now Scanlon was standing in front of me and spraying something sticky and synthetic on to my face.

He had the grace to look ashamed. 'Spray-on cobwebs,' he muttered. 'For the *atmosphere*. Crawler's orders.'

Strands of it clung to my hair and eyelashes. It made my nostrils itch.

'*Is this an actual joke?*' I said.

'Sorry,' he muttered, trying to wipe some of it away, and failing. 'If it makes anything better, everyone's got to have this, even me.'

I met his eyes reluctantly and a little shyly. I hadn't seen much of him over the last few weeks, apart from a few awkward moments during my training when Crawler shouted at him to bring in a cup of tea and an extra shot of Ghoul Aid.

'Have you seen the others?' I asked.

'Yes,' he said. 'I see them every day. I've been putting them through . . . their moves.'

'How are they?'

'They're . . .' Scanlon hesitated. 'Well, they were quite stunned at first, but now I think they're just happy to be out of their cans and to have something to do. Isolde isn't that thrilled, I don't think, but it's hard to know what she's telling me. And I think the little girl is . . . just confused, and upset. She keeps trying to hug people, but no one has the time. And she's *always* asking for her mummy. But the boys and Vanessa can't wait to get started. They keep telling me how grateful they are, to have a bed and board and a job. It's . . . it's *awful*.'

'Maybe you should have thought about that before you hunted us.'

'You're never going to forgive me for that.' It wasn't a question.

'Does it matter?' I said. 'We're here now. Perhaps Vanessa and the boys have a point.'

It felt as if my head was full of dust. Tired all of a sudden, I moved away. Outside, the excited chatter of the crowd swelled and burst.

'You'd better leave,' I said. 'Go and do your thing.'

He moved towards the double doors and looked back over his shoulder. He'd smartened up for the occasion and was kitted out in a red tuxedo, like something a lion tamer might have worn. It made me almost miss his horrid lime and pink T-shirt.

Scanlon bunched up his lips and gave me a flash of those ratty teeth. 'Good luck, Frankie.'

For a moment, there was a responding flicker of something inside me, something softer. I could just *leave*. Wait for the door downstairs to open, and slip out, into the woods. And I could take Scanlon with me. Neither of us was in chains. Really, when you looked at it, we could leave any time we wanted. That was the genius of Crawler – he'd persuaded us all to stay because it was *best for us*. But we *could* leave, if we really wanted.

But was it what I wanted?

I felt a vast, nameless longing. I *had* known, once, but I didn't now. This place had wiped it out of me.

'Scanlon?' I said, throwing out his name like a lifeline.

But in the split second before he turned around, I'd already rejected of the idea of breaking free. *Where* would we go? Where would be right? I'd seen how little either of us fitted in out there. Besides, it wasn't like we were *friends*.

Anyway – I thought about all the training I'd done – I was kind of looking forward to putting on a show.

Scanlon lingered at the doorway. 'Did you say something?' he said gently.

'Nope,' I muttered.

A few moments later, he had gone.

Then all the lights in my room went out, and the spooky organ music started up. Somewhere from the depths of the building came the clatter of the ghost train as it brought me my first audience.

In the dark, I felt my lips stretch back, and heard a strange, dry chuckle, which scared me for a second till I realised it was mine. I moved my neck to the left, then the right, rolled my shoulders, circled my wrists. Felt things

    pop and snap

        and

            tweak and wake.

GURTAIN'S UP.

- 54 -
WILD SUCCESS AND DANCING MONKEYS

DESPITE THEIR FINE clothes and fancy handbags, the crowd at the Crawler Lane Haunted House and Ghost Train™ (with Real Ghosts! And Live Performances from the Dead! Every Night!) all seemed quite ugly, somehow, and not just because they were often grey, bleeding from their eyeballs and vomiting over the side of their carriages. No: it was the delight in their eyes as they came clattering in, fresh from spearing Isolde and ogling orphans and watching people die for their viewing pleasure. They just seemed like not very nice people.

But they were a total picnic compared to the sad ones. The ones who'd lost relatives and loved ones, who stared at me with their desperate eyes, seeking comfort from me. I grew tired of them trying to grab me from their seats, begging me to tell them if I'd seen their little boy, or had any word from their sister, or come across their best friend anywhere, anywhere, had I? Could I possibly look for them? Would I mind? They'd be ever so grateful.

'*Leave me alone,*' I wanted to snap at them. '*If you've lost someone, they're lost for ever. Deal with it.*'

I ignored them instead. No way would they interfere with my performance – I was too trained, too slick for that. And eventually they'd leave, with terrible strained smiles of grief, dabbing tears away, and I'd think, *Phew*. But then they'd come back. It was a nightmare. They wouldn't give up.

In the end, Crawler, never one to pass up on an opportunity, made me lie to them, and say I *had* seen their loved ones. And, for an astronomical fee, I'd relay a message for them from their great-auntie Barbaronka Majonka or whoever. (Which I'd make up.)

Yes, I much preferred those who just wanted to stare at me, who treated me like a firework display of sorts, went *oooh* and *aaah* in all the right places. They wanted me to perform – that's what I did, and then they left me alone. Nice and straightforward. Dead easy.

And Crawler was right about something else as well. I *loved* being seen. Whenever I heard that announcement over the speakers that let me know the ghost train was winding its way up the track towards me ('And now, ladies and gentlemen, the star of the show, the ghost with the most, your very own ghoul with the killer-watt act, it's *POLTERGEIST TIME!*'), I'd get all excited and shivery. And once everyone had gone, I'd lie on my bed and stare up at the ceiling and go over my performance again and again, working out what went down well, and refining what wasn't so effective.

Within a couple of weeks, my whole attitude towards Crawler changed. Whereas before I'd thought of him as the very devil himself, now he seemed more like a benevolent benefactor. After all, before he'd come along, my whole existence had been about what I *couldn't* do. My temper had been a curse – it had made people cry, not to mention wet themselves.

I mean, in essence, ever since I'd been born, and certainly since I'd died, everyone I'd ever known had seen me through a filter of *can't*. '*You can't lose your temper at your little sister, Frankie. You can't set fire to the village hall. You can't scowl at Thea Thrubwell like you hate her guts, even if you do. You can't roam around unaccompanied if you've died.*' Even my so-called friendship with Scanlon only started once he'd told me what I *couldn't* do.

But Crawler wasn't like that. He wasn't interested in limits or what I couldn't do. All he was interested in was what I *could* do. I was *allowed* to get angry. It was my talent. It was the big draw. He saw me through *can*. He saw me through the filter of *do it again, and do it worse*. He saw the storm inside me, and he encouraged me to let it out.

It was kind of refreshing.

Even the spooky organ music that played all day, every day, began to sound quite jaunty and welcoming, in its own eerie, discordant way. I hummed it when it wasn't on. I missed it when it wasn't playing. And I only really felt like myself when it began again. It was my soundtrack. It was my theme tune. It made me come alive.

After a couple of weeks, I didn't recognise the people in the photo on the wall. I knew I'd lived somewhere else, once, and had a life, once, but that meant nothing to me now. There was nothing, absolutely nothing in my heart, apart from the ambition to make even more of a mess the next time that ghost train came clattering through my door. I had become something wonderful.

I had become a professional, full-time, all-consuming poltergeist, and there was no longer any room for anything else.

I smashed things. I broke things.

That was who I was.

- 55 -
BIRTHDAY SURPRISE

SCANLON APPEARED AT my door. 'Frankie,' he said in a frazzled, tight voice, 'Crawler says to let you know that you're heading out this morning.'

'*Out?*' I said, confused.

I didn't like the sound of *out*. I preferred *in*.

'Why? Have I done something wrong?'

'No, nothing like that. You're not being *booted* out. You're being *hired* out.'

I stared at him dully. 'Huh?'

'It's a private booking. We're doing those now. There's a Lady Someone-or-Other who wants you to put in an appearance at her daughter's twenty-first birthday party. Dad thinks this could be a lucrative side business.'

I shrugged. 'Okay. Hey, what's happened to your teeth?'

His cheeks went pink. 'Dad paid for them to be

straightened and whitened,' he said. 'I'm front of house now. I greet the guests, and I'm in charge of corporate booking and international sales. He said my smile was frightening the punters. Or, as he put it: *"You're not part of the show, Scanlon. You can't look more frightening than the spooks."'*

'What does corporate booking and the other . . . thing mean?'

'International sales? Big bookings for large companies,' he said. 'Lots of business people have started coming for their office parties. People are travelling here from all over the world, and you wouldn't believe what they're paying.'

'So you're doing well then, I take it? I mean, the teeth whitening and the private bookings and the money?'

Scanlon busied himself straightening his cuff. 'I guess.'

'Are you still living in the caravan?'

'Not any more. We've got a penthouse. A big one. With a pool. And staff. Someone cooks for us.'

'That must be nice,' I said.

His eyes met mine. After a pause, he shrugged. 'S'pose.'

'So it's worked out for everyone then. I mean, you

and Crawler are set up for life, and everyone's happy downstairs?'

There was a flash of something in his face then, and for a second I was reminded of the scathing awkward boy I'd once known.

'Depends what you mean by *happy*, Frankie.'

He had a confessional look. There was something inside him, I could sense, that he wanted to tell me, if I would only ask the right question. Some secret of his that he wanted me to break wide open, like a clam. But I'd lost the habit of friendship. Besides, why should I waste my energy on another of his riddles? Asking questions of Scanlon only led to disturbing answers.

So all I said was: 'Are we going to this party then, or what?'

Scanlon closed his eyes for a second. When he opened them again, that look had gone.

'The limo's outside.'

A few hours later, our flying car lowered over a vast field before parking neatly outside a creamy stately home. We stepped out on to a crunchy path edged with twigs.

'This way,' said Crawler.

The ground was black with frozen leaves. A bird tried

fruitlessly to peck at the hard ground. And a startling question flared into life inside me, for a moment.

'Scanlon,' I hissed.

He looked over his shoulder.

'How long have we been open? The Haunted House?'

'About eighteen months,' he said, regarding me quizzically. 'Why?'

Eighteen months? It didn't feel like eighteen months – a month at the most. I stumbled on the path.

'Are you sure?'

'Yeah,' he said. 'What's—'

'No whispering,' snapped Crawler, knocking on the wooden door in front of us.

It swung open.

'Good morning,' said Crawler. 'I'm Mr Lane, from Lane and Son Spectre-cals? We're expected.'

'Yes,' said someone.

We were ushered into a cool hallway.

'Follow me.'

I had just enough time to observe how many dead stuffed animals were mounted on the walls before we were whisked off down a wide corridor, lined with portraits of men and women and inscribed with their lifespans. *The Right Hon. Fancypants of Posh House, 2056–2117,* that sort of thing. More dead people on the walls.

I rolled my eyes. Same old. *You might as well take them down, chum. The people who live here can't see them anyway. Trust me.*

A vast ballroom lay before us. Overhead curved a domed turquoise ceiling, studded generously with golden cherubs. They reminded me of something. We regarded each other a moment, but their blank gold faces gave nothing away.

The smartly dressed crowd of young people within the ballroom chatted lazily, admiring each other's clothes. Around them circulated catering staff, pouring drinks and dishing out snacks. At first glance you would have mistaken the waiters for humans, until you spotted the whirring silver discs that made up their lower halves.

Our escort said discreetly, 'Madam?'

A tanned, red-haired woman with a wide, freckly face looked over unsmilingly.

Crawler gave a short bow. 'Lady Craven,' he said. 'I have your order.'

'How perfectly fleck,' she said, clapping her hands

together a little too loud. 'Drixie! Drixie Tink! Mummy's got you a birthday surprise.'

The young woman that slowly materialised from the crowd was even more tanned than her mother, and very thin, with big round eyes fringed by delicate pink feathers.

'Mum, I thought we agreed – *no more surprises*,' she said. 'I still haven't got over that ten-tonne tightrope walker you booked last year. No one sitting underneath him stood a chance. I still hear their screams in my nightma—'

'This surprise is different,' said Lady Craven quickly.

'*How?*' said Drixie.

'I'll show you,' said Crawler.

At a nod from his father, Scanlon walked slowly around the ballroom, pouring out the poison.

- 56 -
WHAT ARE WE DOING?

To Scanlon, Crawler said: 'Get it in position.'

Scanlon looked at me, his cheeks reddening. 'Fran—, er, *Poltergeist*, do you think you can go and stand on top of that box, over there?'

'What?' said Drixie. 'Who is he talking to?'

'You'll see in a minute,' said Crawler smoothly. 'Now, has everyone got their Ghoul Aid ready?'

Scanlon was pointing to the middle of the ballroom. I saw a tiered plinth, the sort you'd find under a statue in a museum.

'That box,' said Scanlon again.

'What – you want me to break it?' I said.

'All you've been booked to do is, erm, stand on it.'

'Really? That's all? But I could throw it! Or chuck it at the window?'

He shook his head, checked the form in his hand. 'Our client was very specific about ticking the "No

Destruction" box when she booked. Doesn't want any of the antiques broken.'

'Certainly not,' said Lady Craven. 'They're priceless.'

So she is happy to poison her daughter, but watch out for the furniture? Er, okay.

To Scanlon, I said: 'But what shall I do instead?'

'Just . . .' Scanlon looked awkward, 'stand. You're a display. You're just here to be looked at.' He gave me a strained smile. 'Please.'

I thought of those animals on the walls, the deceased people in their frames. These people, I thought abruptly, seemed to like their dead that way. Hanging about. Part of the furniture. Not quite around, not quite free.

'Smash *nothing*?' I checked, flustered and a little rattled. 'You sure?'

Scanlon nodded. 'Think of it as the easiest gig you'll ever do. You won't have to lift a finger.'

'And . . . drink!' shouted Crawler, with a flourish.

The guests, as one, downed their poison, swapping excited looks.

Something flapped in my head like a sheet on a washing line. If I wasn't here to show off what I could do, why was I here at all? If all Lady Craven wanted was a dead thing for her daughter to gawp at, why not just buy her a pack of sausages?

Above the usual sound of people moaning with nausea as the first drips of poison trickled into their veins, I heard a terrifying, cold voice of doubt. *Why am I doing this? What are we doing to ourselves?*

What we did in the Haunted House had begun to feel almost routine. If you do anything long enough, it starts to feel normal; practice and regularity sand down any brutal madness into smoother shapes to swallow. But here, in this new place, lit by the stark light of winter? Suddenly what we did seemed very, very wrong.

Life needs to live, I thought wildly, unexpectedly. *And if only the living could make the most of life, then the dead can be set free.*

The sight of Scanlon made me feel desperately sad. My throat grew tight with regret, until I gave myself a little shake. I was forgetting my training. What had Crawler taught me? *'It's better when you don't feel anything. Too much emotion can make you hysterical.'*

'Frankie?' said Scanlon gently. 'What's going on?'

My lips worked but no words came out.

'Is it on the box yet?' snapped Crawler.

'Nearly,' said Scanlon. 'Just making her – its – way now.' He lowered his voice. 'Do you need me to do anything, Frankie? I can try to postpone – ask if they want to reschedule . . .'

My thoughts were still rearing up in fright. I didn't trust myself to answer. Instead I counted to three inside my head, nice and slow. Nothing happened. Everyone's faces seemed to fill with an untold horror, and the world crackled with menace. *What are we doing?* I asked myself again. Madness opened its wings inside my mind, ready to swoop.

With a flash of inspiration, I glanced over at Crawler. Just one glimpse of his arrogant, inscrutable face helped my mind right itself. I remembered what he'd told us, that very first day in the Haunted House. '*Most people really are happiest when they just have something to stare at.*' Why was I even questioning that? Everything was fine. Everything was normal. No need to panic. All I had to do was think of this place as just . . . another haunted house.

'I'm fine,' I told Scanlon, and I began to mount the steps.

Yet a trace of restlessness remained.

They had the only captive poltergeist in the world at their command, and all they wanted it to do was *stand on a box*? I mean, it seemed a *tiny bit* of a shame, didn't it? A slight . . . waste?

Also . . . I threw a critical eye around the place. This party, not to put too fine a point on it, sucked. Lady Whatsit and her guests seemed ever so *stiff*. And I suddenly shivered all over. You know when you find a frozen puddle in a field and stamp all over it, just for the pleasure of hearing it crack? I wanted to do that. I wanted to do that *right now*. Things needed to break in here.

'Look, whatever you're thinking, Frankie, just . . . don't,' said Scanlon.

'I don't know *what* you mean,' I said, sticking my nose in the air.

'Yeah you do. You've got that look on your face. Listen, Dad's been planning this booking for months. He's *really* touchy at the moment. If we don't do what he says—'

'Chill out, Scanlon,' I muttered, getting into position.

I patted my salt-crusted hair and faced the crowd, making sure to smile widely enough so that the cuts on my face split open a little. *A nice touch.*

'I'll give them what they want,' I said.

- 57 -
AN UNWANTED PRESENT

A FEW SECONDS later, the guests began to nudge each other.

'Look,' they said. 'Over there.'

The poison had entered their bloodstreams completely, and the show was on.

'Wh-what's that, Mother?' said Drixie faintly, squinting in my direction.

'Ah, it's the latest thing, darling,' said Lady Craven. 'You're standing right in front of the Cliffstones *poltergeist*. My treat.'

Drixie's bloodshot eyes widened as she entered death's waiting room, and at last her eyes took me in. 'It's . . . *dead?*' she said.

'Very,' said Crawler loudly, from the other side of the room. 'Drowned. But somehow stuck on earth. Isn't it brilliant? Take a look at her injuries – awesome bit of detail . . .'

Any minute now, I thought complacently, *she'll start*

to shriek with excitement, just like they do back in the Haunted House.

But Drixie didn't look excited. Drixie had spent approximately one nanosecond taking my appearance in before she averted her eyes, looking . . .

. . . disgusted. She actually *flinched*. As if I was a plate of something going off in the fridge. It was a small expression, not much more than a nose wrinkle, and she composed herself rapidly – it was all manners, manner, manners with this lot, you couldn't fault that – but all the same, *I saw it*.

'What do you think, my presh? Is it the best thing you've ever loaded?' said Lady Craven hopefully.

Her daughter delicately spat into her hanky. 'Not really, Mum. It's just . . . depressing?'

An awkward silence filled the ballroom. The young people next to Drixie nodded their heads in agreement.

Her words were like a slap. *Depressing?*

'Bit of a thrill kill,' said someone in the crowd. 'Not what we're into.'

'Major unlike. Please swipe,' spluttered someone else. 'Or wipe? Just make it stop.'

Drixie nodded. 'Can you delete, or something?'

'*Delete?*' said Crawler. 'But . . . you've got at least

four minutes left before you need to take the antidote.'

Drixie shrugged and turned back to her friends.

An involuntary gasp left my lips. Had she literally just turned her back on a poltergeist? Did she not know how dangerous that was? I stared around the room. Shock and embarrassment erupted on my skin. My limbs twitched with frustration. I was the star attraction. But she thought I was *depressing*?

Lady Craven had turned to Crawler. A defeated smile fell out of her face, as empty as a nut thrown by a squirrel. 'Looks like I got another surprise wrong,' she said softly. 'I'm sorry, Mr Lane, but you might as well take it away—'

'Nope,' I heard myself shouting. 'Big fat nope to that.' My voice flew around the ballroom and its echo came back at us like a gunshot.

Scanlon gave me a warning glance.

I glared back at him. 'Scanlon, we've come all this way, I've barely been on this stupid box for more than a minute, and now these . . . these icy puddles are telling us to *leave*?'

'Icy what?' he said.

'If you insist,' Crawler was saying to Lady Craven. 'We'll administer the antidote right now.'

'Oh no you won't,' I shouted. And then I located the source of my anger, and raised my voice even more.

'Oi, birthday girl.

YES, I AM
TALKING
TO YOU

Don't even act like you

can't hear me,

cos I know you can.'

The tiny tanned teenager turned around from her friends, surprise and pain carving up her face. She seemed to shrink a couple of centimetres as she finally registered my fury.

'The poltergeist is shouting at me,' she gasped, her lips white and trembling with sickness and indignation. 'She's fleck *shouting* at me. Can't she see I'm not well?'

'Tell it to stop,' said her mother. 'Right now. How disgraceful.'

'Oh, get over yourself,' I snapped, jumping off the box on to the middle of the marble floor. 'You wanted me to entertain your guests, didn't you? Well, now you're going to get what you paid for.'

I mean, come on, Lady Big Bucks. *Think a little*. You don't invite a poltergeist to your party and then not expect it to get angry. It was like stroking a sabre-toothed tiger and being surprised when it bit off your arm. Wake up and smell the ectoplasm, yeah?

- 58 -
PARTY TRICKS AND BIRTHDAY CAKE

THE PARTY GUESTS began to back away from me slowly, their hands out in a placating gesture as if I was a rabid dog. The few that weren't doing this weren't being polite or anything – it's just that they were too busy slipping into unconsciousness.

For a second, I almost forgot where I was. A tiny, strangled cry came from my left, and I whirled upon it almost gratefully. Ah, yes. Drixie. Drixie *Tink*. I mean, what sort of a name was that, for starters? That was enough to make me lose my temper right there.

Anyway, Drixie Tink was swaying violently, still on her feet but barely, and quite purple. Erratic gulping noises escaped from her mouth as she took in that unnerving proximity between *her* and *me*. Her eyes widened with horror at my battered, bloody, salty corpse, the gaping wounds on my cheeks, the yellowing bruises, those awful nailless fingers that spoke of my last scramble for life.

Grinning, I took a small step towards her.

She fell to the floor, moaning. Her heels drummed out a weak beat on the floor as she tried to inch away from me.

'Stop,' she spluttered, wriggling like a woodlouse. 'Please!'

'What's wrong with *you*? Worried I'll stain your dress?' I said.

She'd turned her back on me. She'd made me invisible. It was like dying all over again. Sometimes not being seen is the most violent thing in the world. *But I'd make them see me whether they liked it or not.*

I didn't even need to smash anything in that room to destroy it. I mean, I did, obviously, you know me, but actually I caused the most damage just by being there. In their *home. Their lives.* That was the most destructive thing of all.

Because I showed them *what they'd become* one day.

At first, I chased them. That was fun. They scattered like weak little pigeons and crammed themselves into corners, crying and whimpering. That was when I sat next to them. I patted their hair. Moved my fingers tenderly up and down their cheeks, and watched as they cried and flinched and – yep – had tiny little accidents.

Crawler ran over and tried, half-heartedly, to stop me by making vague, hugging movements with his arms, but he hadn't taken the Ghoul Aid so it was easy to dodge out of his reach. He didn't seem that desperate to stop me either.

When I got bored of prodding them with my clammy fingers, I began to fling china plates at the walls right next to their faces, which was really satisfying. Then I ripped the robot staff in half, which was much trickier than I'd first thought, and sort of like pulling a massive television to bits – so many wires. But when I had about five of those silver spinny discs at my disposal, I plopped five conscious guests on top of them and pushed them, screaming and wailing, down the marble floor and out through the double doors.

Scanlon kept running around the room, darting between the flying crockery and the guests on wheels, giving out the antidote, and shooting stunned, surprised glances in my direction.

I turned my attention to the trestle table, laden with party food, and began to grab great handfuls of it, a vague plan of smearing it in Drixie's hair formulating in my head. I'd just grabbed some squidgy chocolate cake when my anger disappeared as quickly as it had arrived, replaced instead by a small, sad realisation.

The life I could have had, I thought abruptly. Who would I have been, had I not died? I felt the cold, dead weight of all those days I wouldn't know, like damp logs that would never burn.

Somewhere in the room, although it might as well have been a million miles away, a boy was saying a name over and over but it meant nothing to me. My brain felt as if someone had thrown a huge towel over it. I peered around the room but all I could see were thick white snowflakes falling, coating the world around me until there was no one there but me. *Had it started snowing inside the ballroom?*

Or was there something else going on? I felt so blank all of a sudden, tired and drained.

The cake slipped out of my hand and on to the floor.

'Okay, I'm done,' I said. 'Can we go home now?'

There was a muffled sound of crying, and broken china being swept away. Then slow, wary footsteps. Through the white fog stealing over my vision I saw Scanlon and Crawler appear. While Scanlon looked pale and shocked, Crawler was beaming in delight.

In a quiet, discreet whisper, he uttered: 'That was the best show *yet.*'

'Dad, she destroyed millions of pounds' worth of serve-tech. Those waiters on wheels cost a *bomb*. Lady Craven is demanding a refund. There is *wee* all over the floor,' said Scanlon. 'And she – it – the poltergeist looks one udder. I mean, worse than usual. Sorry. It was a disaster.'

Crawler waved his words away with a flap of a hand. 'It was ten udder. The publicity from this alone will keep us sold out for years.'

'Dad, look around you. We're going to be in so much trouble—'

But Crawler merely rolled his eyes. 'Our contracts are watertight. When Lady Craven booked us, she *knew* there was a risk of harm, pain and damage. That's why she booked us, even though she won't admit to it.'

Scanlon and I looked at each other uncertainly. But Crawler was delirious with confidence. As the guests continued to limp out of the ballroom, shocked and crying softly, he spoke feverishly, as if to himself.

'There's nothing more on-brand than an unpredictable poltergeist. Wish I'd thought of it myself.

If they know you're going to explode like that, they'll want you even more. I mean, people like running with bulls, even though they might get gored to death.'

The truth, at last, dawned on me. If I did what I was told, that was good. But if I broke the rules, that was even better. Everything I did, everything I thought, belonged to Crawler. And the more I struggled, the more I was caught in his binds.

I gave one last look at the cherubs above us. Finally I realised what they reminded me of, stuck up there in that plaster. Like little golden flies, trapped in honey. Their helpless heads seemed to swivel in my direction as we left. And by the time we'd got outside, that white snow blizzard inside my head was falling thick and fast.

- 59 -
PACKAGE D

I BLINKED.

I was back at the party. Had they asked for an encore? After everything I'd done? Looked like Crawler was right; they *had* loved it.

But the crowd seemed quieter, and the walls and ceiling had shrunk. The cherubs had vanished – *maybe they freed themselves, after all* – I thought feverishly. Bright balloons hung from the ceiling instead.

'They must have redecorated,' I said through a mouth that was thick and slow.

Scanlon looked at me strangely. 'Huh?'

'The *ballroom*. Redecorated. Right?'

He gave me some serious side-eye. 'Er, Frankie . . . we're here for Nate?'

'You what?' My words sounded like they'd been stuck together with toffee.

'Nate,' he repeated.

I checked in with my brain. Meant nothing.

'What's that?' I asked.

Scanlon looked over his shoulder. Standing there shyly, like an overwhelmed toddler meeting Father Christmas for the first time, was a small thin boy with sticky-out ears.

His T-shirt read:

I GOT FEISTY WITH THE POLTERGEISTY!

The boy looked not much older than nine or ten, and his skin had that grey-purplish tinge I had come to know so well.

'*Nate.* Our client? He's still waiting,' said Scanlon softly. 'I don't think he has long left with the poison. So can you get on with it?'

Oh. We *weren't* in the ballroom. We were in a cramped, stuffy lounge, with quite a lot of things competing for space within it. Two large sofas, one cat hissing in my direction, this mysterious Nate – *whoever he was* – two grown-ups, one whimpering baby and at least six other boys.

I felt strangely jagged, bright and brittle, a broken bauble strung up on a tree.

'*Right*. Course. *Nate*,' I said.

Scanlon turned to the boy. 'So then, birthday boy. What do you fancy doing *first*?'

'I dunno,' said the small boy to the carpet.

'We paid for Package D,' said the scrawny-looking man nearby, in a tight, strained voice.

The woman next to him shifted the snivelling baby on her hips absent-mindedly. 'No high prem extras,' she added.

Scanlon nodded discreetly. 'She – it – knows. It's been briefed. Haven't you, Poltergeist?' Those green eyes of his bore into mine. 'Package D?' he said through faintly gritted teeth.

For a moment, I had a sensation I was spinning wildly on a small planet, only big enough for me.

'Sure,' I said automatically. 'Package D. Gotcha. Say no more.'

What was Package D?

I glanced at Scanlon's face for clues. He looked different, I thought distractedly. His body, once so slight, had filled out, but not with softness. It was like he was carved from slate.

Nate and his friends looked as if they were going to black out.

'Look, is it going to do it or not? It's just, we've dug deep for this,' said the boy's father.

'Of course it will,' said Scanlon in his new, deep voice. 'Get on with it,' he murmured to me. 'You know what to do.'

I didn't, but something told me we'd gone beyond questions. Improvising, I reached out for Nate and threw him, hard, across the room and into the wall opposite. He landed with a soft 'oooof' on the floor, where he lay a moment before stumbling to his feet.

Scanlon opened his mouth, then shut it again.

Nate looked as if he was about to cry.

'How was that, son?' asked the man eagerly. 'Was it what you wanted?'

For a second, the boy's eyes darted to his mother's arms, as if he wanted to run into them. But then he smiled listlessly. 'It was tent,' he said.

His mother and father's shoulders relaxed, and they gave him these awful, bright smiles of relief and love.

'Go on then,' said the dad proudly to the other boys, who were nervously eyeing the dent on the wall Nate had left. 'Your turn. You *all* get a turn, lads. On us.'

I took in the man's bitten fingernails and the woman's pallor, saw the threadbare carpet and the crying baby. I realised what booking me had cost this family, and if *I* saw it, I bet Nate saw it too.

In a voice that spoke of blind and noble sacrifice, the dad said, 'Have another go, if you like. Would you like that, champ? Would you?'

'Course he would,' said the mother lovingly. 'Look at his little face. He can't *speak*, he's that excited.'

'Only the best for our lad,' said the father.

'He'll never go without,' said the mother.

'Not on our watch,' said the father. 'Off you go, son. Enjoy yourself.'

Nate hesitated, nodded with resignation, and limped to the back of the queue.

- 60 -
HAVEN'T YOU GROWN, SCANLON?

LATER, ONCE I'D thrown all the boys as hard as I could, dislocated a few shoulders and thrown the cat too for good measure, a meagre sponge cake with nine scrawny candles stabbed into its icing was brought into the lounge.

The boys stared at it with dazed eyes, rubbing their arms, not quite looking at each other.

'And many happy returns,' I said cheerfully, heading for the door.

Once outside, Scanlon turned to me. He looked angry. It almost suited him.

'*That* was your Package D?' he snapped. 'Dislocated shoulders and unconscious family pets? Care to give me a download? Cos that's not what we discussed this morning.'

I shrugged. I felt lightheaded suddenly, so dizzy I could faint, had a head full of brain snow, and to top it all off that revolting smell of Scanlon's was back too, that sickly stench of rotting fruit.

'Did you hear any complaints from that lot? No, me neither. So can we go back now please?' I said.

'Not right now,' snapped Scanlon. 'We need to sort this out, Frankie. That was an absolute embarrassment back there.'

Never had I felt the chasm between us so strongly. It was as if I'd never met Scanlon before in my life. He loomed over me in a way I couldn't remember either. Once, we'd been roughly the same height. Now he seemed five inches taller than me.

'Have you been taking growth hormones or something?' I mumbled.

'Frankie.' Scanlon ran a hand through his short stubble. 'Look, you've been doing this more and more. Saying random things that make no sense. Losing concentration in the middle of a booking and deviating from the agreed terms of destruction. You *know* that Package D is the cheapest Birthday Party option and doesn't *ever* involve throwing young children around or breaking any bones – we haven't done that for ages, not since that lawsuit—'

I gritted my teeth and waded into battle. 'Wait. Huh? Slow down. *What* are you talking about? What even is a lawsuit? We've *never* talked about Package D – I had to literally guess on the spot. It wasn't fair to land that on me right in the middle of the party and make me look stupid. You're the one saying random things that make no sense, I think you'll find, *pal*.'

I was quite proud of that one. I carried on.

'*Also*, next time I'd like a break between bookings, okay? I was whisked straight from that ballroom to here in a matter of minutes, which was a bit too much for me. It compromised the depth of my performance, and . . . okay, can you stop looking at me like that because it's creeping me out.'

Scanlon's stare was very unsettling.

'Er, what ballroom?' he said finally.

My laugh sounded high-pitched and strained, but we both ignored it.

'"*What ballroom?*" Um, how about the ballroom we were at literally *this morning*? Like, an hour ago?'

'Frankie,' sighed Scanlon, and his voice lost that anger and became very gentle, but also exhausted and flat. It was as if, whatever he was about to tell me, he'd told me many, many times already. 'That party didn't happen this morning. It was two years ago.'

- 61 -
NOT JUST ME, NOT JUST YOU

'Sure, Scanlon,' I said, breaking eye contact and scanning the sky for our lift back.

When is our limousine going to come? I'm tired.

'Two years ago. Hilarious. You're killing me. Ha. Ha. Stop it, I'm breaking a rib.'

'You never believe me, at first,' he muttered. And then he exhaled deeply, and stared at the ground, leaving me no choice but to glare at him with frustration.

And that was when I realised the alarming truth. He wasn't joking. How did I know? It was literally written all over his face. More than a morning *had* gone by since the ballroom. His face was the proof. It was undeniably two years older. That wider jawline, deeper frown lines between his eyebrows, those five extra inches he'd gained in height . . . for a moment an odd mournful feeling crept over me as I remembered, softly, those stolen afternoons we'd shared in the tree house.

This person in front of me wasn't the same person who'd cycled over on a rusty bike to see me. *That* boy had been slowly but carefully painted over by time's relentless brush when I wasn't looking. *Two years.* It had felt like a blink to me.

'The weird thing is,' said Scanlon, 'you always seem totally fine when you come in for a briefing. You always nod and say you understand, but . . .' His voice spluttered out and he looked away.

'What?' I urged him.

'I just feel like there are parts of you that are shu—'

He didn't even have to say it. It was easy to guess the rest.

Parts of you that are shutting down.

Hadn't I been warned? Someone had told me. I couldn't remember *who*, but I remembered their words: '*You won't rot. But your memories might.*'

Now I realised there was nothing the rot wouldn't touch. Blankness was falling inside me, and one day my mind would become completely buried.

'Don't blame yourself,' said Scanlon gruffly. 'It's not your fault. It's happening to the others.'

'The others?' I said thickly.

His eyes grew wide then. 'Yeah. The *others*. The

other ghosts. Back at the Haunted House?'

'Oh, yeah,' I said, suddenly afraid.

'They keep switching off too. Right in the middle of shows. They just stop whatever they're doing and stare into space. It's happening more and more. Dad's not happy about it, obviously, but it's not their fault.' He rubbed his eyes and said, sounding oddly self-conscious, 'It's a challenging time at work, to be honest.'

Work?

Carried softly through the air just then came the sound of the boys singing 'Happy Birthday'. It was the saddest version I had ever heard, but it at least injected a jolt of energy into my sluggish thoughts.

'Scanlon,' I said, caught up within a strange realisation. 'If two years have gone by . . . does that mean you're fourteen now?'

He looked taken aback, but shook his head. 'No,' he said. 'It's three and a half years since we opened—'

We? I thought distractedly.

'—so I'm going to be sixteen next month.'

Whoa.

Like a pebble rolling down a beach, a memory slowly spun out of the haziness in my brain. 'So why aren't you at school?'

'What?'

'Well, didn't you tell me once that only rich kids go to school now?'

He raised his eyebrows. 'Yeah.'

'And you *love* Skool Tools,' I went on with a sluggish determination.

'Well—'

'I never saw you look so happy as you did when you shared your plug-in lessons with me. So if you're rich now, why aren't you making the most of it? Going to college, like you always wanted to? You can more than afford it, right?'

He shrugged. 'Yeah.'

'So why aren't you there then? Why are you here, with me?'

There was a movement beneath his skin, as if he wanted to bring something huge within him to the surface. But then it dropped back down quickly, like it was an anchor too heavy to lift.

'What's with all the questions, Frankie? Why do *you* care all of a sudden?'

I was taken aback by the emptiness in his voice. 'Just wondered.'

'Yeah, well, don't.'

As if aware of how harsh he sounded, he produced a mollifying smile.

'You just concentrate on getting better, okay?'

Abruptly, he fished a pair of keys out of his trouser pocket, beeped a button, and fidgeted until a flying car came to a hover just next to us.

'*You* drive now?'

'Yep,' he said, grinning for the first time that day. 'I do. Perk of the job.'

He opened the passenger door for me. I moved to get in, and stumbled on the way. Accidentally, I tripped into Scanlon, and winced with discomfort as his upper torso moved through mine before popping out again.

That was when I finally discovered what that rotting smell – the one that had been emanating from Scanlon since the day we'd met – was coming from. And realised, at last, what it meant.

- 62 -

LIKE FATHER, LIKE SON

THAT FESTERING, STALE smell which had bothered me ever since I'd met him? I'd *tasted* it. It came from inside him. And it was the worst thing in the world – the rancid taste of a life going bad. Scanlon might not know it, but he was dying inside. He was wasting his life away.

We got in the car. Scanlon pressed buttons and we slowly rose into the sky. Clouds and cars whooshed past us.

As a light drizzle began to fall past our windows, I threw him a puzzled look. *What's in your brain, Scanlon Lane?*

Scanlon wouldn't go to school. That stubborn look on his face made that clear. Even though learning stuff had been the only thing he'd ever talked about with any enthusiasm.

What would he do instead?

Well, now I knew. Scanlon would work for Crawler until Crawler died. And then Scanlon himself would take over the Haunted House. He'd become the Lane in Lane and Son, and probably have kids himself, and they'd all follow in his footsteps. I would watch him grow old, and his kids grow old, and I'd work for them all.

I understood all of that as plainly as if it had happened already.

What I couldn't understand was *why*. For the first time ever, Scanlon had *opportunities*. If he went to school, he could do anything he wanted . . . he could learn in classrooms, not from that battered old laptop . . . have proper friends for the first time in his life. And in time he could do something he loved, if he was lucky, something more rewarding than taking poltergeists to birthday parties and spraying fake cobwebs on ghosts.

Why was he turning his back on all of that?

That terrible taste of him squandering himself away.

I noticed the glint of satin on his trousers, the shine of gel on his stubble. He negotiated the clouds quite skilfully, it seemed, a small smile on his lips, like he was enjoying it.

I went very still as an unsettling idea uncurled in my mind. Was he staying for the money?

Was he staying for the car?

Maybe he *wanted* to take over the business. Maybe he *loved* the idea of being in charge. Maybe Scanlon was becoming more like Crawler than Scanlon?

And suddenly, any pity I might have had for him and his potential vanished. So what if he was rotting away inside? He only had himself to blame.

'Fancy listening to some music?' Scanlon said, after a while.

'Whatever,' I said, staring out of the window. 'Knock yourself out.'

- 63 -
DEFECTIVE

BACK AT THE Haunted House, Crawler appeared.

'We need to chat,' he said to Scanlon. 'Get the others.'

Once Isolde, the Girl With No Name, Theo, Obediah and Vanessa were gathered in Vanessa's fake boardroom, Crawler fixed us all with his usual empty stare.

'A few of the regulars are starting to complain.'

'Oh *no*,' said Vanessa, looking worried. A people-pleaser, she always fretted more about feedback than the rest of us.

'Let's face it, you're all getting a bit . . . glitchy,' said Crawler. 'You keep switching off. It's not what they want. It's not what they've come for. They have a taste for high drama. They want you to bring the house down, night after night. And you're not doing that. You're forgetting your lines, your moves. You're just standing there like lemons, giving me a bad name.'

We threw each other uncertain glances.

'Look, I think you've all still got a lot to offer,' said Crawler. 'But I have to listen to my regulars. I don't want to lose them. So you're going to have a little power-down.'

'Dad,' said Scanlon quietly, 'where are you going with this?'

'I'm giving them early retirement.'

'Retirement?' said Scanlon. 'What do you mean?'

Crawler casually inspected his nails. 'I'm going to can the malfunctioning ghosts. Keep them in storage. Indefinitely. Make space for new stock. Ghosts that don't go glitchy.'

We were all completely quiet as this sank in, and then the most awful thing seemed to happen to Scanlon. He began to shake uncontrollably. Honestly, it was like watching someone get electrocuted. And the more he tried to stop it, holding one hand over the other and pressing down on it hard, the worse it got. He wouldn't look at any of us.

I remembered what he'd told me about his childhood – hunting for ghosts, making friends with them, knowing he'd have to betray them. Over and over. And now he'd have to do it again.

'Please . . .' his lips had gone completely white, his teeth chattering as if he had a fever, 'can't we work something out? I'll find a way to fix the ghosts, I know I can. Maybe we could put them in different rooms. A change of scenery might work miracles. I can try a few mind exercises with them – keep their brains active.'

For a second, I saw that horrified boy he'd been back in the storeroom, surrounded by his unwanted spoils.

'No. I've made my mind up. Once the rot sets in, you have to act fast. I think we'll put the workhouse brats and the Girl With No Name in their cans tomorrow,' Crawler went on, as lightly as if he was discussing what to have for dinner. 'They've been a total let-down recently. And Virginia—'

'Vanessa,' said Scanlon.

'—too. The poltergeist and Isolde can remain. For now.'

For now? I thought I was the star of the show.

'Then we'll head off to Italy. Pompeii. Tragic eruption, lots of death. Lots of dead, gorgeous dark-eyed bambini wandering around. I wouldn't mind exploring Germany, France and Poland either. I bet they're *heaving*. Oh, try to look more excited, Scanlon.'

Scanlon continued to shake.

Theo, the younger workhouse boy, went over to his big brother and very quietly nestled into his shoulder. Obediah put his one arm round him, and closed his eyes for a moment.

Vanessa had put her hands up to her face.

'Back in our cans? How long for?' said Obediah.

'And who will cuddle the Girl With No Name?' said Theo, his mouth all twisty and sad.

This was making me extremely uncomfortable. I needed to get away. Longingly, I contemplated my silent, empty room upstairs. I stared at the table.

Crawler spoke about flight times to Scanlon.

Isolde began to pace around the room with agitation, stopping occasionally to try to force the bars of the window wide open while muttering her long-dead language, as if she wanted to escape.

'Good luck with that,' I said, yawning. 'If you wanted to prise open those bars, you'd need to get *properly* angry.'

For a fraction of a beat, a familiar voice, as soft as a moth, began to speak in a part of my mind I'd forgotten existed. I squinted up at the ceiling, wondering what it was saying, but it fluttered away as softly as it had arrived.

Just when I thought everything had been wrapped up, a hopeful look appeared on Scanlon's face.

'Dad,' he said hesitantly. 'I've got another idea. It might solve the glitchy ghost problem. It could be the boost this place needs. And it wouldn't cost you a penny.'

'Oh yes?' said Crawler. 'Nice of you to take an interest. Fire away.'

- 64 -
SCANLON'S PLAN

WHAT SCANLON SAID was this.

'What if *I* took some poison, and became a ghost too?'

Obediah and Vanessa gasped in shock.

Even I frowned at Scanlon for a second. *Why was he suggesting that?*

Crawler, however, cocked his head to the side, the better to consider Scanlon's business proposal.

'Explain,' he said.

'Well, if I was a ghost here, then . . . then I could be with all the ghosts all the time.'

Scanlon spoke in a light, reasonable voice.

'And what's in that for me?' said Crawler.

'Well, if I was here all the time, I could spot any technical difficulties and deal with them straight away. I think I'd be able to stop the ghosts from shutting down, if I was with them more. If I was . . . dead too.'

Scanlon's voice was very steady and very firm.

Crawler raised his eyebrows as he considered his only child. 'Mmmmm,' he said finally. 'An interesting idea. Not entirely without merit. And I'm certainly impressed at your commitment to the business, that's for sure.'

I shot puzzled looks at them both. This was *bonkers*. Scanlon was offering to *die* just so he could fix the glitches? Had he *lost his mind*?

But by the earnest look on Scanlon's face, it was clear he thought this was a logical, sensible idea. 'I'd also be able to keep the ghosts trained, and running smoothly. You wouldn't have to can them, or put them back in storage. Problem solved.'

'But why can't you train them efficiently now?' Crawler sounded suspicious.

'Oh, I *do*,' said Scanlon smoothly. 'But I'd do it even better if I was *one of them*. I'd be like a . . . live-in manager. Your supervisor. On the ground.'

'Yes, I can see that,' said Crawler, sounding excited. 'You'd be my man on the inside. Very handy, actually. And think of the *drama*!'

'Yes,' said Scanlon, matching his father's voice exactly, in one of his uncannily brilliant impersonations.

'The drama. Imagine how much more punters are going to love this place if *your only child is a ghost as well.*'

'Oh, I'd be devastated,' said Crawler, after a pause.

'Naturally,' said Scanlon.

'And I would choke back the tears in a manly, dignified way—'

'A nice touch,' said Scanlon.

'And they'd all say how brave I was.'

'They'd lap it up,' said Scanlon quietly. 'And bring all their friends.'

'They really would.' Crawler sighed happily. After a moment, he eyed his son. 'Are you sure? When you're dead, you're dead. It seems rather extreme. I'm happy to *replace* the glitchy ghosts instead – stick to the plan. If you want. Never let it be said that I pushed you into this . . .'

Scanlon nodded. 'I'm sure.'

'Fair enough,' said Crawler easily. 'Well, you had a good innings anyway. A good life. Right?'

Scanlon looked away.

'Well, when do you want to, er . . . ?'

'How about tomorrow?' said Scanlon quietly.

'Okey doke,' said his father, and he put a hand, for a second, on Scanlon's shoulder, before lifting it up and heading for the door. 'Well done, you. A Lane through and through, eh?'

Scanlon flinched, then nodded.

'Oh, you can lock up tonight. I'm just off for my facial,' said Crawler.

'Okay,' said Scanlon. 'Bye, Dad.'

Once Crawler had gone, Vanessa, Obediah and Theo stared at Scanlon.

'Scanlon,' said Vanessa quietly, 'are you *sure* about this? You realise that you'll be ending your life if you take that poison? To stay in here?'

Emotions scuttled around in Scanlon's face, like wary crabs in a rock pool, reluctant to be seen. 'I think it's a good idea. It feels . . . like the right thing to do. Now, can you go to your rooms by yourself? I'll be around later to lock up.'

Obediah and Theo lingered outside. When I walked past them, Obediah grabbed my hand with his one arm.

'We're moithered about Scanlon,' he said.

'*What?*' I snapped.

But it was no use pretending I didn't understand. They looked at me desperately.

'Please try to change his mind. He'd listen to you.

He's making a mistake. It's the worst idea we've ever heard—'

I shook Obediah's hand away. 'He can do what he wants, okay? It's not like we're friends. It's not like we're family.'

'Maybe not,' said Theo softly, as I mounted the steps to my room. 'But who else has he got?'

- 65 -
JiLL THE DEATH GUARDIAN

BACK IN MY room, I made myself as comfortable as I could and closed my eyes, but the dull calm I'd been hoping for did not magically materialise. The air around me had become too quiet, too watchful, to be truly restful. The world began to thrum with a peculiar, unsettling energy.

And then, from outside, came a strange, scraping, rasping noise. Like bald tyres grinding painfully over a dirty track. Was this another crowd, coming for their entertainment? And why did I have the weirdest feeling of being watched . . . ?

'Hello again.'

Standing in front of me was a woman in a shapeless beige suit. From behind the biggest pair of glasses I'd ever seen, two huge eyes blinked at me, like a scandalised owl.

I looked at her hazily.

'Jane?' I said through a cloudy head. *The death guardian?* From the bus? From a long, long time ago.

'Jill,' she said wearily. 'Forgotten me, have you?' She pushed her glasses up her nose, and they fell straight back down again. 'I told you I'd look you up, didn't I, when I was in your neck of the woods? Well, here I am. And in the nick of time too, by the look of things.'

I eyed her suspiciously. 'How did you know I'd end up in a wood? And . . . how'd you get in here anyway?'

'Never mind that,' she said firmly. 'There are more important things to consider, and we haven't got long. You've got some thinking to do. Not to mention some feelings to feel – and that's going to be hard, because you haven't done that for a while, have you?'

I jutted my chin out. 'No,' I said bolshily. 'I haven't.'

'And how's that working out for you?' she said, raising one wispy eyebrow.

There was something unusually comforting about being told off by an adult with a kind voice. It reminded me of a world I'd once been part of, where my actions mattered, where I could tell the difference between right and wrong.

I hung my head, horribly lost. For a brief second, I was overwhelmed by an urge to cry.

Her face softened. 'There, there. Don't take on. I've come to help. Now, what did we talk about last time we met? Do you remember?'

Suddenly, I wanted to lie down on the cold hard floor and never get up again.

'No,' I said finally. 'There's so much I can't remember. I'm forgetting everything.'

I don't know how Scanlon and I met. Or what my name is, or how I got here. The only thing I'm really sure about is that I'm here to lose my temper and break stuff, and then I get left alone. And I've got used to that, and now it's all I want.

I stared at my hands and turned them wonderingly. They looked as if they belonged to someone else. *They do. They belong to Crawler.*

One day soon, when everything inside me has turned to snow, I'll just be Crawler's wind-up poltergeist, nothing more. And when he cans me – which he will, I see that now, because he'll grow tired of me eventually, that's just the sort of person he is, and anyway I can't do this for ever, my brain is shutting down – well, it won't even matter. I won't know it's happening. I'll just sit there in a tuna can, staring in the dark, and then I'll start humming, and it will be like that for ever.

The shadows around us seemed unfixed, curiously alive.

'It's funny,' said Jill. 'I always had you down as someone who'd work it out.'

'Work what out?'

Her face grew sly with knowledge. 'What you were meant To Do.'

I stared at her dully. 'Do?'

'Yeah,' she said. 'Do.' And she raised her eyebrows again.

'Um, I don't know what you mean. I get angry on command. I smash stuff. I break stuff. I'm very good at it, actually. What else is there?'

In answer, she strode to the wall of my room, and beckoned me over with a long, surprisingly elegant finger.

'Look,' she said, tapping on the rough wood.

And, because her voice had a certain firmness I didn't want to mess with, I did as she asked, and peered through the rough timber slats.

Beyond us, far away, at the very edge of the horizon, just past the end of the forest, was a small grey cloud. As we watched, it grew bigger and darker, and a quick white arrow darted out from its underbelly.

'A little lightning baby,' Jill said. 'They're so cute when they're that age.'

'Huh?'

My thoughts moved like treacle dripping off a spoon. It felt like a million years since I'd been flinging small boys around a stuffy lounge, and the last few hours had been very strange indeed, and now I just wanted to lie down and close my eyes. Why did people have to keep *pestering me*? Why couldn't I just be left alone?

'What's out there, duck?' said Jill softly.

Reluctantly, I forced my eyes open, and looked out at the world.

'It looks like a storm.'

She pulled away and fixed me with those leached eyes again. 'Yes, it does, doesn't it? The question is: *whose storm is it?*'

For a tiny beat, her face seemed to fill with a disturbing wisdom, and I became extremely cold.

'Jill,' I said, frightened, 'are you . . . are you definitely not . . .'

She shook her head. 'Who I am is not important. It's also fairly complex and difficult to explain. And we're running out of time. This is about *you*. You – and your destiny.'

She pushed her glasses up her nose. They fell back down again immediately.

'Now, you've got a choice,' she said. 'You either get on the bus and come with us or you stay here, and do what needs to be done. And to do that, girl, you're going to have to explore and release that anger of yours *properly*. You've got to show us what you've got, and you've got to do it with love mixed in. Because that's the answer to everything, isn't it? Do what you're best at, even if it frightens you, and do it with love. What's the flip side of anger, duckie? What can you turn it *into*?'

I heard the distant rumble of thunder. Shadowy memories ran through me, like birds flying across the surface of my bones. *'And sometimes I think a bit of that storm's been stuck inside you ever since.'*

The dusk and the cloud had darkened the sky and the light inside my room, turning Jill's face almost liquid, hard to distinguish. She could have been anyone. She could have been an ancient monument who had been around since the beginning of time. Her face continued to ripple and shift, and her eyes were black pools of secrets.

'You've got a storm inside you, haven't you, Frances? Isn't it time you let it out?'

'But . . .' my throat ached with frustration, 'I let it out every day.'

'No, you don't,' she said softly. 'That's just a pantomime. It's not real. It's just a few smashed plates. That's not proper anger, is it? And it's not for the people that need it either.'

'I don't know how to make it any different.'

'Yes, you do,' she said.

And just like that, I did. Dizzy with the surprise of it, I regarded her for a second, and my eyes grew wide with understanding.

'*Oh*,' I said wonderingly. '*Oh.*'

Life needs to live. *Then the dead can be set free.*

Scanlon, I realised. And the others. They were why I was still here. I had to do something for them. And for me too.

And that soft voice I'd heard became a bit louder in my head. '*Sometimes I wish you'd find something more important to get angry about.*'

Jill blinked at me, slowly. And then she reached out her hand and laid it for a moment on my face, cupping my cheek as if it was something precious, and worth holding.

'Between you and me,' she whispered, 'the tricky

ones are always the best ones. In my experience. Which is . . .' she produced the briefest of smiles, 'considerable.'

She cocked her head to the side as if she heard someone calling her name. And then, just as mysteriously as she had arrived, she was gone, leaving an odd smell in the air, like burnt toast, and one single white feather dancing in her wake.

- 66 -
WHO AM i? WHO ARE YOU?

I RAN OUT of my room and pounded the winding, narrow corridors.

'Scanlon?' I shouted. '*Scanlon?*'

In answer, I heard a faint hiccup.

Confused by the gloom, disorientated by the growing rumble of thunder, I stumbled on the ghost train tracks and fell through a doorway, which led to . . .

. . . the little girl's room.

When she saw me, her little face twisted in fear, and she flung herself on the mattress.

'Oh, don't do that,' I said helplessly. 'I . . . I'm sorry I haven't been very, um, friendly.'

She raised herself up from the tousled blankets and regarded me for a moment. 'Ma. Ma,' she said.

There was a sharp pain just behind my breastplate.

She held out her arms. 'Ma,' she said again.

I eyed the doorway nervously. I took a step towards it.

But I couldn't leave the little girl alone in that horrible place.

It wasn't a room. It was a cell.

So I walked over slowly and lifted her up with shaking muscles.

I hadn't held another person without subsequently throwing them for the longest time. Every muscle in my body automatically tensed. *Throw, hurt, smash, wreck,* went the training in my head. I swallowed, hard, until the voice disappeared and my muscles softened. Then I gulped, and reached right back to another time, another place.

My hand lifted and I found myself stroking her cheek. It was so soft. The room seemed to peel away from me for a moment.

There was a small scrap of a nametape sewn in the back of her cardigan. I squinted at it in the gloom.

'Mary,' I said aloud, as if in a daze.

The little girl clapped her hands in delight. 'Mary,' she said, nodding emphatically as if hearing something important.

'*Mary?*' I gasped. 'You mean . . . all this time, you were trying to remember your *name?*'

She looked around the cold fake nursery, its corners that pulsed with silence, and shivered. I held her more snugly, safe from the gloom, and she gave a shuddering sigh of contentment.

'You needed help remembering, didn't you? Cos you'd forgotten a bit, right? But now we know. You're Mary. That's who you are.'

Suddenly I saw the room through her eyes. How frightened she must have been, stuck in there, day after day, trying to remember who she'd been once. She was so small, so alone. She needed someone to stick up for her.

They all did.

I moved my brain in directions it hadn't been in for a while. I thought about *other people* – the others who were here with me. Sweet Vanessa, the pleaser, who willingly let people laugh at her, who thought her death was her fault. Isolde, who'd never been inside in her *life*, and was now trapped for ever, yet longed to feel the fresh air once more. Obediah and Theo – pain flew across me – who had never known kindness, not in their lifetime, not from the adults who should have protected them when they were at their most vulnerable, and certainly not now, and didn't even think to question that.

And then, finally, I turned my thoughts to Scanlon Lane.

He'd always been able to see me. But had I ever properly seen *him*? Had I looked into his heart, and seen the love floundering around in there, with nowhere to go, no one to lavish it on?

I'd got him all wrong. He wasn't sticking around for the money, or the condo, or the flash cloud-car. He didn't want to be *in charge* of us. He wanted to be *with* us. He wanted to make amends. That was all he'd ever wanted. And now that was drawing to a deadly conclusion. It had turned into guilt. That was why he'd offered to take the poison: to stay with us for ever. It meant he wouldn't have more ghosts on his conscience. He was willing to sacrifice himself for us.

And just like that, something warm began to move through my frozen corpse. He *loved* us. And I had to set him free. I had to set us all free.

Mary jabbed a little finger in my cheek. 'F . . .' she tried. 'Fer. Fankee.'

'Frankie?' I said experimentally.

She nodded and stuck her thumb in her mouth, her eyes swimmy with comfort.

'Yeah,' I said softly. 'That's me.'

Frankie. It sounded good. It felt like home.

I'm Frankie, and the only person I belong to is me.

'Come on then, Mary,' I said. 'Let's go make some trouble.'

- 67 -
ALL THIS WILL FADE AWAY

He was in the office, staring into space, looking completely lost. I felt suddenly shy, overwhelmed, at the sight of him. *There's so much to say. Things I should have said earlier.*

At the sight of us, he sat up and rearranged his face.

'Everything all right? Why are you carrying the little girl? That's not like you. I mean—'

'It's okay. I know. And her name's Mary.'

'Oh,' he said slowly. 'That's a nice name. What are you doing up? Is the rain getting in through the roof, or something? I told Crawler we needed to fix that . . .'

'No. The roof's fine.' I bit my lip. 'I just wanted to talk to you.'

Speaking and thinking was getting harder by the second.

In the end, I just blurted out: 'Oh, *please* don't take the poison.'

Scanlon shuffled some papers around on the desk

busily. His face went tight and still.

'It's fine. I'm actually fine about it—'

'But you shouldn't be fine about it! You're making a massive mistake!'

Finally, he met my eyes, and his glare was frightening, because it was the look of someone who had made up his mind. '*Am* I? The more I think about it, the more I realise it's perfect for me.'

'How can you say that?' I gasped.

'Look, I haven't had the life you had.' He sounded exhausted. 'And I know you had a wonderful, loving family, but not all are like that. So it's sweet of you to care, but you don't have to. I won't miss anything, I won't miss my happy life, because I never had it to begin with.'

For a terrible, empty second, I wondered if he was right. And then a beautiful word popped into my mind.

'Fudge,' I blurted out. It felt so right I said it again, like a prayer. '*Fudge*. Proper, crumbly, melt-in-your-mouth fudge. From Devon. Have you ever had that type of fudge?'

He gave me a quizzical look. 'Er, no. I can't say I have.'

'Right. There you go then. You *can't* die till you taste that. You literally can't – it's a rule of the universe. I'm surprised you didn't know that – all babies get told that in the womb. You must have not been listening. Anyway, that's the rule, so there you go. Also . . .' my words began to come more easily now, 'dog's ears. The actual feel of a dog's ear. Have you ever stroked a dog's ear?' I was rambling, but at least I had his attention.

'No,' he sighed. 'I told you, I haven't had the life you've—'

'So you can't die until you've stroked a dog's ear. They're very soft, you see. You can't, in fact, die until you have owned a dog. Because you will love them, and they will love you a hundred times back, even when you're a complete ratbag, and they'll make you happy. And then you can spend entire evenings stroking their ears and rubbing their tummies. So you can't take the poison till you've done that for at least five decades, okay?'

A minuscule smile played around his lips.

'Waking up on the very first day of the holidays,' I added, after a moment's thought. 'It's like waking up in paradise, and you can't—'

'—die until I've had that?' said Scanlon.

'You're catching on. Well done. When you see a fox at night, and it looks right at you. Reading in bed when it's raining outside. Sitting by a fire in the winter. Cats purring when you walk into the room. You might not have had those experiences *yet* . . .'

Scanlon's whole forehead creased with pain, so I quickly added, 'But you will. I know you will.'

That snow blizzard inside my head stopped and I saw everything then, saw my life as if it had happened yesterday, saw it in glowing, beautiful clarity. That short sweet miracle I'd had. And I gave thanks for it, and then I passed it on.

'Hot bubble baths. Putting on clean pyjamas. Trees in autumn. Horses in fields. Cinemas. Sweet peas.'

I paused, swallowed. 'Swimming in the sea.'

Scanlon gave me a quick, surprised look. 'Really?' he asked.

I nodded. Everything inside me ached, but it was a good hurt, like a wound finally healing. 'Totally. When you dive under a wave, and come back up again, and all you can see is the sunlight, darting off the water in front of you. It's . . . it's . . . the most amazing feeling in the world.'

He blinked.

And then my voice changed, and grew deeper, and I gasped as I realised that I was speaking in Dad's voice, as he said: 'Standing in a field when the sun goes down, waiting for the band to start. Meeting the person you want to marry. Holding your children—'

Then that voice changed into Mum's: 'Blackbirds outside your window, kissing your babies, dancing—'

And finally, I spoke as Birdie. 'Holding hands across the hammocks and waking up on Christmas morning!'

Scanlon's eyes widened, and he pressed his lips together very tightly.

And then the voices of all three of them joined together, and they said the same thing. To him. To us. To me. 'It wasn't your fault. Everything that happened wasn't your fault.'

They forgave me. And because they did that, I could forgive him.

'Please don't take the poison,' I said to him softly, in my own voice. 'I was wrong to blame you. You were only a boy, Scanlon, when he made you start hunting. Please don't throw your life away because you feel guilty. The only person who needs to feel guilty around here is *him*. *He's* the real poison. And you're going to make someone an amazing friend one day. You're going to have *loads*. Because you're awesome. You're loyal, and kind, and clever . . . And with any luck, your friends will become your family, and then all of this will fade away, Scanlon. I *swear*.'

Scanlon took a deep, shuddering breath, brushed his eyes roughly and looked down at his desk.

'Fudge?' he said, after a moment. 'Is it that good?'

- 68 -

WE NEED TO PRACTISE OUR MOVES

I LAUGHED.

'Totally,' I said. 'It's like angels having a party on your tongue. It's all that is divine in the universe condensed into one beautifully crumbly cube.'

'Wow,' he said.

'Start with vanilla first – the classic. Then try salted caramel. Some people like rum and raisin, some don't. Experiment. All I will say is this: *be picky about where you buy it from*. Remember that, and you will be okay.'

'Got it,' he said. *'Thank you.'*

'You're welcome. I just wish I'd said it earlier. About the fudge, I mean.'

His smile faded. 'The only thing is – I can't leave this place if you're all still here. I'd feel like I was abandoning you to him. To them.'

'Ah,' I said, finally. 'Well, that's all right, cos I've got a plan. And it will free us all.'

I hope.

His lovely eyes lit up then, and for a brief moment, I simply basked in relief. That horrible smell had finally gone. His life was safe.

I longed to sit down and close my eyes. That cold blank snow inside me, that sense of closing in, closing down, was ever present now. But I wrenched my brain back to what needed to be done. It wasn't over yet.

'Get the others,' I said. 'And hurry. We haven't got long, and it's going to be a long night.'

'What do you mean?' said Scanlon.

I grinned. 'Crawler wanted us to bring the house down, didn't he? Well, we'd better start practising.'

AND THE
THUNDER OUTSIDE
CLAPPED APPROVINGLY.

- 69 -
FiNAL ACT

WHEN THE TRAIN finally slammed into my bedroom the next morning, I was exhausted. We'd been up all night. I'd spent hours teaching the others what I knew. I'd also had to *unlearn* my training, and dig deeper, locate a different kind of anger, one I'd never used before. I only had one chance to make it right. *Was I up to the job? Were they?*

For a sickening moment, as the customers sat and watched me expectantly, gasping for breath as the poison worked on them, I hesitated. *Am I doing the right thing? What if it all goes horribly wrong? How would he punish us? How would he punish Scanlon?*

As if in answer, that low thundercloud outside gave a deafening crack. It was so close now, I felt it was circling the building, looking for me.

The audience began to murmur. 'This isn't what we paid for.'

'Looks like it's half asleep.'

'Thought this was meant to be the highlight of the show?'

'Oh, hi,' I said casually.

The whispers started up again. 'Didn't realise it would *talk* to us.'

'Bit arrogant, if you ask me.'

'What are we meant to do, answer back?'

'Absolutely not,' I said. 'You just sit back, and let us take over.'

This time, bringing my anger out felt completely different. It wasn't like following a script. It was like digging a hooked claw into my heart and hauling it out through my skin. Pain and grief burnt in every single part of me, and I nearly blacked out from it. I gritted my teeth, threw my head back and screamed. For an awful, still moment, nothing happened.

And then the storm finally fell.

Fury ran up and down my body like flames licking wood. I unscrewed the rivets in the beams above. They swung pleasingly from the centre of the room for a second, before falling with a clatter to the floor, missing the people in the ghost train by millimetres.

With difficulty, they all clapped.

'Oh, wonderful,' I heard someone gasp.

'Real sense of *peril*,' said someone else, grey and shaking.

'Great build-up of tension,' panted a third. 'Masterful.'

'Thank you,' I said politely, picking up my heavy single bed and throwing it, panting, at the window.

As it smashed, and the glass fell into a neat little pile at my feet, and the window frame groaned and collapsed, the people in the ghost train made admiring noises, although a few gazed in confusion at each other.

'Did any of you feel that?'

The roar of the thunder overhead was too loud for us to hear much else, but we could easily sense the shift within the building – a feeling of things being loosened, of coming undone.

'Oh my,' said someone. 'The floor is shaking. I felt a tremor.'

'It felt like the *building* was shaking too,' added his companion. 'From side to side.'

'That is possible,' I said reasonably. 'After all, the others are wrecking their rooms too.'

They looked at each other.

'I thought there was only *one* poltergeist?' said a woman slowly, forcing her words out with difficulty.

'Not any more,' I said. 'We're all at it now. We had a chat last night. Turns out, there's a lot for us to be angry about. They're all furious downstairs. You should see them – it's quite beautiful, really.'

Underneath the sound of the thunder you could just about make out a crashing, banging noise coming from elsewhere in the building, and peals of wild, jubilant laughter.

'We're *so* angry,' I said, taking a hammer to the wooden floor and banging at it until I could see the room beneath. '*I'm* angry at what they suffered. We're angry at Crawler, and what he did to us. And to his son. But we're also angry with you. You should be ashamed of yourselves.'

The floor beneath our feet began to groan and splinter. I saw someone swallow nervously.

'If too many beams and planks and joists get damaged,' I explained carefully to the aghast audience in the train, happily remembering everything I learnt during the Sea View restoration, 'then the integrity of the entire property will be compromised.'

'What does *that* mean?' spluttered a purple-faced

man from the ghost train.

'It means *run*.' I grinned. 'Honestly, you lot have more money than sense, don't you?'

Forty grown-ups got up with a gasp and began pushing and shoving each other in their rush to get out of my room.

Crawler burst in.

'What on earth do you think you're doing? Setting yourself free? You'll hate it out there, Poltergeist. They all will. They'll have *nothing* if they don't have this place.'

Even though I knew he couldn't hear me, I answered him anyway, just for the joy of saying the truth.

'Maybe, but that's a risk we're prepared to take. Oh, and by the way? You've been wrong all along, Crawler. It's so much better when you get angry with feeling. *So* much more powerful. You've been missing a trick all this time.'

And for a second, I could have sworn his eyes looked at me, properly, in surprise and frustration.

'Crawler?' I said slowly. 'Did you hear me just now?'

Something about the way his pupils contracted at the question seemed very suspicious. He'd gone completely still.

'Crawler, can you *see* me? Have you only pretended

you couldn't see ghosts all along? So that your son had to do all the dirty work for you?'

So he didn't have to get tangled up in their emotions, and their lives. That's what Scanlon was for. Crawler had used his child as a sponge, to soak up all the guilt he should have been burdened with instead.

'Crawler? I know you can hear me.' Once I'd spotted it, it was so obvious.

His jaw went very tight then. And, as if he was *relieved* that he didn't have to keep up the pretence any more, he looked straight at me. It was like being given an electric shock.

'*Fine,*' he said, gesturing to the wrecked room. 'Pull it down if you want to. I'll rebuild. We can rebuild together. Something bigger. Something better.'

The sound of crashing and splintering seemed, for a moment, to fade under the ferocious persuasion in his face. I gulped. His smile was almost gentle, nearly loving.

'Come off it, Poltergeist,' he said softly. 'Stop pretending. You *love it here*. And listen, I'm impressed that you've orchestrated this, er, little uprising, really I am. You've gone up in my estimation. I'll give you anything, anything at all. What do you want, a bigger room? A whole Haunted House to yourself? Or – better yet – how about a poltergeist theme park, completely dedicated to you? Consider it done. We can be business partners if you like. You and me, frightening the world. How about it?'

My body went limp with longing. *An entire theme park?* I could see it all. 'Poltergeist' in lights. The adulation. The total licence to misbehave, my temper swelling like a nightmare, growing bigger every day. I *could* stay. And together, it would be a total cinch for Crawler and I to persuade Scanlon to stay too. The other ghosts could go, but the three of us would grow old together. Like a family. A twisted, weird one, admittedly, but a family nonetheless, if you didn't look too hard at it.

Crawler could sense my weakening, and he cocked his head to the side slowly, with something a lot like tenderness.

'Stay,' he said. 'You need me. I need you. Together, we can build something incredible.'

'Wow,' I said. 'I'll give you this, Crawler, you always seem to know exactly what I want.'

And we smiled at each other.

In that shared glee, I made up my mind. I felt a stab

of regret, but who was I to fight my destiny?

I knew what I wanted, and now I had to take it. Someone might be hurt, but that was the price I'd have to pay. And I had to act fast, before I changed my mind.

- 70 -
CURTAIN CALL

I STEELED MYSELF to say the next bit. 'But the answer's no, Crawler. No more.'

I placed my hand in front of his chest.

He winced. 'What are you doing?' he said.

'Trying to find your heartbeat,' I said solemnly. 'It's funny, really. All the ghosts in this building have more heart in their little fingers than you have in your entire body. You might as well be dead inside. And deep down inside your wasted soul I think you know that too, don't you?'

His eyelids trembled slightly, and he almost – *almost* – nodded.

'I'm tempted by the theme park, not gonna lie,' I said. 'And there'll always be a part of me that likes to break and rage – but I'm not going to do it for you, not any more.'

'Everything you are you owe to me,' he said.

'Everything?' I frowned. 'You made me into nothing. You *erased* me. You stole my name. I don't owe you anything.'

'I saw what you wanted to be,' he insisted. 'I brought it out of you.'

'You saw one part of me, and you ignored everything else,' I replied shakily. 'You distorted me to line your pocket. I'm *not* going to stay. I *don't* need you. And you know – you *know* – that this is over.'

He looked away. Suddenly, he looked old, and afraid, and I almost felt sorry for him.

'Leave him alone now,' I said. 'Leave *all* the ghosts alone too. They've done their time. This is your chance to do some good, for once. No more hunting.'

His nod was barely perceptible, but it was there.

CRASH! The wall next to us slipped and fell to the ground, making us both jump. And for a minute, as the dust and the wind flew around us, as the thunder shook the forest, we gave each other tiny smiles, bound by the same irresistible thought.

'Nice touch,' I muttered.

'Yeah,' added Crawler. 'Would have been better with—'

'Someone screaming,' I said.

We nodded together, imagining it.

Our eyes met. A wicked, lingering thrill flickered in both of us – a recognition.

Even now, I could almost hear that spooky organ playing, could only *imagine* how brilliant it would sound as it played across the vast expanse of Poltergeist Land . . .

I ripped my attention away from him then.

'Go,' I said. 'Please. Go.'

And he went.

Then I waited. *I'm meeting an old friend, you see.*

A few seconds later, there was another resounding CRASH! as the three remaining walls fell away, leaving me standing on only some rough floorboards, surrounded by a darkening sky.

Lightning skipped towards me, darting through the treetops like an excited child. I thought of my father. '*I wanted to paint the storm. Stand inside it. See its colours.*' Well, now I knew what the fuss was all about. It was dark. It was glittery. It was unpredictable. It was the most beautiful thing I'd ever seen.

I tipped my head back. The first drops of rain began to fall. They carried the blood and salt and dirt away from my face and body, and I was washed clean.

And now it was here, now the storm swirled above my head. *We meet again.*

I opened my mouth and heard myself laughing loudly, with delight, and the storm laughed right back with me, and as it did so it took that tiny bit I'd swallowed as a baby, back up into itself.

Take it. I'm done with it now. Take it. I loved it. Thank you.

Lightning flashed.

Thunder boomed.

And the rain, and the ghost train, came tumbling down.

- 71 -
LET THE LIGHT IN

I RAN DOWN what was left of the staircase, raced through the corridors as glass and nails and old pallets hammered down.

Scanlon was in Mary's room, preoccupied in a frenzy of destruction.

'Scanlon,' I shouted. '*Scanlon!*'

But he couldn't – or wouldn't – hear me, busy as he was smashing Mary's cot to pieces, a wild, almost terrifying look of relief on his face, while Mary egged him on, stamping on the floor with unrestrained delight.

'Scanlon, we've got to go. Now. Get the others.'

Just as I was beginning to worry, his eyes finally cleared. I picked up Mary and we made a run for it, gathering the boys, Vanessa and Isolde on the way.

Just a few minutes later, the top floor collapsed on to the second, and within seconds Crawler's Haunted

House was nothing more than a pile of rubble.

The storm hammered down on its remains mercilessly, as if to prove a point, before abruptly ceasing.

All the tourists had made it out alive, folded themselves into their helicopters and limousines while frantically sipping the antidote, and fled.

There was no sign of Crawler. His absence was the best apology he could have made.

The dark clouds rolled back, leaving just a dampness in the air around us, and streaks of blue sky appeared overhead. The trees around us seemed to sigh with relief that the atrocity in their midst had been pulled out like a rotten tooth.

We stood in a circle on the outskirts of the wreckage and looked at each other proudly. Sunlight stretched like spilt cream across the forest floor.

Dazed, I watched Isolde standing in a beam of light, making soft exclamations of relief as the warmth hit her skin.

I felt pleasantly tired, fuzzy around the edges.

'What happens next?' said Vanessa, smiling faintly.

'I'm not completely sure,' I admitted.

'Doesn't matter,' said Obediah, yawning. 'It feels *good*.'

Scanlon stood slightly outside our circle, as if an invisible force was keeping him apart from us.

I looked over at him. 'Are you okay?'

'Yeah,' he said softly. 'I'm good.'

'Why haven't you gone yet?' Panic fluttered in my heart.

'I'm going to stay here with you,' he said, 'until you're all safe.'

And something unspoken passed between us. He could see something was happening, and he would keep us company until it was over.

'And then I'm going to do all those things we talked about – and more,' Scanlon said. 'I promise.'

'Fudge,' I said sleepily.

'That first,' he said, and his voice cracked a little bit.

My head felt so heavy. I looked at the others. Isolde had sat down against a tree, and her head rested on its trunk. Mary was clapping her hands as if she could see someone just beyond the circle. Theo and Obediah and Vanessa were simply gasping in surprise as the soft green light around us healed their injuries.

I glanced at my body. My hands were nearly transparent, my edges hard to spot.

All around me there was a great vibrating stillness,

a sense that an entire universe was near, and by the happy, inward-looking smiles on the ghosts around me, I could tell they felt the same – that their times, and their people, were close. My eyelids were longing to fall. I could sense a golden time within me – my final journey.

With what energy I had left, I looked at Scanlon one last time. He was smiling and trembling all over.

'It's . . .' My head kept dropping, but I kept my eyes on his. 'It's nearly here, isn't it?'

'I think so,' said Scanlon. 'You're fading.'

'I'll miss you,' I said. 'My friend.'

He blinked. 'I'll miss you too. Goodbye, Frankie Ripley.'

We shared one final grin, and I thought: *He has the loveliest face I have ever seen.*

And

        then

            I

                closed

                    my

                        eyes.

- 72 -
I'M READY

THAT CHILL, THAT dampness on my body, began to fade. In its place I felt a warmth, and outside me, a stillness that thrummed with magic. I wasn't even sure any more if my eyes had closed, because instead of darkness, there was a dappled, shimmering light.

I was no longer aware of whether I was standing or sitting. The air had become very soft. Nothing caused me pain; no tension remained. A huge grin spread across my face.

This, I suddenly knew, was peace.

Out of the stillness, a bird began to sing, high up in the tree above me. And a voice said: 'Are you ready, Frankie?'

'Yes,' I said softly.

Whatever happened next, I realised, I was more than ready for it. I *accepted* it.

Then there was the sound of footsteps walking over pine needles.

I squinted into the golden realm around me and, finally, I saw them.

Smiling at me, their arms outstretched.

Mum.

Dad.

Birdie.

And I went to them.

Thanks to:

I could not have written this book without the help of my editor, Nick Lake. You are a story shaman. Thank you for your wisdom and open-mindedness.

Flavia Sorrentino for her beautiful cover. It honestly is one of the best things about writing a book, when you see its face for the first time. One day I will come to Italy and eat all the pasta with you as a way of expressing my appreciation.

Polly, for your brilliant 'ten-tonne tightrope walker' joke. And for complaining about difficult button holes. And for basically being you, which you really are very good at.

Dr Kate Beeching, Director of Linguistics at UWE, Bristol, for meeting me to chat through how language might evolve over the next hundred years. Can we meet again in a hundred years and see how it all panned out?

The lovely folk at HarperCollins *Children's Books*, chiefly: Jess Dean, Samantha Stewart, David the designer, Louisa Sheridan, Elorine Grant, Harriet 'no one ever thanks sales' WELL I DO, HARRIET, Peter with the Nice Shirt, Sam White, Philippa Poole, Jo-Anna Parkinson, Beth Maher and Ann-Janine Murtagh. Without you this book would only ever be a terribly formatted Word document. Thank you for getting stories into children's hands.

May all your storms be loud and glittery and dramatic enough to be useful. Failing that, to just be *extremely* exciting.